LOTUS GARCíA

TALES OF ESPERANZA

LISA CHEWNING

ISBN-13: 978-1480284654
ISBN-10: 1480284653

LLCHEWNING9@gmail.com

For Geoff, Charlie, and Chuck

who provided unflagging

encouragement, support, and love.

ACKNOWLEDGEMENTS

I send profound gratitude to the many writers I have met along this journey. Thank you for your extraordinary guidance and inspiration. I cannot name all of you but you have all had a hand in this book.

I am indebted to Shirley Jones, Paula Todd King, Nina Smith, and Robin Strong for their keen and wise editing.

Thank you, David Regina, for help in matters of the Catholic church.

Thank you, Elizabeth Martinez Gibson, for help with the Spanish language.

Thank you, Mary Sojourner, for teaching me to know my character's shoe size.

Thank you, Chuck Kinder, for teaching me to put myself on the windshield of the story.

Thank you, Buddy Nordan, though no longer on this earth but still in our hearts, for teaching me to break a reader's heart.

Thank you, Miss Floor, my first grade teacher, for teaching me to read and to love doing so.

CHARACTERS

LOTUS GARCíA – healer

VERDAD PACHECO – mother of Segundo

IFIGINIA VARELA – best friend of Verdad

MATEO MORALES/PADRE MATEO – priest

MARISOL MORALES – daughter of Mateo

MIRAH MORALES – mother of Marisol

SEGUNDO GARCíA – child of Verdad and Silvio

SILVIO SALAZAR– son of Leopold, father of Segundo, husband of Rosalba

ROSALBA CORON – wife of Silvio

CUERVO – a raven

LEOPOLD SALAZAR DE LA VEGA – father of nine boys, grandfather of Segundo, owner of Leopold Bus Line

GRACIELA – wife of Leopold

CARLOS VARELA – father of Ifiginia, drug lord

MILENA VARELA – mother of Ifiginia, wife of Carlos

DOMINGO DOS OJOS YEBARA – bodyguard of Carlos

CLEMENTE PACHECO – father of Verdad, caretaker of church

MARíA TERESA PACHECO – late mother of Verdad

CHARACTERS (continued)

MARCO AND RAFAEL VARELA – twin brothers of Ifiginia

TITO BRAVO – novio/husband of Ifiginia

LUIS CORON – father of Rosalba

ALMA SALAZAR – daughter of Silvio and Rosalba

MARíA FERNANDA MILENA BRAVO – daughter of Tito and Ifiginia

SANTIAGO CLEMENTE YEBARA – son of Domingo and Verdad

PALOMA TURQUESA/PAMELA TARKOWSKI – painter, rich widow from USA

ROB TARKOWSKI – late husband of Pamela

EUSEBIO MEDINA/SHEBO – driver of PeMex truck

TACIANO ZARAGOZA – owner of gas station

SERAFíA – friend of Lotus

JUAN PABLO PANIAGUA – doctor of Esperanza

LOTUS GARCíA

TALES OF ESPERANZA

MEXICO

PART I

Lotus García, the 51 year old virgin with the club foot and mother of 14, had always wanted to be famous. She dreamed of being a dancer. Oh, to gracefully plié and pirouette, to tap and twirl, to stomp and slide, to float and foxtrot, to grapevine and glide in front of an audience. She wanted the world to know her name, to see her name emblazoned on marquees, to hear it whispered in awe as people left the theatre after yet another of her dazzling performances. She dreamed of stepping out of the shadows.

7

Her mother must have had grand dreams for her daughter, or so Lotus thought. Why else saddle her with the name Lotus? But, Lotus blamed genetics and economics for her more than slightly barrel silhouette and vertical paucity. And, of course, her club foot.

In the school library, Lotus found a book of baby names.

> LOTUS: With its roots in the mud, the lotus rises
> through the murky water to blossom clean
> and bright, symbolizing purity, resurrection
> and the enlightened being who emerges
> undefiled from the chaos and illusion of the
> world.

Lotus had always felt anything but clean or bright as she stoutly clumped along, her right foot turned inward, her leg considerably, noticeably, and frustratingly shorter than her left. School became a place of loneliness and torture as she had to endure the stares and giggles she evoked when the teacher called her to the blackboard to solve a division problem. She was the first in the class to master the function and the children teased her even more unmercifully for being smart. On the playground, she sat alone, trying not to draw attention to herself as the other children chose sides for their often malevolent games. She knew she was ungainly, that her footsteps made an unholy cadence: ONE thump, ONE thump, ONE thump. She chose to remain in the shadows.

When she was 12 she began to stay behind to help out at home. She took care of her unflawed sisters, hung wet laundry on the line in the miniscule dusty yard, peeled mountains of potatoes, turnips, and carrots for the Sunday stew that was stretched out and consumed all week long, water and onions added daily to try and disguise the dwindling flavors and nutrients. She thought she might as well gather pebbles from the barren yard and boil them for all the good the sodden vegetables were. Thus, Lotus learned to cook.

She was the invisible child, the good one, the one her aunts and female cousins shook their heads over, and passed their cast-offs to. If someone took notice of her at family gatherings, that someone would inevitably comment on her eyes – how soulful – or her blue black hair, the color of a wing of a raven. Not just once did Lotus hear some such references to her concluded with, "¡Qué lástima! What a waste, what a shame".

Lotus bided her time, a Cinderella of sorts to her family of sisters while they ran off to their games, their sweethearts, their weddings, their lives. Most of the time she did not mind; she wanted to be left behind, left to her own slow, plodding and thumping devices.

One day her sister Marcela came back to Esperanza, the little Mexican town whose name means hope, to visit her mother. She was unhappy at home, her rich husband not paying enough attention to her. She brought along her colicky baby, Harold. He was two months old. Upon crossing the threshold, she shoved him into the arms of her sister where he stayed the entire visit. He did not fuss but settled in with a solemn and steady gaze, his dark eyes into her dark eyes. She walked him tirelessly from room to room, back and forth, ONE thump, ONE thump, ONE thump.

"Look, look! He does not make a sound when she holds him! He is so peaceful."

Marcela left him for longer and longer periods of time, claiming it gave her a chance to get her hair styled, to find a new dress for her post-pregnancy figure, to win back her gringo husband who had lost interest in their marriage bed shortly after her belly began to grow.

Harold stayed overnight. Harold stayed for a weekend. Harold stayed for a week here, and another there. Lotus found herself in charge of his care as if he were her own. Harold only cried when he had to leave Lotus who taught him to play Patty Cake and to count, who witnessed his first steps, taught him the names of the birds and of the stars in the milky sky. Together they planted seeds and watered the tiny plants that struggled through the thin soil in the sad little garden in the backyard. She taught him not to be ashamed of whom he was.

Harold stayed with Lotus until he was six, until his father remembered he had a son. It nearly stole away her very being when Lotus had to say good-bye. In her best sixth grade hand, she wrote his name on an end paper from the family Bible, the only paper she had. She added his birthdate, then she burned it in the old kitchen stove. As the paper curled, turned brown, then ignited, she prayed for his health. As the smoke rose, she vowed, "No one will hurt me like that, or take something I love away from me again." Harold was her first child.

By then, word had spread about her great love for children. Las monjas, the nuns, directed young mothers to Lotus, tearful women carrying swaddled infants who refused to grow, who refused to sleep, who never seemed to be content. Lotus would take the squalling babies, hold them tight to her mighty heart, and croon lullabies, tell them tales of enchanted forests with secret waterfalls, and happy babies who played with the golden fish. The restless babies would gaze up into her soulful eyes, listen to her soothing voice, and drift off to sleep. Lotus held them and walked them, ONE thump, ONE thump, ONE thump, gazing at their rosebud lips, seeing their blue-veined eyelids flutter and move back and forth. She wondered if babies dreamed. Did they dream of the safe shadowy cavern where they floated before their birth? Or, did they dream of angels and mermaids?

Time passed for Lotus García and the dreaming babies grew, grew into men and women who moved away, had babies of their own that they sometimes, but more often rarely, brought back to visit Lotus. She would walk the new babies, hold them in her safe arms, and the lullaby of her footsteps eased into the rhythm of their hearts, ONE thump, ONE thump, ONE thump. Each time she returned the babies to their parents, she repeated the ritual of sending an incantation upward with the smoke of their names.

Lotus rode the local bus, a creaking, wheezing rusty thing, into town to do her marketing. A basket, una canasta, hung over her arm to carry her purchases. It was one she took particular pride in. Family lore said it had been made by a long ago relative. It had been in the García family forever, used for gathering vegetables, carrying eggs and wool to market, left out in the rain, forgotten in the back of the shed until Lotus salvaged it, scrubbed it softly with warm water and soap until it looked good again. Lotus knew the basket was strong; it had been made so many unknown years before and survived hard use, then neglect, and now, it glowed as if it were new on her arm.

The bus was crammed, as it always was, on the trip into the market. Neighbors crowded three to a seat, clutching their eggs, their roosters, and their bounty to be sold that day. The old bus, the only one in the fleet of Leopold Bus Line, smelled of exhaust, gasoline, and sweat. It smelled of old clothes, unwashed bodies, and green onions. Lotus nodded in a half slumber, squeezed into a window seat. Her treasured basket, filled with squash and carrots to sell, was planted on her lap. The bus belched and rattled along, Lotus lulled by the exhaust and the jostling. Only once or twice did she open her eyes to see where they were, to note the other passengers who boarded the bus.

A tall, young girl with something wrapped in a tattered blanket squeezed her way to the back of the bus. Lotus felt an air

14

of desperation in the being of the young woman, saw anguish in her pinched face, in the way she carried her tiny bundle. Ah, look how unhappy she is, sent to market, forced to give up some family treasure, Lotus thought, as she watched the girl make her way to the farthest seat. Several passengers squeezed into each other even more to make room for the girl to wedge herself into the corner.

Lotus closed her eyes again, resting her head against the cloudy window. The picture of the girl lingered in her mind as she tried to doze. Raven black hair and black soulful eyes. They could have been related but no, Lotus had never seen her.

The long, dusty, and bone-jarring journey to the market finally ended and Lotus García tried to stretch away the stiffness in her body. Her neck ached from the uncomfortable position she had been in and she turned this way and that. When she turned her head toward the back of the bus, she saw that the tall, thin girl with the raven hair had already pushed to the front of the crowd, parting the other passengers with a firm but gentle hand.

She hurried off the bus, almost falling down the steps, and disappeared into the crowd of tourists and vendors.

Lotus waited her turn. She knew from painful experience that there was no reason to hurry, to try and push her way to the front. They would all disembark in time. She went over the things she needed to purchase for that week: corn meal, tomatoes, a packet of sewing needles, black thread. Maybe if the price of these things was not too dear, she would be able to treat herself to an apple for the long ride home.

The last passenger in front of Lotus had moved to the door and Lotus swung her left leg into the aisle, dragging her nearly useless right leg and foot behind. She settled her basket on her arm, adjusted her skirt, and with absolutely no idea why, thumped to the back of the bus. She clumped back to the seat the young, thin girl had occupied. She had left behind her bundle. Lotus bent to pick it up, to put it in her basket, hoping she would run into the girl in the market or perhaps on the return trip home so she could give her the forgotten item.

The tattered bundle moved, just ever so slightly. Lotus looked more closely. She heard a muted intake of air before the bundle began to softly mewl. Lotus pulled on the end of the blanket, fought with the tightly wrapped object to open it. All the while, she knew what she would find but prayed she would be wrong. "Please, Dios mío, no. Do not let it be."

Inside the sodden blanket, a tiny baby—she saw immediately that it was a boy--turned his head toward her voice. He had a mop of black hair and coal black eyes that did not quite focus on her face.

"Last stop," the driver bellowed. "Vamos, Lotus. I want to eat my lunch."

Lotus scooped the baby, sodden blanket and all, into her basket, on top of the carrots and squash. She whipped off her head scarf and covered her new cargo. Thumping as quickly as she could and as quickly as she dared, she worked her way to the front of the bus. She glanced at the driver, and for the thousandth time, and for the first time, saw his name written in ink in neat

17

block letters over his heart. Leopold. He tipped his hat to her, gently took her elbow, and helped her down the bus steps. As she made her way to the fountain in the middle of the square, her heart pounded, feeling as if it were trying to turn over in her chest. She began to shiver, though the day was hot and sunny.

What have I done? What will I do?

She dipped an end of her scarf into the fountain and drizzled the water into the open mouth of the baby. He swallowed greedily. She dipped the scarf again. And, again. She wiped his face, cleaned his eyes, and checked to see that all the rest of him was in order. He seemed healthy, just hungry. He waved his arms and legs in the air, freed from the wet confines of his blanket.

Lotus hurried to one of the stalls and traded some of her yellow squash and carrots for a bit of brightly woven fabric. She rewrapped the baby in it and settled the remainder of the squash and carrots around him. She moved from stall to stall, until she had secured her needs for the week. She took the coins she had brought with her and convinced a young mother to give up the bottle of her baby filled with milk. Lotus forgot about the apple she wanted for her treat. She had all of the treat now that she needed. She looked around for the girl who had left the baby on the bus. Nowhere. Lotus García sighed with relief. Already, the baby was hers.

Lotus fed the baby the milk, crooned to him as they swayed and bumped on the ride home that seemed to go on forever. It was always the same bus, the only bus that carried people to and from the market. The ride home was never as crowded as the ride into town and Lotus was able to stretch her aching legs out on the seat. She kept vigil over the baby, not daring to drift off for fear of the basket with him inside rolling off of her lap. She watched nervously as each person boarded the bus until they were far enough away from the market that Lotus relaxed just the slightest bit. She smiled to herself the rest of the way home.

At home, dark haired and dark eyed Segundo slept in the

market basket. Yes, she had named him. Segundo Leopold García.

The day after she found Segundo, she awoke to find a goat tied up out in the yard. While she waited for the owner to come and claim her, Lotus and Segundo enjoyed her milk. No one ever came for the goat.

Lotus continued to go to market once a week, the tiny Segundo in the basket over her arm. Each time the Leopold Bus Line vehicle halted in front of her house, Leopold the driver stepped down and helped her up into the coach.

"Buenos días, doña Lotus," he would say as he tipped his hat. She had never noticed how his hair curled around the nape of his neck. "How are we doing today?"

His new attention and courtesy confused her. No one ever paid attention to her; they most often looked away when they saw her coming. Now, this man acted the gentleman, helping her onto his bus, addressing her with respect. Why? Every week she stretched out her hand to drop coins in the collection box, and every week Leopold covered it with his big hand. "No, doña Lotus. Your beautiful smile is payment enough. Is enough."

Segundo grew and other people began to notice him. When he outgrew the confines of the ancient basket, Lotus had to carry him on her shoulder. Suddenly, there was an empty seat for her each time she boarded the bus, always the same one. The other passengers smiled and nodded to her. All the while, they wondered where the baby had come from.

In their small minds in this small place, they knew he had not come the normal way. No one, no man, had ever shown the slightest interest in Lotus, and besides, was she not past the age of child bearing? Yet, he had to be her child; did he not look exactly like her with his hair the color of the wing of a raven? His eyes? Had there been a miracle they had not witnessed? Or, had she conjured up the child?

Their attention, too, confused her. In time, the guilt she carried eased but she was always wary that the young, tall girl who had left the gift of Segundo would one day board the bus and demand that Lotus return him. She often looked up to see Leopold watching her in the long mirror over his seat. As he expertly wrangled the bus around curves and up the steep hills, grinding gears and swooshing open the bus doors, he spent a great deal of time observing her. When their eyes met, he would often smile at her. She would look away, finding something outside of the window to stare at. One day when she took her usual seat, she saw that her window was clean and free of streaks, inside and out. Only hers.

Life continued and Segundo grew. Lotus García returned from her marketing one day to find a small sack with eggs waiting at her door. She looked around but saw no one. She let them remain outside until evening came, thinking that whoever had left them there would realize their mistake, return, and take them where they belonged. As she locked up for the evening, she saw the sack was still there. She took them inside and she and Segundo enjoyed them for supper. Another day when she and Segundo returned, the missing window in the front room had been repaired, the swollen and splintered piece of wood that she had nailed over the gaping opening was gone and in its place was a piece of glass reflecting the sun. The room inside was brighter and felt more open. There were no more shadows in the middle of the day. She felt exposed. She looked at her shabby belongings and set about doing something about them.

"Segundo, run to my dresser and bring me my church shawl, the one with the roses."

The child was accustomed to the occasional odd thing happening when his mother was around. He knew his mother had special powers with the babies brought to her to be nurtured and loved when their own mothers could not do the same. Hearing the dance of his mother tirelessly moving through the house with the baby of someone else, ONE thump, ONE thump, ONE thump, was as natural to him as birds singing in the trees. He even helped her set flame to the bits of paper holding the names of the children when they returned to their homes. This, though, the new window, a view out into the world, was the strangest thing he had witnessed. With great care, he carried the

23

old black shawl to her and helped her pull it over the threadbare

sofa. The faded roses seemed to come alive in the sunlight.

Lotus tried but she could not get used to the tiny changes

taking place to her house. When did they occur? Who made

them possible? One day there was a pot of marigolds on the

stairs leading up to the porch. Another day it was a coat of paint

on the old shed where she had found the ancient basket. She had

her suspicions as to where these little miracles came from yet,

she could not be sure. No one spoke to her about them. No one

on the bus commented on the improvements but she felt their

knowing eyes on her, on Segundo, and on their house as the

Leopold Bus Line pulled up to collect them on market day. Her

home began to look respectable, less a place where a destitute

and lonely woman lived. Her thin-soiled, sad patch of a garden

now sported neat, tidy rows of herbs and plants, nestled in

stinking, beautiful mounds of manure. A spindly apple tree

provided the fruit she craved; it became the task of her son to

water it each day. A blue ball with yellow stars appeared in the

yard. A battered metal truck. Segundo now had toys. It looked like a family lived there. Life had somehow become easier for Lotus García.

These small gifts and anonymous gestures brought a change to Lotus García. Now she did not feel relegated to the shadows. She began to take pains with her appearance. The night before market day, she gently soaped and rinsed her old but nicer skirts and blouses until they shone. Now instead of plaiting her heavy black hair to keep it off of her neck, she let it hang loose, the wing of a raven that she brushed and combed until it glistened around her shoulders. The small changes she made to herself were subtle but they made her feel new and worth something, no longer someone to be ignored and overlooked.

And, she paid even more attention to Segundo, snipped his tight black curls so they would behave and lie down, mended the knees in his trousers, taught him to scrub his nails every night so he would not look like a campesino, a peasant.

Segundo accompanied the only mother he knew to market each week, running from stall to stall, tasting the samples held out to him by the good-natured vendors.

"Here, Segundo, taste these sweet peas."

"Segundo, try this empanada, this pie."

"No, no, mine is better. Segundo, come over here!"

"Segundo, take this apple to your mother."

When their shopping and trading was finished, Segundo and Lotus would sit by the fountain, in the shade of a tree, and enjoy some small treat someone had given to the boy. Musicians played as the shadows lengthened; Segundo loved watching the men of the mariachi group play their violins, trumpets, and guitars. He especially liked the deep voice of the guitarrón but the rhythmic vitality of the high-pitched, round-backed vihuela also intrigued him. On some days, if they were lucky, there would also be someone playing a harp. Segundo often told Lotus that he was going to sing in a mariachi band and dress in a silver-studded charro outfit with a wide-brimmed hat. He bragged that beautiful women would swoon over his romantic songs. Lotus would shake her head and laugh; what else could she expect?

One day as they sat in the shade, sharing a bottle of

orange soda, Lotus saw Leopold, the owner of Leopold Bus Line, dancing alone to the mariachi band. He wore his blue bus driver shirt with his name emblazoned over his heart, his cap tilted back on his head, his teeth flashing in a wide smile. Leopold noticed them and motioned them over. Lotus shook her head no and looked away. *¿Yo? ¿Baile? Me? Dance? Absurd.* But as she plumped herself up, resettled on the stone seat of the fountain, she felt a slight flush of pleasure. *Oh, to dance. For it all to be so easy.* Leopold waved to them a second, then a third time. Segundo bounced up and down in front of her, his excited face begging her to give him permission to join the dancers.

"Go, Segundo, go. Dance with that crazy man."

Segundo darted through the crowd until he reached the bus driver. He took his outstretched hands and they stomped and twirled to the music.

A tall, thin woman stepped out from the crowd and moved close to Leopold and Segundo. It was the young woman

27

from the bus so many years ago. The bus driver held out a hand to her and she took it and one of the hands of Segundo.

Lotus watched the trio in amazement: Who was this woman who looked so much like her and like Segundo? Did she know Leopold? Her heart pounded in her chest. They glided to the marriage of instruments: the plaintive resonance of the violins, the thumping bass of the guitars, and the blaring of the trumpets. The woman smiled down at Segundo, then looked to Lotus. She beckoned to her with her head. *Come, come join us.*

Lotus tried to look away, to shake her head no, but just as that day on the bus, she found herself inexplicably drawn. She rose, settled the old basket on the edge of the fountain, and straightened her skirt. With great dignity, she clumped across the dusty plaza. ONE thump, ONE thump, ONE thump. The three dancers stopped and waited. Lotus took one hand of the other woman and one of Segundo. She joined her body to their graceful movements, and she, Lotus García, plied and pirouetted, tapped and twirled, stomped and slid, floated and fox-trotted, grapevined and glided to the guitars and violins and trumpets.

VERDAD, THE TALL THIN GIRL

Verdad Pacheco made only one mistake in her 15 years of life. That mistake was not walking alone late one night on her way home from the party of a friend. From that miscalculation, a moment of weakness, her life changed into one of stratagem, sorrow, and silence.

The tall, thin girl lived with her widowed father, a caretaker for La Iglesia de la Santa Cruz, the church and the Catholic school who, try as he may, could never provide Verdad with the things she dreamed of and sometimes beseeched him for. How she ached to live a life like the other girls who attended the school in town. She knew she was needy, that las monjas, the nuns, viewed her as a charity case. Her best friend wore new clothes, lived in a fancy sprawling house, went on expensive vacations, and even had maids to keep her life in order. Verdad had only her father and their humble rooms in the casita behind the school. Her desires were not elaborate: Tiny gold earrings for her pierced ears, shiny black patent leather shoes with low heels suited to a girl of her age to wear to church, an embroidered shawl instead of the old tattered one of indeterminate color scavenged from the church jumble sale.

Verdad tried to be a good daughter and studied diligently. A full scholarship to la Universidad in a large city nearby was the carrot that las monjas dangled in front of her. She daydreamed about leaving Esperanza, going to the places she knew only from books. Verdad escaped her life in books; she devoured everything she could find to read. When she lost herself in a book, she could travel to anywhere in the world, to any time in history, and be whoever she wanted.

After school, Verdad worked side by side with her father to keep the grounds manicured and filled with flowers as befitted a holy place, sweating in the sun, resenting the dirt and dust and rocks they constantly battled. Or, she washed the chalk boards, helped to empty wastebaskets, and swept the walkways. She made do with whatever her father provided but she could not help wanting. She was, after all, una adoloscente, a teenager. She noted with great envy as her fellow students marked la fiesta de quince años, la Quinceañera, when they moved from childhood to womanhood. Adorned in a tiara, arrayed in a pink evening ball gown symbolizing their purity, they were allowed to wear elegant make-up for the first time--although most of them had been wearing it for some time when they were with their friends and away from their home. The gifts they received were lavish, such as the cherished gold locket depicting Nuestra Señora de Guadalupe, blessed by the priest. Mariachis played during the elaborate parties their parents arranged for them, some so grand that for these families, the police blocked off streets for the festivities.

The best friend of Verdad, Ifiginia Varela, marked her Quinceañera, her Pink Party, with much of the grandiose fanfare some of the girls and their families displayed, enough to let everyone understand the standing of her family. Ifiginia had siete damas, seven maids of honor, to attend to her and help pass out los bolos, the favors. The mother of Ifiginia, doña Milena, chose fancy dresses for las damas, each one a different pastel color. They looked like confections as they milled around Ifiginia. Verdad was one of the siete damas; she had never had a dress so fine.

Verdad would not have a Quinceañera, her own celebration. Her father was too poor. The Varela family bought her dress and underpinnings. And, they had arranged for Padre Mateo to bless a gold locket for her, identical to the one they gave Ifiginia. In this way, she was able to feel a little like a princess, as well.

Clemente, the father of Verdad, attended the party. While he had managed to buy the patent leather shoes his daughter wanted, he could not do anything more for this important birthday. His heart beat heavily and sadly in his chest. He drank very little, ate nothing, and hovered on the outskirts of the party. Early in the evening, he slipped away. Verdad saw him leave to make the lone walk home, but stayed on with her school friends. She danced to the tejano music cds Ifiginia received as gifts; she made believe that the handsome mariachi singers crooned to her and to her alone, declaring their never-ending devotion and fidelity.

Ifiginia, la festejada, the celebrant and her father, don Carlos, danced to a traditional waltz. He then disappeared and he wheeled out a multi-tiered birthday cake. Dripping in meringue frosting and decorated in pastel hues to match the dresses of the girls, the cake was of such monumental proportions that earlier in the day, the door leading into the courtyard had been removed from it hinges to accommodate it.

The Leopold Bus Line had been hired to take the guests who did not have transportation to and from their homes; it would be too far for them to walk and not at all proper for the young girls to roam the countryside, to risk being found dead on the side of the road, or even worse, raped and tossed from the car of some criminal. That is what las monjas, the nuns, told the girls on an almost daily basis.

SILVIO Y CUERVO

It was not Leopold, though, who came to the Quinceañera to pick up the last guests. His son, Silvio, took the bus out for these kinds of late runs, the ones where nobody minded if he had a bottle under his seat, or that the bottle got passed around, and everyone sang and was happy on the bumpy ride home. Some of them were so happy, Silvio had to hose out the bus before he returned it to his father.

Silvio was 19, wore his glossy hair long and slicked back like the actors on television, the hair tonic he applied doing little to disguise his curls. They were a source of embarrassment to him; he thought they made him look common. None of the stars on the telenovelas sported curls, nor did many of them have beards so Silvio shaved twice a day.

Silvio had a sooty raven named Cuervo that rode on his shoulder. No, Silvio insisted to anyone who would ask, Cuervo was not a pet, even though Silvio had raised him from a fledgling. He came to find Cuervo like this: One day Silvio, then only 12, and his posse of brothers, large and small, were out gathering firewood and came across the nest of a raven in the top of a pinyon tree. While his brothers scrambled to gather the nuts that had fallen to the rocky soil all around the base of the trees, Silvio climbed up the tree and examined the nest. It was a sturdy and bulky nest made of stout sticks. He saw it was lined with bark and hair, fur and grasses. It even looked as though a piece of a white plastic bag had been woven into the nest. Silvio listened for the defensive call of the parents but, strangely, neither of the parent birds was present.

Fragments of brown-blotched, turquoise eggs lay in the nest next to three dead hatchlings, their bald necks and bulging eyes so fragile and weak looking. As Silvio prepared to climb down from the top of the tree, to leave the dead hatchlings to nature, a slight movement caught his eye. There was a fourth bird, concealed under bits of grass. It was alive, just barely.

Silvio tucked the bird into his shirt against his warm skin and cautiously made his way down the tree, careful not to crush him against the trunk. He showed his brothers his prize and they teased him for being so soft-hearted.

"Why did you not leave it up there for the buzzards?"

"What are you going to do with that thing?"

"Birds are dirty, bad luck."

"It will never survive."

Survive it did. Silvio fed it mashed up hard boiled eggs and apples until its thick bill became larger, then it was seeds and raisins, then raw meat, then lizards and newly hatched frogs. He named it Cuervo, a simple name for such a determined little thing. His metallic looking feathers came in. He began to hop and then tried to fly. Silvio feared the day Cuervo would leave him, but it never came. Silvio attached himself to Cuervo and Cuervo attached himself to Silvio. Cuervo slept on the windowsill in a wooden box Silvio had made and lined with sticks and grasses. Cuervo found bits of brightly colored string and added them to his abode.

Leopold watched Silvio and the raven in bewilderment, wondering where this holy terror of a boy had gotten his tender side. This was the child who tiptoed up to his sleeping brothers and roared in their ears to frighten them, who could never sit still or stay silent in school, and who was always being punished for some real or supposed infraction by las monjas, the nuns. Here now was his son, caring for a wild thing that had no business surviving, talking to it as if it could understand! Silvio mimicked the sounds of the raven, the "kaah" when it was hungry. Cuervo bowed his head, as if listening intently when Silvio talked to him. On more than one occasion, Leopold thought he heard the bird say, "Hola", but he mistrusted his own ears because it was not possible for a bird to speak.

Cuervo rode on the shoulder of Silvio and went everywhere he went. If Silvio went into a restaurante or into the casa of a friend where the mother was superstitious (and nearly all were) and would not let the harbinger of bad luck enter with him--"Get that eater of death out of here!"-- Cuervo waited patiently in a nearby tree. Sometimes he would fly off, his broad shining wings carrying him to some secret source of food. Most of the time it was the garbage cans in back of the casas and restaurantes. Cuervo was quite adept at taking the lids off of the cans and helping himself to their bounty. Always, though, when Silvio started for home, Cuervo came flapping overhead, and landed on his shoulder again. When Silvio grew old enough to court the girls of this village, Esperanza, and later of the surrounding villages, Cuervo was always with him. Most of the girls thought it was cute, or at the very worst, eccentric. The presence of the black bird often helped Silvio start up conversations with strangers.

While Silvio had many dalliances, none was lasting. He flitted from girl to girl, much like Cuervo flitted from roost to roost in pursuit of food. Early on Silvio gained a reputation as a playboy, a man who would never stay long with one woman. He was kind but always managed to break their hearts when he moved on. "Naipes, mujeres y vino, mal camino", or "Cards, women, and wine, bad ways" was what he claimed as his credo.

The night of the Quinceañera Silvio was in fine form. He had begun drinking early in the day as the revelers boarded the Leopold Bus Line and he had graciously accepted sips of beer and wine from them. He nibbled on picadillo, spiced beef, rice pudding, cakes and breads at the party itself, while he awaited his passengers, washing the food down with just a little more alcohol. Whatever he ate, he was sure to give Cuervo a taste.

When the party finally ended, when the mariachis staggered off into the night, when the father of Ifiginia bellowed, "¡Basta!", "Enough!" to the last guests, Silvio stood at the foot of the Leopold Bus Line steps and bowed ceremoniously as the party-goers grabbed onto the handrail and tried to pull themselves into the bus. He occasionally offered his hand to a woman who seemed to be in need of his attention.

One such person that he deemed in need of his thoughtfulness was Verdad.

"Señorita, allow me," and he kissed the back of her hand before helping her up the stairs. No, she had not been drinking, not even one sip of vino from an abandoned glass, as she saw her school mates dare. Silvio merely saw that she was pretty.

Intoxicated by the night, the festivities, and the attention of the handsome Silvio, Verdad blushed. No young man had ever paid her the slightest bit of attention, and here was Silvio himself, the man with the raven. She took a deep breath, thrust her breasts forward as she had seen older girls do, smiled, and replied, "You are too kind, señor."

Her encouragement was not wasted on Silvio. He drove the other passengers to their homes, naturally dropping off the closest ones first. He avoided the casita behind the church where Verdad and her father lived, even though he could have easily turned the bus down that street several times to let her off.

He watched Verdad in the mirror over his seat and when their eyes met, he winked. He expected her to look away, to redden, but no, Verdad straightened her shoulders, met his eyes, and resolutely smiled at him. Though surprised by her boldness, Silvio enjoyed the flirtation, and had to remind himself to pay attention to the road.

Verdad enjoyed the flirtation as well. She had never done this before but it made her feel daring. The next time they drove past the casita where her father slept, something deep inside of her seemed to flip over and she found it difficult to sit still. While she had not had her own fiesta to mark her passage into womanhood, she no longer felt that she was a child. After all, she and Ifiginia were born so close together they could have been twins. Playing with the new locket that hung between her breasts, she thought, Wait until I tell Ifiginia about this! She thought she might not be able to bear it until they returned to school on Monday and might have to visit with her friend after church.

Finally, all but Verdad, Silvio, and Cuervo had exited the bus. Silvio pulled the bus over onto a deserted street and turned in his seat to look at Verdad. Her heart fluttered and this time, she did look away. She looked at her hands which had suddenly become very moist. Every part of her body felt moist, especially between her legs, and she felt ashamed.

Silvio rose from his seat. Cuervo hopped onto the steering wheel. Silvio slicked back his hair. He ambled down the aisle toward Verdad.

She swiped her hands on the skirt of her dress.

He sat in the seat directly in front of her. He leaned over the back.

"Did you have a good time at the fiesta, señorita?"

Verdad swallowed and found her voice.

"Sí, yes, it was a beautiful evening."

"But not as beautiful as you, señorita."

Although she blushed, she looked him in the eye.

"Nor as beautiful as you, señor."

Silvio reached over and gently lifted the locket she wore. The tips of his fingers were rough where they grazed her neck and chest. Verdad shivered.

He looked from the locket to Verdad for many seconds, searching in her eyes for an answer to an unspoken question.

She did not falter in her gaze.

"It is late, niñita."

Silvio turned away from Verdad, returned to the front, and started the bus. Cuervo gave a 'tock' and returned to his shoulder. They drove to her home in silence, tears smarting her eyes. When the bus door swooshed open and Verdad disembarked, she turned to Silvio and said, "Me llamo Verdad. Verdad Pacheco."

She hurried into the night, whispering a litany of self-remonstration, "I am not a little girl. I am not a little girl." She knew at that moment she could never tell Ifiginia of the bus ride.

VERDAD Y SILVIO

At school on Monday, all the talk was about the party for Ifiginia.   Verdad was grateful that no one asked about her evening. As the days passed, the sting of her first experience with a boy, a man really, lessened and Verdad returned to the studious and obedient daughter she had been before the party. Each night, though, as she lay in bed, awaiting the dreams that carried her away from the tortures of being 15, of being poor, of living in the sad little town, she played over the events of the bus ride with Silvio.

One Saturday morning Clemente stood in the doorway to her bedroom, hesitant to enter. He had always been a tall and thin man but now Verdad saw how stooped he was becoming. As he told her that he needed to go into town to buy supplies for cleaning the church, he looked at the crack in the ceiling, out the window, at the scuffed wooden floor, at the hat in his hand, but not at her. He had been like this since the night of the party. It was as if he sensed a change in her, as if her womanhood had become a reality, and he was uncomfortable. He did not know how to talk to her, she thought, how to be her father any more.

"Papi, may I come with you? Ifiginia and some other girls are going to el cine and she will get a ticket for me." Verdad was not sure that was true but she felt she would go crazy if she did not escape the confines of the casita and school.

Clemente nodded and dug deep into his pocket. He handed her a few coins and said, "For the bus. For after. It is not safe for you to walk home that late. But, now, we walk."

Verdad met up with her school mates at el cine in town. It was owned by don Carlos. They saw a film they had all seen before but that did not prevent them from sighing over the elegant dresses of the leading woman and giggling over the bumbling romantic attempts of the leading man.

Don Carlos also owned la lavandaría, the laundromat, next door and the thumps and vibrations from the washers and dryers could be heard through the theatre walls during the quiet scenes.

After the movie, they sat on the edge of the fountain in the plaza, el zolcalo, and sipped Diet Cokes.

"It is always the same. The man and woman like each other, the man does something stupid, the woman gets mad, she does something stupid, he rescues her, and they fall in love," Verdad said.

"Yes, it is always the same. But did you see the beautiful shoes she had on when they danced? Her hair? I want romance and love! I want someone to buy me pretty clothes and I want to live in a big house!" Ifiginia noisily finished her drink.

"You already live in a big house," Verdad said.

The girls laughed yet they all agreed that they too wanted that kind of romance and love. A long, black car pulled up and don Carlos leaned across the seat.

"Verdad, do you want a ride home?"

Without hesitating, she said, "No, thank you! I am waiting for Papi."

Papi had walked home hours ago.

After the girls said good-bye, Verdad sat and sipped at her flat soda and she watched the people hurrying home to la cena, to their dinner. Vendors packed up their unsold goods. Shopkeepers turned out lights and locked their doors. With a heavy sigh, she stood to begin the walk home. She would save the coins Clemente had given her for her next trip to town and perhaps, then, buy her own ticket and Diet Coke.

A shrill whistle cut through the air and she turned to find its source. A black bird corkscrewed in a barrel roll above her head. She fell backward onto the edge of the fountain as the bird sailed past her, nearly brushing her hair with its wings.

Another whistle. She saw Silvio standing in front of her and felt more than saw Cuervo whoosh in for a landing.

She began to laugh and Silvio bowed to her, the bird atop his shoulder.

"Señorita, please pardon my bird. He has no manners."

So, she was señorita again. Or, had he forgotten her name from that night on the bus? She began to walk in the direction of home. Silvio and Cuervo walked with her.

"May we accompany you? It is not safe for such a beautiful woman to walk alone."

She nodded and thought how much he sounded like her father and las monjas, the nuns. They began walking, but in the opposite direction of her casita. She went willingly. What went on at night on this road? She did not think everyone was referring to los linces rojos, the bobcats who roamed at night.

She could not think of anything witty to say to Silvio, so she asked him how he came to have Cuervo. Silvio gladly told her the story of climbing the pinyon tree. Verdad was acutely aware that there was little light on the way home.

"Maybe he will kiss me," she thought. They walked and talked, Cuervo occasionally taking off to investigate something in the twilight woods. On one of his absences, Silvio stopped and turned to Verdad and said, "Do you mind if I kiss you?"

Verdad wanted to laugh out loud; finally! But, she contained herself and said, "No, Silvio, I would not mind."

Both of them wetted their lips. Silvio gently held her face between his rough hands and leaned in. He brushed her lips with his in a whisper of a kiss. A thrill rushed through Verdad, melting the very center of her body. She wanted more. She wrapped her hands around the back of his head and pulled him into her. As their lips met again, she could feel him smile.

51

Silvio took her by the hand and they stepped off of the road into the woods where Cuervo had flown. As they picked their way through the underbrush until they found a small clearing, Verdad smelled dry leaves as they crunched underfoot, the green of the vegetation as they brushed up against it, and the air felt cool and damp. It was so quiet in the woods she thought she could hear the trees breathe.

He pressed his lips into hers so hard that his teeth scraped against her tender skin. He slid his hands down her back until he cupped her nalgas in his hands and pulled her against him. Her breasts were smashed so hard against his chest she could barely breathe.

His tongue slid into her mouth and she recoiled. She had never imagined this. He pulled her head to him and continued to kiss her, his tongue slowly tracing the outside of her lips, her teeth, then again, finally, inside her mouth. This time she welcomed it and found herself letting him kiss her as deeply as she had ever dreamed of. Her own tongue seemed to have a mind of its own and it darted in and out of his mouth, first touching the tip of his tongue, then dancing away, back to his tongue, and again dancing away.

Silvio was breathing heavily and loudly. His hands glided up her sides. She wanted to squirm away from him. She wanted to press herself harder into him. When he caressed her breasts, they both moaned. That she felt such heat and such wanting shamed her, but only ever so briefly. Silvio gently touched her breast, sliding his fingers into her shirt onto her bare skin. He reached into her bra and found her nipple. She was afraid to move.

¡Dios mío! Beginning at the collar, one agonizing button at a time, Silvio unbuttoned her blouse. She heard the slight sound of his rough fingertips abrade the smooth fabric. He pulled one of her breasts out of the cup of the bra and covered it with his mouth. No boy or man had ever seen her unclothed. No man or boy had ever touched her breast. No man or boy had ever put his mouth on her, anywhere. Silvio pulled away and looked her in the eyes. She felt the evening air touch her skin, cool where his wet mouth had been. The locket of Nuestra Señora de

Guadalupe hung between her senos, her breasts, and he lifted it and gently placed it behind her neck.

Her blouse hung off her arms at her waist, her bra was askew, and Silvio was unbuttoning his own shirt. She let her blouse drop to the ground. She unhooked her bra and let it slide down her arms. She was uncovered from the waist up. Silvio grinned at her as he wrestled with his shirt. As she unbuttoned her skirt, let it fall to the ground, then stepped out of it, she was mystified by her boldness. She had thought she would be shy, standing in front of a man the first time, but she found she liked it. She enjoyed the look in his eyes, his clumsy haste in removing his shirt, and the knowledge that right then, perhaps only then, she dominated him. He spread his shirt on the ground, smoothing it over the sticks and rocks, and pulled her down to lie with him. The feel of his chest against hers was like velvet and satin. She had never felt the thrill of the skin of another on hers until that night. Silvio kissed her lips, her breasts, her belly, and he began to slide his hands up under her skirt. He hooked his thumbs under each side of her panties and slid them down her legs, past her knees, and over her feet. She lay motionless.

Starting at her knees, he laid gentle butterfly kisses on the inside of first one thigh, then the other. As he came closer and closer to her wetness, she froze in shame. What was he doing? She had never imagined a man would want to do this. What if he went higher? She worried about her scent, knowing it would be heavy and musky. He parted her and kissed her very essence. She did not know what to do. Should she be doing something to him? Should she lie still and wait for him to finish whatever it was he was doing? She could not lie still. She found herself arching, moaning in pleasure.

Silvio leaned over her and kissed her on the mouth again. Again, she recoiled when she tasted herself on his lips and tongue but accepted his kiss, drinking him in. She felt him fumbling with his belt, felt the rough fabric of his jeans against her bare skin, and then felt something smooth and at the same time rigid press against the uppermost part of her thighs, where her legs came together and her womanhood began.

Silvio drove into her. She gasped at the pain. He covered her lips with his, his tongue driving into her mouth almost as insistently as the rest of him did. This is it, she thought. I am no longer a child.

Then it was over. He shuddered then collapsed on top of her, panting into her neck and hair. Again, she did not know what she was supposed to do so she lay still underneath him. She wished he would get up. He finally raised himself up, still joined with her. He smiled down at her and kissed her. It was a loving and gentle kiss without his tongue invading her mouth.

He rolled off of her and she dared to look at him. Surely the thing that had been so urgent, pressed up so hard against her, could not be what she saw now. Then she saw blood! ¡Sangre! Had he hurt himself doing this to her? Then she remembered what she and her friends had talked about, about the first time. It was her blood.

Silvio offered his shirt to her to clean herself with. He looked away as she dabbed at the stains on her legs. She hurriedly dressed and handed him his soiled shirt.

56

"I am sorry, sorry for the . . ." She could not finish the sentence. Her heart swelled in her chest and she felt as if she might cry.

Silvio shrugged on his shirt and pulled her into his arms. "Do not be sorry, querida. It is only natural. Never be sorry."

Cuervo sailed onto his shoulder with "Hola" and holding hands, Verdad and Silvio continued to her home in silence. Silvio occasionally gave her a chaste kiss as they walked. Verdad ached inside and her thighs felt sticky.

They said good night before they reached her casita. She scurried into the yard; no light glowed from inside. She would bathe in the morning, she decided. She did not want to risk awakening her father. She heard Silvio whistle for Cuervo as she slid into bed. Again, her heart swelled in her chest and this time, she let the tears come.

VERDAD

Three months had passed since her night with Silvio. She occasionally saw him in town or driving the bus but he only waved to her. She waited in el zolcalo Saturday evenings but he never appeared as he had that one time. Her heart thumped when she heard the 'krak' of a raven but it was never Cuervo. Any dreams she had carried about a life of romance and love like the ones she saw in the movies slowly faded away. The reality of what she had done and how foolish she had been revealed itself every day as she watched the calendar, waited for her blood to flow. It did not.

She could never tell her friends, not even Ifiginia, about her time with Silvio. She was ashamed that she had done the very thing las monjas, the nuns, had warned the girls about, falling for the charms of a man who had only one thing on his mind.

The days passed, Verdad continued to go to school, to study, to help her father with his tasks, and to appear as if nothing had changed. Yet, she knew all was changing and would never be the same. Her breasts became more tender and swollen than she had ever experienced; the other girls teased her about stuffing her bra. Her waist thickened and she could not fit into her favorite clothes. She began to wear the work shirts of Clemente. She spent more and more time in her room, buried in her beloved books. Reading gave her the only escape and comfort she could find any more.

One day, many months after her evening encounter with Silvio, Clemente announced there was going to be a wedding in the church and he had to get things ready. There would be a large party in the church hall afterward and he asked her to bring some of her friends to help with the preparations

Padre Mateo had left money with Clemente and he sent Verdad to the gasoline station to buy sodas for the girls. Verdad never liked going there. The station was two streets away from the plaza and often, no one was around. Dirt devils swirled around the barren and uninviting lot. The owner, Taciano, made her uncomfortable. His beady eyes seemed to bore right through her. Today was no different. He stood in the office where the sodas were kept in a cooler and watched her every move. The tip of his tongue continually darted in and out of his lips. When he put the bottles in a paper bag and handed her the change, he held onto her outstretched hand and lightly ran a dirty finger over the palm. He smirked at her discomfort. She hurried with her purchase and scurried back to the church.

Ifiginia and two other girls joined Verdad. They chirped to each other while they swept and mopped the floors, tidied the bathrooms, spread linens on the folding tables, and put white roses in vases on each table.

"So, who is the lucky bride? Is it anyone we know?"

"Rosalba, somebody, from the next town. What is the rush? And why not have the wedding at her own church?"

They giggled.

"You know why. So no one would be able to see her belly under her wedding gown!"

"White roses, ha! They should have plucked weeds from the roadside."

Verdad worked silently as the other girls exchanged slurs about the unknown bride. Her work shirt inched up as she swatted at cobwebs in the corner.

One of the girls pointed at her.

"Look at Verdad, what a gordita she is becoming! Verdad, you look like a slob any more. What is wrong with you?"

Verdad could say nothing in response.

"I wonder where the groom will get the 13 gold coins, the arras, for Padre Mateo to bless."

"Silvio does not have a coin to his name. I doubt that he has trece monedas de oro or 13 of anything!"

Verdad stopped what she was doing and listened intently.

"I heard don Leopold and doña Graciela are paying for the whole wedding and fiesta, a kind of a bribe to her parents to keep everything quiet."

"This baby made their decision to get married for them. I do not know how much romance and love they will ever have."

Nausea swept over Verdad and she ran to the bathroom. Colored dots swam before her eyes and she felt as if she were floating. She did not seem to have control over her arms and legs. She tried to call for help but could not hear her own voice over the deafening ringing in her ears.

A few moments later she awoke on the floor where she had crumpled. She felt odd, as if she had taken a long nap and had awakened suddenly. The face of her friend, Ifiginia, was white as she looked down at her in alarm.

"What happened? Are you sick? I am going to go get your father."

"No! Not my father."

Verdad struggled to sit up. She knew tears were ready to spill but took a deep breath.

"Estoy embarazada. I am pregnant. By Silvio."

The two girls held each other and cried.

"What are you going to do? He is getting married this afternoon! Have you told him?"

Verdad shook her head no. "I can never find him alone. He has not come around since, you know. It was such a huge mistake. Poor Papi. It will kill him when he finds out."

"He will not have to find out, Verdad. I will help you. We will figure out something."

Ifiginia and Verdad returned to their chores and worked in silence for the rest of the afternoon.

Many girls had made similar mistakes and disappeared, either running away or sent off to stay with a relative until the baby arrived. The ones who ran away never returned and no one had to guess why they had left. Verdad had no desire to do that to her father.

Verdad managed to hide her mistake from las monjas, the nuns, and from her father. If anyone suspected why she was gaining weight, why she stopped skipping rope in the school yard, they did not say anything. The school year was soon over and Ifiginia arranged for Verdad to stay with her family for a few weeks, saying that Clemente would be busy with the grand renovations Padre Mateo planned for the church.

"We do not have to stay in the main house with my little brothers. We are old enough now that we can do whatever we want." Ifiginia and Verdad hatched a plan to tell everyone they were preparing for the entrance exams to la Universidad, that las monjas, the nuns, told them that the more often they could take them, the better their scores would be. "I will tell Mama that we are moving into the guest house, that we are studying, and no one is to bother us."

One day, shortly after school ended, Verdad took a long bus ride to nowhere. She boarded the Leopold Bus Line, paid her fare, and sat in the seat behind Leopold. She looked out the window as they travelled to the farthest houses on the route. She felt Leopold watching her. When the bus was empty and they were headed back into town, she said, "Buenos días, señor. May I speak with you?"

Verdad decided she would give birth in the clinic established by los Americanos. They were friendly and kind and welcomed her when she went to see it. They answered her questions and did not press her for details about why she was asking them.

"Do you wish to see the doctor? Do you have questions of him?" the woman at the desk asked.

"No, no, I do not want to see a doctor. I was just curious," Verdad answered as she edged to the door.

The woman looked Verdad over, saw the over-sized shirt, the slight swelling of her abdomen. Her height and slim build helped hide her secret but the woman had seen many girls like this.

"Wait here for a moment – I have something for you." And the woman went into another room. She returned with a bottle and handed it to Verdad.

"These are vitamins, for your, for your skin and hair. They will make everything strong and healthy. Be sure to come back if you need anything else. There is always someone here, all day and all night."

Verdad and Ifiginia sat in the shade of a tree in the plaza, sipping freshly squeezed limonadas, when suddenly, Verdad felt a pool of liquid forming under her and spilling to the ground. She grasped at her friend and nodded to her. The day for the birth had come earlier than expected. Verdad and Ifiginia were only slightly panicked that the labor had begun.

"Oh, no! Look at how clumsy I am. I spilled my drink!" Ifiginia tilted her cup and her limonada cascaded onto the lap of Verdad.

Verdad and Ifiginia walked as best and as fast as they could, Verdad hunched over, grasping her belly, her shawl wrapped around her waist in an effort to disguise the wetness. The front door of the clinic was open to allow whatever little breeze might be wandering by to enter and the woman at the front desk, the same one who had given her the vitamins, spotted them coming down the road. She ran out to meet them. She whisked Verdad into an examining room, quickly assessed how far along her labor was, and called for the doctor.

Ifiginia waited for what seemed to be days but it was actually only hours. She tried to block out the desperate sounds she heard from behind the door where Verdad was.

"Nunca nunca nunca, I am never going to have a baby," she swore silently to herself.

Finally, a weak mewling, and the woman who had met them at the door came to Ifiginia. An older woman waiting for the doctor crossed herself.

The woman from the clinic leaned over her and whispered, "It is fine. All is good. She has a boy. Go home, now, and let her rest. Come back tomorrow and bring her some fresh clothes."

Verdad lay on the narrow cot, wrapped in blankets, shaking with exhaustion and fear. She had never known what de dar a luz, giving birth, entailed. Las monjas, the nuns, had glossed over everything beyond the evils of having sex. They had repeatedly and sternly warned them that it was a sin, a stain on their honors and on their familias, to produce a baby outside of marriage. Verdad had tried to look up childbirth in the library but the one book there was outdated and very parochial in its information.

A nurse brought the tiny baby to her after he had been examined and cleaned. She tried to get Verdad to hold him, to put him to her breast, but Verdad turned away and closed her eyes. Hot tears slid down her face. "You must name him, so we can write it on the birth certificate," the nurse told her. Verdad was mute.

Verdad fell into a deep sleep. She did not dream of angels and mermaids, wedding gowns and happily ever afters. She dreamed of a sinister place, a place where she was trapped, and where she ran and ran and ran but could not find her way home. This place was full of briars and brambles and thorns. They tore at her clothes, they pierced her skin, they made her bleed.

She awoke the next morning and the day was already hot. Her sheets and blanket felt clammy with her sweat. Her body was sore and she felt soiled. The nurse changed her bedding and the pad between her legs. She showed her how to keep herself clean. She dabbed at the tears Verdad shed with a damp cloth, then tried again to get her to hold her son and to feed him but Verdad turned away. "If you do not feed him, either with your own milk or with a bottle, we cannot let you leave the clinic," the nurse cautioned her. Still, Verdad could not take him into her arms. She thought only of Papi, of the shame she would bring to him.

The thick walls of the clinic sheltered her. She heard a dog bark, a few lazy yips. The sound of old, rumbling trucks arriving at the market and the voices of women drifted into Verdad. The world was getting ready for another day; no one knew she lay in the clinic, no one knew she had a baby now, no one knew her shame. Why could she not stay here forever? Stay in this safe place with the people who had helped her, people who seemed to care and not judge? Her face was constantly wet with tears, tears she did not even know she was shedding. They simply slid down her face. She thought of her father, wondered what he was doing right now; she thought of Ifiginia and wondered if she would come back to visit her; she thought about Silvio, how he did not even know. Should she try to find him and tell him? Thrust his baby into his arms and watch his face? Would he welcome his son? Would he welcome her?

No, he would not. She knew he could not. He was married with another baby due to be born any time now. He could never acknowledge this child as his son. And, she would not give him the opportunity to reject them.

She looked over at the tightly swaddled child in the bassinette in the corner. She saw how tiny he was, how helpless.

Outside, she heard the Leopold Bus Line make its way through the narrow streets. She heard the grinding gears, the laboring engine, the merry voice of Leopold calling out to people on the street.

It was time. She got out of bed and gingerly walked over

to her baby. She lifted him up –he weighed no more than a feather!– and held him against her heart. He nestled into her. She sighed. It was time to feed him.

LEOPOLD SALAZAR DE LA VEGA

When Leopold the bus driver learned what his son, Silvio, had done to Verdad, he wanted to do to him what the ranchers did to the horses, so he could not make any more babies. Here was Silvio, married under duress, and now soon-to-be father of the baby of another girl. The girl was a child herself! Yes, it was true that he, Leopold, had fathered many children, but it was under the mantle of marriage.

Leopold and his Graciela grew up together, on adjoining farms. Their mothers bathed them together and they often swam naked in the stream that divided their properties. They were nearly inseparable from birth. They spent time with no one else their age and no one was surprised when they were both 16 that they announced they wanted to marry. Actually, their parents breathed a sigh of relief.

Graciela and Leopold dreamed of having a house full of children. And, a houseful they had! First came Onofre, the most peaceful of the children. He was followed by Hector—a sickly baby who blossomed into a strong, healthy child. Santana came next, a gentle baby who smiled and never seemed to cry, then Fidel, faithful and loyal to his brothers. By the time Fortuno arrived, Leopold had started the Leopold Bus Line and had great plans to become wealthy. He envisioned a fleet of buses, all driven by the sons. Graciela, a little chicken of a woman, was becoming tired and their next baby was named Ultimo. But a picnic in the woods soon produced Silvio. Noble Basilio, and finally, Lucero, joined the brood. That was when Graciela banished Leopold from their marriage bed and said, "¡No más!" Even after bearing Leopold nine sons, she still caused him to have lustful thoughts. He respected her wishes, though, and tried to leave her alone.

He often joked that he was building his own fútbol team, that it was a good thing that he had the bus so he could take everyone to church. The Leopold Bus Line was a great source of pride for Leopold, almost as much as his family.

While many men shined their shoes every night when they came home from work, Leopold tended to his bus. Just as other men daubed on polish and buffed their shoes to remove the soil and wear of the day, Leopold swept out the bus, brushed the seats free of crumbs and litter, polished the hand rail, oiled the hinges on the door, checked that the air freshener that hung from the dashboard was fresh. He often found things that the passengers had forgotten, even had discarded, on the bus. If the items were in good shape or possibly beneficial to his large family, he presented them to Graciela, who in turn distributed them to the boys or found some use for them in their house. Jackets, shawls, an occasional toy truck, even an occasional chicken found their way home with him. It was rare that he

75

found money or anything else of great value; those things were vigilantly attended to in the small, humble community. Yet, one day he would find a necklace of la Virgen de Guadalupe.

Despite the enforced abstinence, Graciela and Leopold were still very affectionate with one another. Leopold would grab her from behind while she was cooking and dance her around the small kitchen, and often out the door into the yard. Graciela feigned annoyance but inside it charmed her that he was so light-hearted. When they danced it was often the only time they had to talk and discuss the events of the day.

Leopold and Graciela watched their numerous sons grow and become men. A few moved away when they married, a few went to la Universidad in a neighboring town and became respected members of the community after they returned with degrees in law and medicine and commerce. And, yet, there was Silvio.

Silvio was not quite a golden child for he ever hovered on the brink of being blessed and being damned. He drifted along, not seeming to have a care or a goal. It was enough for him to enjoy life. Over and over, Leopold advised him to find a trade and become a productive member of their family and of the town. Leopold always cleaned up after his son, fixed the messes he got himself into. Whether it was when appeasing Graciela after Silvio pretended he was a bullfighter with the clean laundry from the line in the back yard, or repairing a broken window shattered from an overly enthusiastically kicked balón de fútbol, or as now, juggling the dilemma of two girls with babies on the way, Leopold accepted that Silvio would always present him with problems.

On an evening when the sun seemed hesitant to say good-night, when the sky glowed amethyst, and the moon capered behind the trees, too shy to rise wholly in the night sky, Leopold danced Graciela out the kitchen door into the yard. With great solemnity of purpose and with more than his usual courtly manners, Leopold waltzed with Graciela. He wrapped his arms around his bride of 27 years, hummed an anonymous melody, and gazed into her eyes. He took in the lines that had begun to spread from the corners of her eyes, saw the strands of silver that seemed to have appeared overnight in her once black black hair, and he felt his heart swell with his old love for her. It hurt him to say what he knew he must.

"Graciela, mi corazón, we have a problem with Silvio."

She sighed and nodded.

"There is a young girl," Leopold said as they traversed the yard.

"Sí, and Silvio married her. He and Rosalba await the birth of their child."

"Claro, surely, sí, but it is not just Rosalba now that we must be concerned with. This one is a school girl, the daughter of Clemente."

Graciela barely knew who Clemente was, other than the thin man of few words who tended to the church and school. She remembered he had lost his wife when their child was born. Other than that, she could not even picture the girl.

"¡Cielos! Heavens! Another niño. What is wrong with him?" Graciela sighed; it seemed her heart would explode from her chest. She sighed for the baby, she sighed for Clemente, and she sighed for the young girl.

"So, what do we do with this one, Leopold? She cannot come to live here. We cannot take the baby in as our own. You and I are too old for a baby. Everyone would know I did not have another."

Leopold tightened his hold on her waist and stepped forward with his left foot. As he moved around his wife, she pivoted to remain in front of him. They moved easily and almost without thought, even without music.

"We need someone who will take the child and raise it as her own," he said. "And, we will tell no one."

"¡Por supuesto, Leopold! Of course! But who would that be? Let me think on this."

Leopold nodded. "Do not think too long; this baby will be here before the other."

Graciela knew it would be pointless to speak with Silvio about this matter. Beyond learning he had another child on the way, she knew he was in no position to solve the predicament. His wife, Rosalba, was a buxom and raucous girl from Matamoros but with a sweet smile like dulce de leche. Graciela never saw her that Rosalba was not complaining about her swollen feet, her sparse maternity wardrobe, or some other woe connected to the pregnancy. Graciela suspected she would be pressed into service as a nanny for the baby so Rosalba could visit with her friends and take long naps. She did not have much sympathy, if any, for Silvio. He got himself into this added problema and there was not much she or Leopold could do now. And, she had a bad feeling that there would ever be other problems such as this.

On Sunday, waiting in line to give her confession, she heard the soft melodic murmurs of a woman ahead of her in the confessional, punctuated by the deep bass notes of the voice of Padre Mateo. The thin curtain did little to afford privacy and she tried not to eavesdrop, covering her ear with her hand. She smiled and nodded to the other men and women, mostly women, ahead and behind her. Buenos días. Buenos días.

Finally, the curtain was pulled back and out stumped Lotus García.

Lotus looked serene as she moved away with her awkward steps. She nodded to Graciela and went on her way. ONE thump.

What a strange woman she is, Graciela thought. Always keeps to herself, no family to take care of her any more, barely getting by. And that foot— qué lástima. What a shame. Yet, she always seems content and at ease with her lot. What could she possibly have to confess?

Graciela had heard the rumors that Lotus García was a curandera, what with her herbs and waters. Yet, she also was purported to employ holy water and saint pictures. Not one of the women who turned to Lotus would talk openly about it so no one knew for sure but she did indeed have a special way with los niños, ones who could not be fed, could not sleep, or could not grow. Graciela knew many of the women of the town took their babies to her for help, when all else seemed to fail. They always came away smiling with peaceful babies in their arms. It was not wise to call someone a curandera; the church frowned upon such things. So, Graciela thought, perhaps Lotus was just someone with the ability to know what a baby needed.

Why not?

Graciela returned home to Leopold and told him she wanted to dance that night when all of their chores were done. As they twirled around the moonlit yard, kicking up little puffs of dust with their shoes, Leopold asked, "What is troubling you?"

"Why not La Extraña, Lotus, the Strange One? Why not give the baby to someone who never had one of her own, but so obviously has an enormous and good heart?"

It did not take much for Graciela to convince Leopold. Yes, Lotus García would be their answer.

Graciela wanted to put aside little things for this other baby, but Leopold convinced her that it would be safer not to do so. They might be traced back to them and then to Verdad, and then everyone would know their story.

One day, only weeks after their initial conversation about Silvio and Verdad and the new baby, Ifiginia rode the bus to the end of the line. She sat behind Leopold and when he looked at her in the mirror, he recognized her as the friend of Verdad. He thought he knew why she was there. Like the other time with Verdad, she waited until all of his passengers had taken their bundles, their clucking roosters, their baskets of fruits and vegetables, and disembarked from the bus. When the bus was empty and they were headed back into town, the girl said, "Señor, may I speak with you?"

Leopold pulled the bus over and turned in his seat.

"I know why you are here, chiquita. Was it a boy or a girl? How did Verdad fare?"

She told him about the baby boy and explained that Verdad was waiting in the clinic.

"Ah, a grandson." He paused and for a long moment, stared at nothing. "Pues, well, tell her to be ready in the morning. She will get on the bus with the baby and go to market. It will happen then."

Ifiginia returned to Verdad and told her what Leopold had said. Verdad nodded. It must be done.

After a wakeful night where the infant squalled restlessly and Verdad shed silent tears, she arose before dawn to bathe him. She had only the diapers provided by the clinic, a thin cotton t-shirt to cover his body, and her old shawl. She wrapped the infant in the shawl and kissed his tiny head. She removed the necklace blessed by Padre Mateo and tucked it inside the shawl. It was all she could give him. She thanked the nurses and the doctor and scurried from the clinic to await the Leopold Bus Line.

That night, when she had returned to the house of Ifiginia and when Leopold returned to his own home, Leopold walked through the bus, sweeping out debris, checking for lost and forgotten items, and came to the back seat where Verdad and el nieto, his grandson, had sat. He sat in the corner, in the exact same spot. This time the birth of a child was not a thing to celebrate; it was not a time for joy. His heart beat heavily and sadly in his chest. As he rose to exit the bus and join Graciela for their evening meal, he saw something shining on the floor under the seat in front of him. With a great deal of effort, for at the end of this long day Leopold was more tired than usual, he bent down and retrieved it. He saw the gold chain and the gold locket with the image of Nuestra Señora de Guadalupe. He turned it over, saw the letter "V" inscribed on the back, and realized at once it belonged to Verdad. He slipped it into the pocket of his pants.

PADRE MATEO Y LA SIRENA

Before Padre Mateo became a priest, he lived a less than sacred life. That life begins to explain the tattoo of la sirena, a mermaid, on his forearm. There were often murmurs among the many people of the parish who believed the tattoo was a desecration of his body, a slap in the face of God for the priest, a holy man, to have a mythological being permanently inked on his skin. Some said that he should keep the tattoo covered with long sleeves. Some even went so far as to suggest that he get another tattoo over that one, one of la Virgen María that would disguise this heathen portrayal of an imaginary woman. Why not the Queen of Mexico, Nuestra Señora de Guadalupe?

Padre Mateo demurred, and when pressed by the people of the pueblo who suggested it was a travesty to carry the emblem of a sea creature, a fairy tale at that, merely said, "She is there to remind me."

Padre Mateo came to the pueblo via los Estados Unidos. Though born in Mexico, his family moved north when he was very young. Upon entering the priesthood, he returned to Mexico to be of service to his people.

No one knew much about his life in the north other than the whispered rumors that he had been married before he received his calling. The women of the pueblo, girls, women, and grandmothers alike, often found themselves staring at the handsome, yet deferential man who looked like a movie star. Attendance at Mass increased steadily, especially among the female parishioners. Going to Confession became a double-edged sword—to confess their sins before God through the ears of this handsome holy man was undoubtedly a trial for many.

Padre Mateo worked with the people of Esperanza to improve their lives. He brought practical knowledge of how to raise stronger and healthier crops, of how to increase their herds, and how to live in harmony. Literacy and employment were principles he strongly believed in, and he urged schooling for all, no matter their age or station in the village. He also worked with the people to temper the many Indian customs that they clung to, especially the ones revolving around health care and medicine. For centuries, many Catholic patriarchs had tried and many, if not all, had failed to get them to surrender their so-called pagan ideas entirely. Padre Mateo was a wise man and understanding of their needs. He truly respected their customs and beliefs and did not want them to renounce them. He knew that for many, these ancient values helped to soften and even resolve the harsh lessons of daily life. He simply wanted them to see there might be other ways than only the ancient ones.

So, what was the story of Padre Mateo? What was the story of the mermaid? Before becoming a priest, Mateo Morales had lived with Mirah, and their daughter Marisol in east Los Angeles, California. He had moved to the United States with his family when he was only six to escape the hardships and poverty and violence of their home in Mexico. He went to college and majored in Chicano Studies at UCLA, with the goal of teaching in the barrios. Rather than escape violence and poverty, he planted himself firmly in it.

He met Mirah at UCLA in the Chicana and Chicano Public Interest Law course. They studied together, frequently meeting at the Darling Law Library. It was not long before they became lovers. And, it was not long before Mirah became pregnant. Each day as he saw her waist thickening, her breasts growing heavier, and the shine in her eyes, Mateo Morales wanted to marry her, to give the baby his name and to make everything easier for the child but Mirah wanted to wait. She wanted to be sure he was marrying her for love, for forever, and not just for some outdated notion of honor, she said. He did and said everything he could think of to convince Mirah but still she refused. Mirah was so very serious and tense.

Mateo had chosen the name of their baby. Marisol meant sea and sun. He wanted her to always know happiness and light. He was a good father and he tried to spend as much time with her as he could.

From the time she was four years old, Mateo took Marisol on the Metro Line to MacArthur Park. He wanted her to learn how to fish, not to be afraid of the water. He had never learned to swim and going into any water, other than a bath tub, was unnerving. He would slowly venture out until the water was up to his knees and then his legs would refuse to go further. The idea of not being able to see what was in the water with him, not knowing what might be swimming around his body was his greatest dread. He did not want Marisol to have the same ridiculous fears.

Marisol loved to feed the ducks and they spent long hours watching the fishers catch trout. One day, Marisol began to cry when she asked her father what happened to the fish that people caught. Mateo gently told her why the fish were there, so people could catch them and take them home to eat for dinner. He tried to explain to her that everything was connected, that everyone and everything had a purpose and that was the purpose of the fish.

Marisol would have nothing to do with it. She wailed and thrashed at Mateo. The people around them at first laughed at her anguish, nodding and smiling with understanding, but after many long minutes went by and still she wailed, Mateo saw their smiles turn to frowns. He heard a few people say she was scaring away the fish and he knew they were becoming angry.

In desperation, he gathered her up and ran to the boathouse and rented a paddleboat. He thrust his money at the kid in charge and got Marisol safely into a little boat.

"Come, Marisol, let us see if we can find a mermaid." And they set off from the shore. Mateo sat in the center so he could pedal on both sides. Marisol buried her head in his side and sniffled. The novelty of the little aqua-colored boat and the feeling of gliding across the lake began to calm Marisol, and soon she was only making an occasional hiccupping sound. Mateo wiped her snotty face. A fish flew from the water and made a small splash as it reentered.

"Look, Marisol! Look! It is a mermaid. Right over there --do you see her?" Mateo pointed to where it had been and Marisol, seeming to forget the other fish, looked. There were only ripples in the water.

"I did not see it, Papa. I want to see a mermaid," she pleaded. Mateo gulped when he realized how deep the water was where he pedaled the little boat but, he kept on. Another splash and a flash of a tail. This time, Marisol saw it.

Her delight in the mermaid carried all the way home. When she told her mother that Papa had found a place where the mermaids lived, Mirah fussed at Mateo for filling her head with such lies. Mirah was a practical woman. While she could not deny her origins, she tried to distance herself, and Marisol, from superstitions and fancies of the old ways. Sometimes her pragmatism frustrated Mateo.

"What is the harm," was his reply. "Our children today do not have enough make-believe. Too often, they see first-hand only the hardships of life. Let her have fun with this."

From that day on, Marisol would not go to bed without a story about a mermaid, whether from one of the books Mateo found at the second hand book store, or one he made up. Marisol knew that mermaids simply and surely must exist. Her favorite story was the one his abuelita, grandmother, told him when he was small. Marisol loved to hear it as Mateo brushed her hair each night.

"There is a mountain in Mexico called Nevado de Toluca. Toluca is where my abuelita is from. The mountain always wears a mantle of snow. It was once a volcano. There is a lake at the top in the crater of the volcano. The water there is very, very cold. A beautiful young girl climbed to the top of the volcano with her father one day. He wanted to take some snow back to his village. The girl waited patiently for him to collect the snow but soon became bored and decided to go for a swim. She splashed and swam, and then tilted her head back and began to wash her long hair, hair that was much like yours. But, something began to pull her down into the murky lake. She disappeared under the water.

"Her father hunted for her but never found her. He sat down at the edge of the lake and began to cry. He heard her voice saying, 'I am safe, Papi, but I cannot return to you. I have become a mermaid. I am half human and half fish. I will live in this lake forever.' And he never saw her again."

"But you would find me, right, Papa, if I turned into a mermaid?" Marisol always asked.

And, Mateo always said, "Claro, Marisol, claro. Of course. I would search for you until I found you."

Mirah would not engage in their fantasies.

Mirah came from a family of superstitious old women and she was determined that Marisol would grow up differently.

94

Mirah was afraid of so many things and she blamed her childhood. She grew up hearing about the Evil Eye, mal de ojo. Her mother and aunts believed that a child who became ill with a fever or nausea or just about anything was cursed with mal de ojo. They insisted Mirah wear a red bracelet, just as they all did, to protect against it. When Marisol was born, instead of diapers and dresses, Marisol received enough red bracelets to last a lifetime. Mirah threw them all away. She knew the Evil Eye was a belief bound up with jealousy. Yet she lived with the irrational belief all of her life; her mother told her that her very name meant "look". The women in her family would never walk beneath a ladder, never cross the path of a black cat, never start a journey or anything of import on the day of bad luck, Tuesday. They were aghast that Mirah cut the fingernails of the baby before her first birthday; they insisted that because of that she would need glasses. And, if they dropped a tortilla, they announced that they were going to have a lot of company, and would hurry to la cocina to clap out more.

Living with one foot in the Mexican culture and one foot in the American culture, Mirah always strived not to stand out in either and she wanted her daughter to live the same life. So when Marisol begged for a story about la sirena, Mirah always corrected her. "The word is mermaid and mermaids are not real."

Mateo sighed in frustration when he heard her comments.

"And neither is Santa Claus or the Tooth Fairy but every other child in Los Angeles, in the entire United States, believes in them. You have already taken those away from her. What more?"

Mateo signed up Marisol for swimming lessons at the local YMCA. He was hesitant to tell Mirah but when he needed to buy a bathing suit for his daughter, he had to ask her for help.

"Why should we waste money on these lessons?" Mirah asked. "When will she ever need to know how to swim? We live in the center of the second biggest city in the United States. It is not like we live in Florida or something." But she took Marisol shopping and bought her a modest ruffled, one-piece suit. Tears formed in his eyes when he saw the skinny legs and arms of his little daughter, as if for the first time.

The day of the first lesson, Mateo and Marisol waited with the other children and parents in the bleachers by the cloudy pool at the Y. Mateo was not sure who was more nervous, he or Marisol. Twice already, she had run back to the locker room to go to the bathroom.

Every week, the young female instructor took roll. When she called out "Morales", both Marisol and Mateo lined up on the edge of the shallow end of the pool. The instructor never seemed to notice. Mateo heard several of the parents snicker but he stood proudly. He too was going to learn to swim. When the instructor blew the whistle, all of the children and Mateo jumped into the pool. They blew bubbles in the water. They learned to float on their backs, then on their stomachs. They learned to move their arms and kick their legs. Marisol won a prize when she sat on the bottom of the pool long enough to hear the song the instructor sang under the water. Marisol bobbed to the surface and shouted, "¡Feliz Navidad!" Not even Mateo was brave enough to do that.

At home, Marisol spent hours in the bathtub. She insisted that Mateo time how long she could hold her breath.

"See, you are already becoming a mermaid!" Mateo would tell her. If Mirah heard him say that, she insisted that Marisol get out of the tub.

One day, early in the morning after Mirah had taken Marisol to school, Mateo took all of the furniture and toys out of her tiny room. It did not take long; it was really no bigger than a closet with room enough for a bed and a small dresser. He painted the walls a beautiful aqua color, almost a deep blue, called Ocean Soul. He painted the ceiling a lighter aqua, Mermaid Song, and pressed starfish he cut out of grocery bags into the wet paint.

When Marisol returned from school, she shrieked with pleasure. "Mommy, come look! Now I AM a real mermaid. I live under the water!"

Mirah said nothing and turned away.

In the days that followed, Mateo felt Mirah pulling away from him; Mirah became stingy with her affections toward him but lavished more and more attention on Marisol. She insisted on taking over nearly every facet of the care of their child, pushing Mateo out of the picture in inches and feet. He felt the distance between them grow into miles. He knew there was something else behind her dread of superstitions but it was all he could latch onto. She no longer allowed him to take Marisol on their outings, the swimming lessons ceased, and he spent more and more time alone.

One afternoon, Mateo returned to their apartment in East Los Angeles, the City of Angels, to find Marisol and Mirah were gone. Every trace of their existence had vanished. A stack of mermaid books sat on the floor in the under-the-sea room. Atop was a note that simply read, "You will not find us. I am sorry." He called her mother, her aunts, her cousins, but they all hung up on him. He frantically went to each of their houses, but no one would open their doors to him.

Mateo spent days, then weeks, then months searching for Mirah and his daughter. He haunted MacArthur Park, hoping that some miracle would bring Marisol there to feed the ducks and quest for mermaids. They had disappeared. The loss of his child and of his life with Mirah was more than he could bear. One morning, after a night of sleeplessness and torment, he stumbled into a tattoo parlor and had a chaste but ornate mermaid inked onto his forearm. He barely felt the pain as the needles drove repeatedly into his skin. In his anguish, it was no worse to him than a thousand cat scratches.

He could not continue to live in the place of constant reminders. He took the vows of poverty, chastity and obedience, and entered the Seminary. He spent the required time studying and praying, searching his heart, and learning the will of God. When he was ordained, the Morales family was proud to have a shepherd of souls in their midst, though they knew what it had cost him to reach this holy place in his life. And, he never stopped looking for Marisol.

Mateo returned to the land of his birth and became the second priest in a small village where the current priest was failing rapidly. The people of Esperanza were a bit skeptical of a new, younger priest. They were also wary of someone coming from the Los Estados Unidos, changing their pueblo and more importantly, their beloved church, with modern ideas. They liked the way things were and did not want change.

The eyesight of the old priest was nearly gone and he was becoming forgetful. When he lost his place in the homily, Padre Mateo politely stepped in. It did not take long before everyone seemed to welcome the handsome young priest who looked like a movie star. He gently took over more and more responsibilities, first with house calls to the elderly and the homebound, administering the rites of baptisms and communion, then last rites and confession. Within a few months, the elderly priest was no more; he graciously died in his sleep and Padre Mateo had his own parish, La Iglesia de la Santa Cruz.

CARLOS VARELA

One of the more colorful members of the parish was the father of Ifiginia, Carlos Varela. Carlos was a narcotraficante, a drug lord. Plain and simple. And, everyone over the age of 12 in Esperanza knew it.

Except Ifiginia. She stubbornly believed her father, the man who always wore snakeskin boots, was a respectable business man with many interests in Esperanza and Matamoros. It helped her to accept his long absences from home, followed by his longer stays in Esperanza. They lived in a big house on top of a hill overlooking the pueblo, one with a pool and a guest house, all surrounded by an electric fence. When he was at home in Esperanza, working at a large, ornately carved desk in his cool shaded office, his business partners came and went, some staying for several nights in the guest house.

Carlos chose to live in unpretentious Esperanza for his family. He knew he could not put a price on the safety their seclusion offered and he treasured his family over everything. In Esperanza, he avoided the violent turf battles over control of the smuggling corridors, and never would he have las drogas or illegal guns in his possession. Carlos had a modest entourage of attendants. He called them his aides; yet, the people of Esperanza recognized them for what they were—enforcers, sicarios.

He chose to eschew the seedier side of the drug trafficking world and maintained his kingdom from a distance. For him, the movement of cocaine and marijuana, and occasionally, firearms, was a business. Nothing more, nothing less.

Ifiginia and her brothers knew to stay out of his office and away from the men who came and went. While Carlos Varela was a very important man, not to be disturbed, he loved his family and went out of his way to involve himself in their lives. He often abruptly cleared an entire day of appointments so he could take Ifiginia and her mother shopping. Or, to take his twin sons fishing and camping.

Carlos took his family to La Iglesia de la Santa Cruz each and every Sunday; he received the Sacrament of Penance, though no one but the old priest, and later Padre Mateo, and Carlos knew what he confessed. He made large charitable contributions to the church and the school, usually anonymously. Sometimes after a visit from Carlos, Padre Mateo found a thick envelope on the kneeler. Other times, a mere mention of needed repairs for the church brought trucks filled with building materials.

The stone church with the twin towers was the center of Esperanza and Carlos was especially proud of the old structure. This pride was recognized by his family and by the other members of the community. It was told that very many generations ago the men in the Varela family helped to construct the church. When Carlos headed the renovation campaign of the centuries old church, parts of it dating back, many believed, to the 1700s, everyone in Esperanza dug deep and donated everything they could, whether in money or in labor. Padre Mateo brought one of his American ideas to them and had some of the students draw a huge thermometer to hang in the church hall. They marked off goals in bold black letters on either side of the huge poster, and as the contributions arrived for the church renovations, the students used bright red markers to fill the thermometer. Carlos monitored the progress of the contributions and often, after a visit to the church hall, when the money was barely trickling in, there would be a significant increase on the thermometer.

Padre Mateo never discussed his generosity with anyone but, he did introduce him as, "Nuestro amigo. Tiene un corazón de oro. Our friend. He has a heart of gold." Carlos liked that.

IFIGINIAY VERDAD

It was Ifiginia who urged Verdad to go to Confession. After the birth of the baby, Verdad had slipped into a silence that worried her friend. Verdad seemed to sleepwalk through her own life. She had lost her desire to go do things with Ifiginia, no longer scanned the movie star magazines at la farmacia, nor did she care to sing along with the tejano cds Ifiginia played non-stop. She continued to wear baggy clothes and did not seem to have any interest in her appearance. All of these things made Ifiginia sad. Ifiginia was not a good student and at times, seemed not to be very bright, but she knew Verdad was terribly depressed.

"Verdad, you MUST talk with Padre Mateo. You must reconcile yourself with God. You will finally be at peace with this whole thing. When you confess into the ear of Padre Mateo, it will ease your soul."

Verdad resisted but only weakly. She knew it was the right thing to do but she dreaded doing it. She continued to attend church but her heart was not in any of the rituals. She had borrowed one of the handkerchiefs from the dresser of her father to wear on her head in place of her shawl. She felt ridiculous doing so but had no choice; her head had to be covered in church.

When Ifiginia next went to Confession, after her litany of sins and the words of absolution from Padre Mateo, she grabbed Verdad and shoved her into the confessional after her. Verdad was so startled that as she kneeled she began to speak.

"In the name of the Father, and of the Son, and of the

Holy Spirit. My last confession was eight months ago." And she stopped. Padre Mateo waited patiently. Nothing further came from the girl.

"Go on."

"I cannot. I have done something so terrible, so wrong, that I cannot even say it out loud."

"You are safe here. God wants to help you."

Verdad tried to stifle the sounds of her weeping. She sniffed and began again.

"In the name of the Father, and of the Son, and of the Holy Spirit. My last confession was eight months ago." She sniffed. "I cannot."

"Do you love God with your whole heart, with your whole soul, with all your strength, and with all your mind?" he asked.

"Yes, I do."

"Then you must do this, no matter how heavy your burden."

"Sí, Padre." She paused, took a deep breath, and spoke. "I was guilty of immodest acts."

"More than once?"

"No."

"What else do you wish to confess?"

Again, Padre Mateo was greeted with silence. He had heard just about every possible sin, real or imagined, over the years. Never had he encountered someone so reluctant, so unable to confess.

"It is obvious that this act that you cannot speak about is causing you great pain. You must go home and pray for guidance. God is always listening and He will answer your prayers. Say three Hail Marys. Give thanks to the Lord for He is good." He made the sign of the cross.

As Verdad, too, made the sign of the cross, she muttered, "For His mercy endures forever."

She scurried from the confessional and out of the cool church into the hot sun.

Ifiginia chased after her friend.

"Verdad, wait, wait!"

Verdad ran on and into her casita, the handkerchief sailing off of her head and into the dust. She slammed the door and Ifiginia was left outside. Ifiginia retrieved the handkerchief, left it at the door of the casita, and turned back to the church.

CLEMENTE PACHECO

The father of Verdad, Clemente, was worried about his daughter, as well. He had no idea what had happened to his cheerful and hard-working girl; she had become a stranger to him. She spent hours in her room, supposedly studying, but when Clemente peeked through the door, he saw her crying or staring out the window.

One morning, when she was moving about the kitchen and making his breakfast, he saw that her necklace with La Virgen de Guadalupe from the Quinceañera was not hanging around her neck.

111

"M'hija, daughter, where is el collar, your necklace? The one Ifiginia gave you."

Verdad had anticipated that he would notice it was missing and had prepared an answer.

"The clasp on it broke and I lost it, Papi. I am very sad but perhaps I am not ready to take care of such a fine thing." She turned back to his breakfast and he thought he heard her sniffle.

Clemente shook his head. Something was very wrong.

That same day, he approached Padre Mateo and asked his advice.

"My daughter is not happy. She never smiles, never sings any more, never visits with her friends. I have asked her if she is sick and she says she is not. I have wondered if it is something at school, if she is having trouble with her studies. Could you please ask las monjas, the nuns, and see if you can find out what is going on with her? I know los adolescentes have crazy moods, las etapas locas, especially the niñas, but this is beyond anything I have ever heard of."

Padre Mateo clasped Clemente by the shoulder. "I will see what I can find out."

PADRE MATEO Y VERDAD

Padre Mateo was very careful in how he made inquiries about Verdad to las monjas. He knew if he dug too deeply, it would arouse their suspicions. And, he already had his own ideas about the girl.

He went to her classroom and as he walked around, he looked at the art work and papers hanging on the wall, pretending to admire the work of everyone. He noted the neat handwriting of Verdad. He started out by discreetly asking la monja about several of the girls, ending with Verdad. He discovered that her grades were what they always were, her assignments done promptly and with great care, but that she rarely volunteered answers in class. She sat mutely at her desk and if las monjas, the nuns, called on her, she simply shook her head and would not answer. It was as if she could not trust her own voice. She often appeared to be close to tears.

The nuns had seen girls act like this before. They knew about the dramatic, complicated world of teenagers and supposed that Verdad was suffering from amor adoloscente. This would pass, they told Padre Mateo. `

He told the teacher that he needed someone to update the donations on the thermometer in the church hall; he asked if Verdad could be excused for a few minutes to do so.

Verdad followed Padre Mateo in silence. She feared there was more to this than just filling in some red ink on a picture. It took all of her resolve not to flee the school and run home. She saw the front door and judged how far it was from them. It would not work. He could catch up to her if he wanted.

Padre Mateo chatted with Verdad as she counted the lines on the thermometer that needed to be filled in. She uncapped a red marker and began to carefully outline the area. Padre Mateo stood nearby, seeming to supervise her work.

"Verdad, I know you need to talk to someone and I wish you would trust me enough to tell me what is troubling you. I am no stranger to personal problems. I have had many in my life. I think most people believe that because the days of a priest are filled with serving God and ministering to the people that they have no problems of their own."

Verdad concentrated on the poster. She did not dare respond. She filled in the lines on the thermometer with more care than she had done in a long time. He continued.

"No one here knows this about me, Verdad. May I tell you something that is very private? Will you keep it confidential?"

She turned to look at him. Her eyes were wide with

surprise. Why would he want to tell her anything? She dipped her head in agreement.

"When I lived in Los Estados Unidos, before I became a priest, I fell in love. I lived with the woman I loved and we made a child. I asked this woman to marry me but she refused.

"We had a beautiful daughter. Her name was Marisol. I gave her the most wonderful name I could, for I was filled with so much love for her.

"One day when I came home, Marisol and her mother were gone. They had moved out and I never saw them again. It nearly ruined me. I looked for my daughter everywhere but I never found her."

There was a long pause. Verdad was afraid to look at him. She wanted him to continue speaking but she also did not want to hear the end of the story. He cleared his throat. "Fortunately, before I did anything stupid, I entered the Seminary. I gave myself over to God and He helped me learn to live with the pain of my loss. I learned how to use it for good.

"I think about Marisol often; she would be about as old as you are now. I imagine you look like her, perhaps more than just a little bit. I can only hope that she is happy and safe. That is the best a parent can do for a child, sometimes."

Tears slid down her cheeks. She cried in silence with a heart full of sorrow for the child of Padre Mateo, for his loss, his broken heart. She cried in silence for her mistake and for her child.

Padre Mateo offered her his handkerchief. He was only too acquainted with her kind of pain and he wanted to embrace the girl and comfort her but at the same time, knew he should not.

"How did you know, Padre? How did you know about my baby?"

"Ah, you would be surprised what I see and what I know. Just because I am a priest does not mean I do not see the body of a young girl changing. I suspected something like this a while back.

"Besides, how else would doña Lotus get a baby?" He chuckled to himself as he thought of La Extraña and the tiny boy she so obviously adored.

"We have both lost a child. But, unlike me, you will be able to watch your child grow and not have him disappear forever. You should thank God for that blessing. And, you have given doña Lotus a great gift."

It took several moments for Verdad to compose herself but finally, she cleared her throat.

"I was very foolish and have been paying the price. I have been thinking only of what I have lost. I could not see any good coming from my mistakes."

Padre Mateo looked at this tender girl and saw a maturity that many women never achieve. Along with the maturity, he saw a sorrow she would carry with her the rest of her life already etched in her face.

"Pues, go to el baño and wash your face. No, I do not want that handkerchief back now! Wash it and wear it this

Sunday. By the way, what happened to your manton? I see you do not use it to cover your hair in church."

"I wrapped the baby in it when I . . ." Her voice trembled and Padre Mateo and she both were afraid she would begin to cry again.

"Claro. Of course. Back to class before they send out a search party."

Segundo thrived in the care of Lotus. He began to walk and he chattered nearly non-stop as he paraded through the market every week with his mother as they made their weekly purchases. His hair was thick and curly and Lotus did not often trim it. He looked like a little seraph, an angel of the highest order. Some said the child fell from the sky. He seemed to have an inextinguishable light and intelligence emanating from him, and it spread to anyone who happened upon him. Even the most cheerless viejo, old person, of Esperanza could not help but smile when he was around.

120

Verdad never got too close to Lotus or to Segundo. She could not risk revealing the fundamental part she played in their pairing. She sometimes had to physically hold onto something when she saw them; she ached to touch him and to talk to him. When her longing became almost too much to bear, Padre Mateo would find her on her knees in the chapel, surrounded by the carved santos. He understood, all too well.

One day, after she had finished praying, he approached her.

"Here, m'hija, I found this in the road. Someone must have dropped it."

He handed her a nearly new manton, snowy white and crisp, with lavender flowers embroidered on the hem. It had a large footprint on it.

"You will have to wash it."

She thanked him. It was one she had admired in the market just last weekend.

"Verdad, what are you going to do after you graduate?"

"I would like to go to la Universidad but as you know, we do not have the money. And, that would mean leaving Esperanza. That would be muy difícil , very hard," she said.

"Comprendo. I understand. What would you like to study, if you could leave and go to a university? If money were no barrier?"

"I have often thought of becoming a teacher, or perhaps of owning a book store. I love books. When I feel I have nothing else, I know I can always turn to a book. They give me great solace. Reading is such a gift and everyone should to be able to enjoy it."

"Claro. Of course. I think that it is very sad that so many of our neighbors do not know how to read. They do not know what they are missing. Or, if they do, they do not know how to go about changing. I believe that everyone should reach their full potential and, when you can read, you can do anything."

Verdad nodded enthusiastically. Many times she had thought long and hard about what she had to say next. She took a deep breath.

"Padre, I know you wish for the people of Esperanza to all become educated. I also know that you cannot achieve this by yourself. We could expand the library, make it a real one, not just a corner of the school with dusty old books. The books we have now can teach nothing. We need new books, books with real facts. We need a way for the people to feel safe and not feel as if they are being judged. They can learn to read there. And, the little ones need to learn how wonderful books can be." She exhaled.

Padre Mateo remembered the wonderful times he had spent with his daughter, the two squeezed into one chair, or onto her little bed, looking at pictures and picking out words. He remembered her wonder when she recognized a word or sounded out a new one. It was something he had treasured. He looked away from Verdad. He did not want her to see his eyes.

Verdad hesitated. The next would be a very daring thing for her to say.

"Perhaps we could take some of the money raised for the renovation and use it for this. I want to be involved. I can learn to run a library."

Padre Mateo tried not to smile at her eagerness. He had cast his line.

"But, it would mean you have to study about libraries—cataloging, preservation, literacy, and anything else like that. You cannot do that in Esperanza. You would have to go away, at least for a while until your studies were completed." Now he would reel her in. "You could enroll at the University of Texas at Brownsville, where you can get your degree in just a few years, depending on how fast you complete the studies. You could always return and I would ask you to run our library.

"It is a lot to think about, Verdad. I wonder if you really want to leave Esperanza, even if it is only for a short time to study. Maybe I should seek someone else."

The air was redolent with incense and candle wax. The moment seemed other worldly to the girl.

"How would I pay for it? And my English is not the best. We have some practice in our classes but English is not emphasized."

He stared up at the ceiling and seemed to think for a moment. "I could practice speaking English with you. You are smart and I know you will pick it up quickly. I truly wish I could convince las monjas that our students of today need to be bilingual.

"And, I think don Carlos would be delighted to help you. After all, you are the best friend of his daughter. He is always looking for things to do for the church."

"And, ¡tiene un corazón de oro!" They both laughed.

"But what about Papi? I am afraid he will not want me to go. And, he is such a proud man. How could we convince him to accept help from don Carlos?"

"I will talk to him. Your father is a reasonable man."

They exited the pew and genuflected in the aisle before turning to leave the church. Padre Mateo saw her huge smile and the bright spark in her eyes again. He knew he had found the answer to several problemas.

CARLOS Y VERDAD

Don Carlos was elated to be able to help Verdad. He had seen her sorrow and asked Ifiginia if there were something they could do to help her and her father, thinking it was the strain of their finances. He had tried on several occasions to help don Clemente with his obligations but don Clemente always politely refused. Over the years, Carlos took Verdad shopping with Ifiginia and his wife as frequently as he thought he could get away with it and made sure she returned home with at least the necessities a young girl needed, if not an occasional extravagance. He viewed Verdad as more than the friend of his daughter; he felt a true affection for her. He knew, too, that his daughter was unlikely to continue her studies after high school. Homework and class room exercises bored her. The only subject she excelled in was English. Ifiginia had no plans for beyond high school; she talked only of her father bringing home a rich husband for her, building a fancy casa, and living as her mother did. She had subscribed to <u>Architectural Digest Mexico</u> since she was 13. Carlos was only too glad to know that Verdad would go to college.

When it was time, he took Verdad and Ifiginia to Brownsville and set up a bank account for Verdad. He explained that he would be in charge of depositing funds to pay for classes, books, food, and even a little extra so she could have fun. They enrolled her in the necessary courses at the college, as Verdad reminded him that it should be called. She would bring him her report card every semester and show him her progress. If she was doing well, he would pay for the next semester, and continue to do so until she had her degree.

Carlos also wisely sidestepped the issue of the pride of her father, Clemente. He let Padre Mateo explain their arrangement and if there was any communication necessary, it was through Ifiginia, or his bodyguard, Domingo.

DOMINGO DOS OJOS

Thick-neck, beefy hands with short sausage fingers,
shoulders and thighs so big his clothes had to be custom-tailored,
and with eyes of two colors, Domingo Dos Ojos, Two Eyes, was
the head sicorio, henchman, of Carlos Varela. He was seen
everywhere, patrolling their compound, holding the door for don
Carlos or his wife and children as they got in and out of their big
black car, or picking up Ifiginia at school. If anyone wanted to
get close to don Carlos and his family, they had to deal first with
Domingo.

He and don Carlos had grown up together. Domingo could not read. He struggled daily with las monjas, the nuns, to please them but he just could not get it. The other children made fun of him, not just because he could not read but especially because he had two different colored eyes. One eye was the color of obsidian, the other of amber. Las monjas wanted to send him to Matamoros to have his eyes examined; surely, the amber one could not see and that is why he had trouble reading. The old padre looked into them and saw nothing wrong. He pronounced Domingo perfectly able to learn and read, just like the other children. He was just lazy.

No one took Domingo seriously but Carlos stood by his side. As the other children grew taller, Domingo grew stronger and broader. He was darker-skinned than the other children, which spoke of his mixed blood. When he wanted to drop out of school, Carlos tried to persuade him to hold on, to just wait another year. Carlos helped him with his homework but was of no use when Domingo was called upon in class to read out loud.

On the day he turned 14, Domingo Dos Ojos stood in the

dirt yard of his house and watched his schoolmates walk down the road to la escuela without him. He had suffered enough. He spent the next years, while waiting for Carlos to graduate, doing odd jobs around Esperanza and increasing his muscles. His hair grew long and he pierced his own earlobe. In it, he wore a very flashy diamond with great gusto. And, he invested in a pair of blue blocker aviator sunglasses to hide his eyes. Carlos teased him and called him Top Gun.

When Carlos became involved with selling drugs, Domingo was right there with him. He personally did not care what Carlos did but wanted his friend, his only friend, to be safe. He stood lookout for other drug dealers and la policia while Carlos climbed the ranks. It was a dangerous business, rife with deceit and violence. Domingo took his job seriously and never questioned the need to intimidate someone. Or even more. Everyone took Domingo Dos Ojos seriously.

Domingo viewed the Varela family as his family. He was a force to be reckoned with when he saw someone anger don Carlos, or get too close to any of the Varela family, and the man never seemed to rest. His sunglasses hid just who or what it was he watched but Carlos knew he missed nothing. He often joked that Domingo Dos Ojos watched over them in his sleep. Ifiginia used to tiptoe down the long hall into the room where Domingo slept. She wanted to find out if he really did watch over them in his sleep. She stood by his bed and peered down at the big man. More often than not, she would find him with his eyes closed but also with a smile on his face.

"Hola, niñita," he would whisper.

She would giggle and scamper out of his room. How did Dos, as she called him, know she was there if his eyes were closed?

One day, Carlos came out into the driveway; Domingo was washing one of the big black cars in the Varela fleet. Carlos watched him go over every inch of it with care and pride, as if it were his own.

"Domingo, I have a special job for you. It is something that requires some delicacy. I am confident you can do it."

133

The big man dropped the soapy sponge into the bucket and gave his full attention to Carlos.

"You know Verdad Pacheco, the friend of Ifiginia? I am going to send her to la universidad in Brownsville, Texas. I am sending you along as well."

"No, don Carlos! I cannot go to school. You know that. Please do not do this to me." His face contorted in agony.

Carlos laughed. "It is not what you think. You and she will live in an apartment near the campus, you will get her to and from her classes every day, and bring her home for visits. I do not want her hanging around todos los sinvergüenzas, all of the riff raff, in that town. I have seen where it is and I do not like the idea of her being alone up there. There is a lot of gang violence and drugs. She would not be safe."

"¡Uf! I thought you were trying to make me go back to that tortura! You know I would do anything for you, don Carlos, but I do not think I could have done that!"

"No, no, mi amigo. I know you will watch over her and I

also know you will make sure no harm befalls her. None. From anyone."

Carlos stared intently at Domingo, making sure his meaning was perfectly clear. "It would cause me great pain if anything happened to her, from anyone. And, I would not hesitate to personally cause that person great pain. To me, she is a member of the Varela family. Understood?"

"Por supuesto, certainly."

So, Domingo took Verdad to school. He stood silently while she bought her books, carried them for her to their apartment. He prepared their meals, surprising Verdad with his efficiency in the kitchen. He sat at the back of the classrooms and the lecture halls while she attended classes. No one quite knew what to do with the big man in the sunglasses but no one questioned his presence. When handouts and exams were distributed, the teachers were sure to pass one to Domingo. Some of the students even greeted him in the hallways and treated him like just another one of them.

Verdad knew Domingo was part of the price for her education. She rarely chafed at her shadow in the town that seemed so large and confusing after Esperanza, and actually welcomed his companionship.

She saw how he sometimes picked up a handout or opened one of her books and stared at it for a long time, as if he were trying to study it. She often saw his lips moving. She knew he could not read much; Ifiginia had told her that a long time ago. It was just part of who Domingo was: big, fierce yet kind, and a little estupido. Verdad often discussed her studies with Domingo Dos Ojos and found that Ifiginia and anyone else who thought he was estupido was wrong. He had a great curiosity and he was able to solve complex problems successfully and quickly. He also understood abstract concepts nearly instantly.

Sometimes when Verdad was studying and Domingo was making dinner, she would read something out loud to him from one of her books. He especially liked hearing the story of unlucky Santiago and the huge fish. He identified with the man with interesting eyes.

"Everything about him was old except his eyes and they were the same color as the sea and were cheerful and undefeated."* Domingo had great recall and often, when he was alone, mulled over what she had read to him, or what los professores taught. So, in this way, Domingo also went to school.

*The Old Man and The Sea, Ernest Hemingway.

EL DíA DE LOS MUERTOS

Verdad went home in late October for a break from her studies, and she was overjoyed to see her father, her friend Ifiginia, and to be back in Esperanza. Brownsville was by no means a city as large as say, its sister city, Matamoras, but for someone unaccustomed to urban life on any scale, Brownsville was crowded, dirty, and intense.

It felt so safe and comforting to sleep in her own bed in the casita, knowing her father was right next door. As usual, Clemente did not know what to talk to her about; he inquired about her classes but while what she told him meant little to the uneducated man, he was very proud of his daughter and he told her so. That made up for much for Verdad.

Ifiginia was delighted to have her best friend back, even if for only a long weekend. They talked nearly nonstop about her classes, the boys she met--virtually none, thanks to the hulking company of Domingo--and what the girls wore. It did not take long for Ifiginia to update Verdad on the goings on in Esperanza. The tidbits of gossip she shared—the wife of Ruben Guzman threw him out, again, after a drunken weekend; María Salinas was seen riding in a strange car, twice now—brought a sense of home and familiarity. In the time she had been away, Verdad felt she may have changed a little but the town of Esperanza had not changed at all.

At first, Verdad was relieved to be allowed to walk freely and to visit with anyone she chose, free of the scrutiny of Domingo Two Eyes. She found herself watching for him, though, when she sat by the fountain in the plaza, or when she bought a ticket to el cine and sat in the cool theatre with Ifiginia and the other girls. I am just used to him, she told herself. I will

be back in his custody soon enough.

During her visit home, it was El Día del los Muertos, a

time for family and friends to pray for and remember friends and

family members who had died. Ifiginia and Verdad jumped into

the festivities with their usual enthusiasm. They gathered

humble orange marigolds to decorate the graves of the dead that

they would visit. One such grave was that of María Teresa, the

mother of Verdad. María Teresa had died from an infection after

the birth of Verdad.

Clemente and Verdad, and often Ifiginia, so like a sister

to Verdad, tidied and decorated her grave. At home they

prepared what Clemente said had been her favorite foods and left

them as ofrendas, offerings as a welcoming gesture for her.

Verdad always made candied pumpkin, Calabaza en tacha, a

traditional treat on El Día de los Muertos. Everyone used the

huge green pumpkins grown expressly for this purpose. She

boiled the sliced pumpkin with cinnamon sticks, cardamom,

cloves, orange zest, and Mexican sugar shaped into a cone. It seemed in the days before the celebration that all of Esperanza smelled deliciously of spices and piloncillo, the brown sugar with molasses, and baking bread.

Verdad also brought out and aired the blanket and pillow of María Teresa, reserved for this day only, so that she could rest after her long journey. She and Ifiginia constructed a small altar in a corner of the casita and decorated it with a cross surrounded by laughing and dancing calacas, La Catrina skeleton figures made out of clay and paper-mache. There was a cup of fresh water to drink after a long dry journey and they surrounded it all with enough candles, as Clemente liked to say, to light all of Esperanza.

All of this was done as a way of luring her spirit to come home for a visit. It is believed that the souls return every year to make sure that they have not been forgotten and to see that their family is well.

Verdad was only a little sad that she had never known her mother. She talked with her often, especially now, and told her what was going on in her life. She tried to remember it was a time to celebrate the loved ones they had lost, to remember and share the good the person brought to the world.

Of course, Padre Mateo also embraced the holiday. He went from home to home, visiting his flock, and admiring the altars made in remembrance of their dead. Some had cigarettes next to bottles of tequila, next to sugar skulls, next to crosses and candles. For the very young, godparents weighed down tables with fruits, a favorite toy, such as a doll or a truck. And always pan de muertos, the sweetened soft bread shaped like a bun, decorated with bone-like pieces that represent the lost ones, los difuntos, and often a baked tear drop on the bread to represent sorrow. And always always always marigolds. Padre Mateo relished the observance of the day, a tradition carried over from the time of the Aztecs. Its joyous celebration of the life of the deceased stood in great contrast to the celebration by the Roman Catholic Church of All Souls Day, a solemn and sober day when the church is draped in black and is devoted to the suffering souls in Purgatory.

By the end of the night, the head and stomach of the priest were rebelling from the many favorite foods he was pressed to sample, the tequila he felt obligated to sip, and from the smell of flowers and melting wax. He saw that many of the people celebrating looked a little done in by the festivities, too.

Domingo Dos Ojos came to take Ifiginia home. Doña Milena, the wife of don Carlos, had sent a message that they were to join them for the evening meal. Verdad and Clemente had already planned to make the long walk to their hilltop house, to deliver gifts of veladoras, candles that would burn for seven days. They graciously accepted the invitation. No one argued with the Varelas. In the back seat of the big car with the tinted windows, Clemente held a blue candle with the image of San Miguel, to pray for deliverance from enemies, for victory and peace and protection against the devil. And, Verdad held a pink candle of la Virgencita de Guadalupe, who had come to comfort, defend, and protect the people of the Americas.

."We are honored to have you as guests in our home,"

don Carlos greeted Verdad and Clemente. Verdad handed the candles to doña Milena. She kissed Verdad on both cheeks.

Clemente twisted and twisted his hat in his hands. "We are honored to be here, don Carlos," he replied. Should he bow? Doña Milena took his hat and placed it on a bench.

"Verdad, show your father where he can freshen up. We are ready to sit down."

Clemente glanced around him as Verdad lead the way to el baño de huespedes.

"M'hija, what a place!" he whispered to Verdad. The house spoke of age and grace, as if it had always been there. It had been built not to look new. Their footsteps rang on the stone floor. He saw sumptuous leather sofas and chairs waiting in readiness for guests, books lining entire walls. The house was simply and tastefully furnished. A slight ash and wood smoke smell from a cold fireplace somewhere contributed to the feeling of ancient welcome.

On their return from el baño, they passed a heavily laden table, la ofrenda. Nearly every photo and item on the table were in honor of the family of don Carlos: Aging photographs with backdrops of potted palms and stone arches showed soberly posed women and men from long ago; little boys in sombreros so big they all but obscured their faces; girls with large white bows and high top shoes; young brides holding lace fans; men in dark suits with stiff white collars, some with large bigotes, moustaches, that drooped over upper lips, sombreros adorned with silver, one hand resting on the hilt of una pistola, the other clamped firmly on the shoulder of a wife or daughter seated before them. La mesa, the table, was burdened with cigars, tequila, sugar candy skulls, candles, candles, candles, atop a heavily embroidered manton, the colors as bright as the mob of flowers in the blue urns and pitchers placed casually around the house. There was even a wash basin with water and a towel to refresh with from the journey from the netherworld to this one, and also to use to freshen up when getting ready to depart.

The whole thing looked like a shrine to half of the puebla of Esperanza. And, it looked as if every marigold in

Esperanza had been called upon to rest on this table. The flowers with their pungent smell gave freely of their seeds so there was never a dearth of flowers for the altars and graves. Above it all hung a pintura de la Virgen in an ornately carved, gilt frame.

Verdad pointed to the table as they passed so that Clemente would see the candles they had brought as gifts were placed on each side of a wooden cross, its green and gold and red paint worn with age and reverence.

Doña Milena and don Carlos waited for them near the table.

"My wife requires only one rincón to honor her family." Clemente noted the lavish and opulent offerings to all of the relatives of don Carlos and so little for those of his wife. There was a faded photograph from the wedding day of her parents propped against a bottle of tequila. It seemed as if la ofrenda was yet another of the areas don Carlos ruled. For the most part, from what Clemente saw, all of the house, elegant and rich, was the house of a man.

Clemente discreetly examined doña Milena and took in her soft-spoken, refined and quiet mien, one maybe not so subservient. He noted her upswept hair, silk blouse and matching tailored pants, low heels so as not to be taller than her husband. A gold peso on a chain hung around her neck. A simple gold wedding band circled her finger. Everything about her was tasteful and understated.

As they entered the dining room, doña Milena asked, "Has everyone washed their hands?" Everyone obediently affirmed that they had, los gemelos, Marco y Rafael, the twins even offering up theirs for her inspection.

"Bueno."

Don Carlos seated his wife to his right and then motioned to Clemente to sit at the foot of the table, facing him. The children took their places around the adults. Domingo Dos Ojos took his usual seat. He ate nearly every meal with the family and sat with his back to the wall, facing the arched doorway to la sala, the living room, so that he could see everyone at the table, into la cocina, and into the rest of the house, all at once. He slid

his sunglasses into his shirt pocket.

It was one of the rare times that Dos Ojos took them off.

He had learned a long time ago never to argue with doña Milena

about it. To wear sunglasses at the table was as crudo as wearing

a hat inside the house or forgetting to wash his hands before a

meal.

Clemente saw why Domingo was called Dos Ojos. His

different colored eyes, one as black as night, one the amber of

the eyes of a wolf, were unsettling. His silent presence and

massive size made Clemente feel as if Domingo were from

another realm.

Before beginning the meal, don Carlos rose from the head

of the table and lifted his wine glass. Perfectly manicured and

clean hands held that glass; a heavy gold chain with a gold

crucifix circled his neck. The Rolex watch he wore dangled

from his wrist like a heavy bracelet. His slicked back hair was thick and precisely trimmed. Everything about Don Carlos spoke authority. He began to speak

The four children seated around him ducked their heads and smiled. They had all heard his speech many times before.

"Death is something that each of us must face, with that of our own passing or that of someone we know.

"Tonight, we honor those who have passed on, and in doing so, we honor our own lives. As we spend this time in celebration of the lives of nuestros difuntos, our departed, we can then be more appreciative and aware of the life we ourselves are gifted with. As we celebrate, we stop to consider that our lives are indeed fleeting and that those we love will not be with us forever. By celebrating with our loved ones, we remember what our elders have done for us."

All four children began to mimic the rest of his speech.

"Sad is the tree which has no roots and sad then would also be the child. For just as a tree needs roots by which to feed itself and to be nourished so does a child have that same need.

We must never lose the value of family and the sweetest gift, life. To life!"

Everyone lifted a glass and repeated, "To life!"

The meal doña Milena had prepared was the best Clemente had ever tasted: cactus cooked on un comal, a griddle, served with a salsa of tomatoes, chiles, onions, and cilantro, blended with lime juice; Mole Poblano with chicken, chiles, almonds, raisins, and unsweetened chocolate; Calabacitas y Elotes con Crema, zucchini and corn simmered in cream; Chiles en Nogada, stuffed chiles with walnut sauce; Frijoles Borrachos, Drunken beans; Arroz Verde, green rice, and plenty of tortillas. For dessert, they, of course, ate Calabaza en tacha, the candied pumpkin that Verdad had made.

It was more than most of them ate in a week but this was for a special night, a night of remembrance. It was a time don Carlos insisted they celebrate with enthusiasm.

The Varela maid had been given the day off so she could celebrate El Día de los Muertos with her family. When everyone had pushed their plates away, Ifiginia and Verdad jumped up and began to clear the table.

Don Carlos groaned. "Milena, mi vida, buenisimo. Siempre."

His beautiful wife smiled but kept one eye on the girls, the other on the twins.

"Niños, go play."

Rafael y Marco obediently rose, went first to their mother and kissed her cheek. They then went to don Carlos.

"Con permiso, Padre." They shook hands with their father before galloping outside.

Doña Milena folded her napkin and placed it on the table. "This is where I must leave. Thank you for honoring us with your presence, don Clemente. You know we love Verdad as if she were our own daughter. Ifiginia, when the table is cleared, bring Verdad to your room. I want to clean out your closet before she goes back to school."

All three men rose slightly in their chairs as she exited. Domingo fitted his sunglasses onto his face. He seemed to instantly relax.

Clemente saw that his daughter was happier these days than she had been for a long time. He attributed going away to get an education with her change. He also saw the ease with which Verdad moved around the Varela casa, as if she had always lived there. She seemed to know where everything belonged. She placed coffee spoons at each place and retrieved heavy crystal ashtrays and set them, too, in front of all three men. Ifiginia presented the humidor, first to her father, then to don Clemente, and finally to Domingo. Clemente knew he could not refuse the after-dinner cigar and brandy but he was totally out of his element now. He mimicked don Carlos as he sniffed his cigar, snipped the end with the proffered cutter, and leaned in to light it from one of the many candles on the table. Don Carlos exhaled a plume of smoke with a great sigh of pleasure. Clemente turned, expecting to see Domingo do the same. But,

Domingo held his cigar in front of his lips. Something else had his attention.

Carlos put his cigar down, took a taste of brandy, and looked squarely at Domingo. Clemente too looked at the big man.

Through a cloud of cigar smoke, he saw that Domingo watched his slender daughter. In a soft voice, don Carlos said, "Cuidado, amigo. Careful."

Clemente looked from Dos Ojos to his host. The sound of the voice of don Carlos made him shudder.

Domingo just as quietly replied, "Sí, don Carlos. Yo recuerdo. I remember. Siempre. Always." He seemed never to take his eyes from the retreating back of the young girl.

When the cigars and brandy had been enjoyed, don Carlos rose and told Domingo it was time to take their guests home. "I am sure they are tired of our company and I have a business associate arriving." Clemente retrieved his hat from the bench in the front hall. Once again, he tortured it as he thanked his hosts and said "Buenos Noches". In the car on the way home, Domingo was silent. Clemente turned to Verdad and said, "I know now why you like to spend so much time with them."

Verdad looked at her father for a long moment. "Papi, their world is fun to visit and I am glad they give me so many pretty things. But, it is not my world. I know that. I am very happy in our casita."

They heard the vibration of helicopter blades as Domingo drove them home.

LOTUS GARCíA Y SEGUNDO

Visiting the graves of the difuntos was a normal part of the life of Lotus, not just on El Día de los Muertos. Segundo joined her whenever it was feasible and he grew up with a healthy understanding of death. He had toy skeletons he played with and so made friends with the very things that give other children nightmares. Lotus taught him that we are always in the presence of death, life is for the living, and it is to be lived ... until the time comes to no longer do so. Death is a matter of course. It is a door we will all step through and making our peace with it will make our time here more precious.

Late in the night, as they awaited the spirits of their loved ones to return, Segundo ran off to play tag in el cementerio in the shadows with some of the other children while Lotus lighted a ring of candles around the family graves. She pulled weeds and straightened the occasional headstone of a relative. Sitting back on her knees, she looked at the markers of her loved ones. She knew it would not be long before she joined them. She called to Segundo to help and they spread rich yellow and orange marigold petals over the grave of her mother. Lotus then spread a blanket on the ground and they ate their meal.

"Segundo, do you remember why we use la calendula, the marigold?"

"Yes, I remember, Mama Lotus. The marigold comes from Mexico. It was a sacred herb of the Aztecs; they used it to decorate their temples. But, when the Spanish arrived here many years ago, the Spanish killed the Indians. Their red blood splashed all over the yellow gold the Spanish stole from them."

"Sí, and that is why we also call them flor de muerto. It is to remember their suffering."

They continued their meal. They chatted with the people at the other graves. For a long time, a large black bird sat high above them in a tree. It seemed to be watching everything Lotus and Segundo did. How strange for a bird to be visible this late at night.

"Look, Mama Lotus, that bird wants to steal our food!" The bird hopped down to a lower branch. Segundo tossed a piece of tortilla to him. Lotus studied the bird. It was a raven, as black as the surrounding sky. There was something familiar about it.

"¡Segundo! Do not waste our food. Besides, I do not think he wants to eat. He wants something else."

With that, the bird swooped down over them, flying so close he grazed the top of the head of the boy. Segundo giggled. The bird flew over other people enjoying their picnic. One man stood up and waved his hat at him.

"¡Fuera! Shoo! Get out of here."

The raven slowly circled and neared Lotus and Segundo. This time it landed on his shoulder. The weight of it surprised Segundo but he sat without flinching. He moved only his eyes and looked at his mother.

"What should I do?"

Lotus smiled and said, "I think you have a new friend. Leave him alone and see what happens."

Segundo remained motionless for a few more minutes until he could not stand it. He slowly rose to his feet. The bird clung to him. Arms raised at his sides, Segundo took a few steps toward Lotus. Still, the bird stayed with him.

"You know, I think this is a bird that used to live aquí, here, in Esperanza, Segundo. A boy who used to live here rescued him and the bird never left his side."

The raven cocked his head at the sound of her words.

"What happened to the boy?" Segundo lowered his arms. He walked in large circles around the blanket.

Lotus looked at Segundo a long moment before she answered.

"He became a man and moved away. He lives in Matamoros now. He is one of the sons of Leopold. You know, the bus driver."

The bird nibbled at his curls, making the boy laugh.

"Come, help me put all of this away. It is getting late." Lotus clumsily got to her feet and began to gather their things.

Segundo took one end of the blanket and together they folded it, corner to corner. The bird stayed with the boy.

"The bird was named Cuervo," Lotus said.

Again, the raven tilted his head, seeming to listen.

"Then I shall call him that, too. Come on, Cuervo. Let us go home."

Lotus was not sure what it meant, that the raven had found them. She did know that an immediate bond between Segundo and Cuervo had been formed and that there would be nothing she could do to separate them.

They walked to the bus stop, Lotus thumping along, carrying their ancient basket with the remainder of their meal, Segundo nearly floating in joy with the big black bird on his shoulder. People stared at the spectacle of the little boy and the raven on his shoulder. Some crossed themselves. Others laughed.

"That bird is almost as big as Segundo himself!"

It was just after midnight when the Leopold Bus Line pulled up and the door opened with a swoosh. Leopold gaped at the bird.

"Buenos días, don Leopold. Mama Lotus thinks this is the bird your son used to have. I am going to call him Cuervo."

Lotus shot a look at Leopold. His mouth still hung open. With Segundo and Cuervo following her, Lotus made her way as gracefully and with as much dignity as she could muster to her accustomed seat.

LEOPOLD

When Leopold arrived at the García casita, he announced

to the few remaining passengers that they had to disembark, and

for the first time ever in all of the years he had driven the bus,

skipped the last few stops of the night. He sped home as fast as

the clunking, smoke-belching bus would go. In the yard he saw

the car of Silvio and Rosalba and he allowed himself a slight

moment of relief. But just a moment.

He burst into the house to find Silvio sitting in la cocina

with his niñita, his little girl, Alma, and his wife, Rosalba, who had grown incredibly fat since the birth of Alma.

"¡Dios, mío, niños!   You gave me such a scare! I saw that crazy bird, Cuervo, and thought he had winged all the way from Matamoros to Esperanza to tell us . . . I thought, I thought . . ."

He collapsed onto a chair next to Silvio. He covered his face with his hands and his loud, gasping sobs bewildered them all.

"Leopold, mi corazón, ¿qué pasó? What happened?" Graciela rushed to put her arms around him.

Alma, with her always smiling face and pleasant personality, now began to snivel. She had never seen a grown-up cry before.

When Leopold could speak again, he wiped his face and looked around at his family.

"That bird . . . I was sure something bad had happened to

Silvio or to one of you girls. Why else would it appear like that? And, on the shoulder of Segundo, the son of Lotus García."

With this he looked at his handsome son. Graciela busied herself with retying her apron strings; she turned her head away as she tucked a piece of hair behind her ear.

Silvio laughed at his distressed father. "As soon as we got out of the car, Cuervo flew off. I suppose he was looking for something to eat. Maybe he remembered the pueblo where he used to live and wanted to have a look around. He will come back to me. He always does."

"No, Silvio, not this time. I think you have seen the last of him," Leopold said.

"That is fine with me," the stout Rosalba said. "I do not care what Silvio says, he is a bird and birds are dirty."

"Si, birds are dirty," Alma echoed. "They eat worms and dead things. I do not like when Cuervo tries to sit on me."

Leopold rose from the chair and embraced Alma. "Hay que bonita, how beautiful you are. No more tears. Your silly abuelo is fine. Just fine." He blotted his face with his handkerchief and turned to his wife. "Graciela, they must be starving."

Silvio and Rosalba stayed in Esperanza until the early hours of the morning when the sun was beginning to lighten the night sky. They visited los difuntos at el cementerio and showed Alma around el pueblo, where her padre had been born. Their trips from la finca, the farm, outside of Matamoros were few. Alma had been a toddler when they last visited. When they returned to the house, Leopold exclaimed over how tall Alma had grown and how smart she was, Silvio stepped outside to search for Cuervo. He whistled for him. There was no krak or whistle in reply and the sky remained empty.

They stayed longer than they had planned, waiting for Cuervo to return. It pained Silvio to leave him behind but he had to work later that day. He proudly told his parents that Luis Coron, his father-in-law, had promoted him and now he was in charge of the maintenance of all of the tractors, cars, and machinery on the soya farm. It meant longer hours but more money. Leopold told Silvio that he would watch for Cuervo, that if he came to their home he would feed him and try to keep him there until Silvio could retrieve him.

Silvio asked, "Do we still have that bed I made for him? Put it on the window sill. Perhaps he will see it and come back."

But Leopold knew he had found another boy. He suspected that Silvio knew it also.

DOMINGO Y VERDAD

Domingo had tried to time their arrival at the border crossing when he expected the least traffic and fewest delays. He approached the old bridge, the Gateway Bridge, over the Río Grande, because don Carlos swore it was the easiest one to cross. It was also only a block away from la Universidad. Domingo and Verdad got out their smallpox vaccination certificates, TB and x-ray certificates, passports and visas; Verdad her student i.d. The "Welcome to the United States" signs seemed to taunt them; they knew they had a long wait.

Verdad climbed over the seat from the back and plopped down next to Domingo. She did this on every trip across the border to the U.S. The first time she had done it, Domingo swerved the car and almost drove off the road. Now, he did not even acknowledge it. Verdad felt awkward when her friends saw her sitting in the back seat; having Domingo as her constant companion made her stand out enough. On the way home to Mexico, she reversed the procedure and slid into the back seat.

From her backpack, she pulled out a magazine and she thumbed through it. The car inched forward.

"Domingo, why do you not like to read?" she asked.

He took a long time to answer and she thought at first he had not heard her. She was ready to ask him again when he said, "I can read a little but it is so difficult for me. I would like to be able to read as much as you and everyone else, but I never mastered it." His voice was raspy with emotion. "I think I have something wrong, that makes me unable to read very well. I know people think I am estupido. It often makes me sad. But, I have learned to live with it." He cleared his throat.

Verdad looked out the window at cormorants resting on a dead tree on the bank of the shallow, dirty river. They preened and flapped, some flying off to dive for fish. She turned to the big man and as she picked imaginary lint from her pants, said, "I could help you, I think. That is, if you want me to. And, I think people are wrong."

It was their turn to get out of the car, show their documents, and let the perros sniff for drogas. While they waited, Domingo said, "Gracias, Verdad. I would like to try. I want to be able to read all of the story about Santiago, El Viejo y El Mar. On my own in Spanish."

They smiled at one another. That is how it began.

SEGUNDO Y CUERVO

Segundo thought he was the luckiest boy in Esperanza, in all of Mexico even. He had a beautiful bird who went everywhere with him. Cuervo executed intricate moves in the air as he flew, circling, rolling, dipping so low that he looked as if he were going to collide with the ground, then soaring straight up like a jet. Everything Cuervo did delighted Segundo. His delight charmed Lotus and everyone who saw them together. There was some talk about the sudden appearance of the bird and his fierce attachment to the boy; it resembled so closely the one that

Silvio had had as a child. Muy curioso, how strange.

Cuervo had a penchant for shiny things and began quite a collection of aluminum foil, sparkly rocks, and bits of scrap metal. He would fly onto the sill of Segundo with something in his mouth. He gently lay it down on the sill and took a step back as he looked at Segundo. It was as if he were presenting him with a great prize. When Lotus went to find her basket one market day, she found instead that Segundo had put all of the gifts of the bird into it. Pues, well, it was time for a new basket any way.

Every waking minute that he was not in school or doing his chores, Segundo trained Cuervo. He wanted him to be the best bird anyone had ever seen. Segundo knew he was smart but nearly every passing day brought him a surprise.

The boy threaded a grape on a long piece of string and hung it from a perch he had secured to the porch ceiling. Cuervo loved grapes and when he saw and smelled this one, he had to have it. He stood on the railing under the grape and looked up.

Segundo had hung it just high enough that he could not reach it. Cuervo hopped and tried to land on the string but it was too thin for him to get a grip on. He whistled in frustration at the elusive grape. After several minutes of hopping, circling, and flapping, Cuervo landed on the perch. He caught the string in his beak and pulled it up, a little at a time, and stepped on the loops to gradually shorten the string. At last the grape was his!

Segundo often took Cuervo to an empty field and gave him a signal to fly away. He would wait for a few minutes until his friend had disappeared then whistle, a skill recently and laboriously acquired for this very purpose. Cuervo would come flying back to the boy and with a barrel roll or two, land on his outstretched arm.

One day Leopold stopped the bus in front of their house. It was not a market day so its appearance brought Lotus and Segundo from inside the house. Leopold wooshed open the door and from his seat, held something out to them.

"This is the bed that Silvio made for Cuervo. It looks like he is here to stay and I thought he might like to use it again."

172

Leopold had cleaned out the box and rinsed it with soapy water. Segundo carried it with great reverence into the house, turned and ran back to the bus, and said, "Muchas gracias, don Leopold", and raced back to the house.

In his room, he opened his window and set the wooden box on the sill. Lotus brought in a rag that she placed in the bottom. Cuervo hopped onto the sill, examined the box from all angles, then began to set up housekeeping. With his beak he moved the cloth until it was to his liking, flew off to find twigs and pieces of straw, then settled into his nest.

Segundo made sure Cuervo was in his box every night when he went to bed. It did not surprise him to see that the bird continually added things—a shiny piece of foil, a bit of fur that he had collected, even once a battered golf ball. Some mornings, Segundo would awake to find Cuervo had thrown out this or that from his nest and discarded it on the ground so he could make room for some new improvement.

Lotus explained how no one can own a bird such as Cuervo, that he was gracing Segundo with his friendship. Los cuervos are the bringers of powerful magic.

LOTUS AND CUERVO

Lotus knew that ravens are among the smartest of all birds. Segundo had taught him to make a sound that was like the bark of a dog. She had seen Cuervo distinguish the people of Esperanza by their voices. He seemed to know and trust the people who had fed him but, she had witnessed him become agitated by the voice of anyone he had never seen before. She also knew he was a thief, stealing food from other birds, and pilfering bright shiny things that were not just scraps of foil or metal, like the dangly earring that Segundo had found in his nest one day. They both hoped he had found it on the road.

Lotus also knew many secret things about plants and animals from the teachings of her madre, her abuela, grandmother, and _her_ abuela, the teachings being passed down from one wise woman to another, on and on without end. From these women, she knew a raven is the guardian of ceremonial magic, and it is the courier of healing. She knew that the magic a raven brings can give one courage to enter into the darkness of the Great Mystery. The Great Mystery is where the Great Spirit, El Gran Espiritu, lives. The color of el cuervo, black, is the color of this place; it is the blackness that holds all the energy of creativity. And, some believe that el c8uervo is a mediator between life and death.

Las viejas, the ancient ones, had taught that the blue-black iridescence in the feathers of a raven often changes the form and shape of what the human eye sees. Change, if recognized and embraced, can bring awakening. El Cuervo carried a message and it was the challenge of Lotus to interpret it, and perhaps help Segundo understand. As Cuervo hovered over Segundo or flew to the back of beyond, Lotus watched him closely. He was buoyant and graceful as he soared, glided, and slowly flapped. Just why Cuervo had come to Segundo, she did not yet know.

VERDAD Y DOMINGO

Verdad continued her studies. She took classes year round. She was anxious to get her degree and move back home. As the demands of her classes increased, her visits home were not as often as before. She spent many weeks and months in Brownsville with Domingo.

Their routine was that of a married couple in nearly every way. They shared in taking care of the apartment, in shopping and preparing meals. While Verdad studied, Domingo watched television in his room with the volume turned low.

She set aside an hour every night to work with Domingo. First, she had him pick out words in the Mexican newspaper that he knew so she could get an idea of just how much he could read. Sometimes she pointed to words for him to sound out and she praised him every time he got a word correct. When she found a word he did not know, he had to write that word in a notebook. When he had 10 new words, they practiced using them in sentences. He had to write the sentences in the notebook.

She suspected he could read better than he let on but he did not have much confidence. She remembered how some of las monjas could isolate and embarrass the slower students when they made mistakes. Domingo told her how he had been self-conscious about his size and about his eyes. Too often when a child stood out for all of the wrong reasons, he or she tried to become as inconspicuous as possible. In his case, that would have been nearly impossible so he remained as silent and invisible as he could. That included not doing homework, taking tests, or volunteering in class. No wonder he had stopped learning—Verdad thought he had shut down in self-defense.

Verdad wrote down his experience with school just as Domingo told her. He told her that his brothers and sisters could read and he was ashamed that he could not. She then typed it up and together, they read it out loud. When they went to la tienda Mexicana, the Mexican store, for groceries, she had him find the items on their list. At first, she made up the list. After a while, she asked him to write the list. When they got home from la tienda, he had to read the words on the front of each can and package before he could put the item away. Slowly, his reading ability improved. Now he read the headlines from the paper to her without her help.

She got a call from the campus bookstore one day; <u>El Viejo y El Mar,</u> <u>The Old Man and the Sea,</u> had finally arrived.

They read it together in Spanish. She translated the themes she had learned in her English Literature class. Domingo had no problem understanding the symbolism of the sea, the flying fish, the lions.

He spent less time watching television in his room. Now, he began to copy El Viejo y El Mar in longhand in a second notebook he bought from the bookstore. It was a laborious process for him. He would not allow himself mistakes. If he misspelled or omitted something, Domingo matter-of-factly tore out the page and began that page again.

This task was more painstaking than it would be for most because of the demand he placed on himself for perfection. But, it was also because he read and wrote slowly. It touched Verdad to see the big man so rapt with his project, so intent on getting every letter, every word, and every sentence correct.

Never did Domingo forget the warning don Carlos had given him about not letting any harm come to Verdad from anyone. Yet, never was Domingo ever unaware of her presence. He was falling in love with the dark-eyed raven woman, a woman so serious yet so gentle, one who always had time for him. He spoke to no one of his feelings.

He began to hunger for her.

VERDAD, DOMINGO, Y CUERVO

Verdad was acutely aware of Domingo, too. At night she could hear him in the room next to hers. She heard when he tossed in his bed, when he turned over, or when he got up to use their shared baño, bath.

Her experience with Silvio had made her careful in her dealings with the male students. She heard stories about drunken parties, casual couplings, bitter break-ups, and she wanted none. With Domingo around all of the time, she knew no one would dare pursue her. Yet, she too began to feel a hunger. Domingo made her feel safe; he was the unvarying constant in her life.

She longed for the familiarity of Esperanza, her friends, the sights, the sounds. T he presence of the big man helped with those longings but it was not enough.

She thought about her child and wondered what he was doing. What did he look like, was he growing tall, was his hair still curly? Did he wonder who he was and where he had come from? She ached for him so much at times that it made her cry. When that happened, Domingo was helpless to soothe her. He had no idea what was going on and attributed it to las hormonas. When she had these moments, he retreated to his room.

One night she dreamed that a black bird came to her. The bird perched on her shoulder, the same bird that had been the companion of Silvio. She could feel his talons as he clutched her shoulder. She was not frightened yet she felt something important was going to be revealed. Her body tensed in anticipation and she clutched her pillow. She also felt very sad. She knew it was because she could not see Segundo.

In a gentle whisper, not much more than the sound of the wind blowing the leaves in a tree, the bird spoke into her ear.

"Forget that you cannot fly, Verdad."

When she awoke she felt confused and out of sorts. Her body felt as if she had been beat up and she dragged as she got dressed. She told Domingo that she was not going to her classes

"Are you ill?" the man asked.

"Quizas. Perhaps. I do not know. Something is not right. Perhaps I just need a break."

"You study too hard, Verdad. I do not think it would hurt to take a day off." He gave her a bashful smile. "We will not tell don Carlos or don Clemente."

Verdad nodded in agreement. "I want to do something different today. I want to have fun."

Domingo wracked his brain for something they could do that might lift her ennui. She was not often like this and it frightened him. While she was his responsibility in Brownsville, she was also becoming more and more important to him.

They drove to the Gladys Porter Zoo. In the parking lot, chaos reigned. Men on bicycles wove in and out of the cars, often getting in the way of the drivers as they directed them to parking spots. Domingo was afraid that it was a mistake to come there but her mood seemed to have improved a bit. As they headed to the entrance, Verdad grabbed his hand to hurry him along. That surprised and pleased him. He was only too aware of how his hand engulfed hers.

The zoo opened up into natural habitats and they saw giraffes, elephants, zebras, flamingos, a peacock strutting along a path, not behind bars, osos—bears—white tigers, lions, kangaroos, and changos—monkeys—everywhere. Little monkeys, big monkeys all swinging, sleeping everywhere. Their antics made Verdad and Domingo laugh. Verdad seemed to be most fascinated by the gorillas. One female lolled in the shade of a big tree, her baby in the identical position on the ground next to her.

"Look how human they look," she exclaimed. "The baby is so cute."

"I do not know about that. They just look like big overgrown monkeys to me," Domingo said.

"They are not monkeys; they are apes. No es el mismo, they are not the same."

"Okay, smart girl. Apes."

Domingo and Verdad both almost gagged at the acrid smell of the gorillas. The stench was nearly overwhelming and stayed in their nostrils long after they had moved on. Domingo saw how happy Verdad was and felt better about her. They stopped at the refreshment area and ate a lunch of hot dogs and sodas. Next to the picnic area Domingo saw a gift shop that looked like una palapa, a hut with a palm roof. He told Verdad to wait there for a moment.

Inside the gift shop, he eyed the stuffed animals. He found a gorilla and quickly purchased it. As he approached Verdad, he hid it behind his back. She saw his grin and wondered what he was up to.

"Un regalo, a gift, to make you feel better."

She hugged it to her chest. "It looks like you, Domingo! ¡Jayán! You are both so big and robust! I am going to name him 'Domingo'."

For the first time in his entire life, Domingo liked being compared to an animal.

That night Verdad hugged the stuffed animal as she fell asleep. She heard Domingo in the next room clear his throat and she whispered, "Buenos noches, Domingo."

Cuervo came to her in her dreams again. It was the same dream as the one the night before. Again, she felt sad but could not place why. Again, she felt something significant was going to be disclosed.

"Forget that you cannot fly."

This time, though, Verdad felt herself rising up and floating on the air. She felt wings, her wings, carry her over Esperanza. She saw the market with the colorful and busy stalls filled with fruits and vegetables. She passed over the Varela compound and saw her friend, Ifiginia, lying by the pool listening to cds. She glided above the Leopold Bus Line bumping along the rutted dirty roads and she saw el paraje, the place where she and Silvio had lain.

Tears ran down her cheeks in her dream and in her sleep. She was so happy to be home, to see all that was familiar. Something was incomplete about her journey, though.

She floated high above Esperanza. There was La Iglesia de la Santa Cruz and her father working in its garden. She continued to fly and soon she recognized the little house where Lotus García and Segundo lived. She dropped down to the porch, to the big glass window that looked into the main room. There was Segundo, sitting at a table, his head bent over a book. Cuervo sat on his shoulder.

She fluttered at the window for what felt like a long time, afraid that Segundo would see her, yet unable to fly away from him. Cuervo turned his noble, sleek head and looked directly into her eyes.

The next morning she rose early and made el desayuno, a breakfast of tortillas, chorizo sausage, huevos, eggs, and coffee, for her and for Domingo. The stuffed gorilla sat at the little table. Domingo came in, fresh from showering and shaving, aviator glasses in place as always.

"¿Qué pasa, Verdad? What is this?"

"Sit down. It is for you, Domingo. It is my way of thanking you for yesterday." As she set a plate in front of him, she gave his smooth, moist cheek a kiss. She pulled off his sunglasses and placed them on the stuffed gorilla that sat on the table with them.

From then on, any time she worried about Segundo, she flew through the stars and clouds and found him.

CLEMENTE

Clemente was proud that his daughter, Verdad, had finished her degree, with honors, in just under three years. They were on their way to her graduation.

He sat in the front seat of the Varela car; don Carlos drove. Doña Milena and Ifiginia dozed in the back seat. He had never traveled out of Esperanza before and did not know if he was more excited to see his daughter graduate or go on the trip. And, a trip to Los Estados Unidos at that! They approached the border crossing in Matamoras. So many cars, so many souls trying to get out of Mexico. He watched the ones crossing the border on foot, inching their way across the foot bridge. La policía and los perros, the police and dogs, and all of the people made him uneasy. He would be glad when he returned to Esperanza.

He took a deep breath as he exited the car for the inspection. Carlos had told him not to speak unless spoken to but Clemente wanted to shout out to the guards and all of the other people around them, "My daughter is graduating tomorrow!"

He stayed in her apartment the night before the ceremony. It was clean and nicely furnished, but it looked like something out of a magazine. It did not resemble their casita in Esperanza in any way.

Domingo stayed at the hotel with the Varela family, insisting that Clemente sleep in his bed. When Clemente tried to argue and tell him he would sleep on the couch, Carlos gave Clemente a look that quickly silenced him.

"How would that appear? The father of the graduate, coming all this way, only to sleep on a couch?"

The next morning Clemente dressed in his best guayabera, the short-sleeved white shirt with the straight hem and many pleats; he noted that when the Varela family came to pick them up, Domingo and don Carlos were dressed similarly. He was relieved that he had chosen the right thing to wear. At the ceremony, they all sat as close to the front as they could. Almost everywhere Clemente looked, he saw only the faces of strangers. Ahead of them sat the seniors who were to graduate. Dressed in black caps and gowns, they looked very somber and serious; they appeared almost mournful to Clemente. It would be a long ceremony with several speakers and several hundred names to call.

One by one the students crossed the stage and shook hands and received their diplomas. Many smiled and waved from the stage. One young woman carried an infant in her arms. There was extra applause for her. Family members and friends whistled, applauded, and shouted words of congratulation to the graduates. While Clemente recognized Latino surnames of many of the students, the rest of the ceremony meant virtually nothing to him. Yet, he awaited the turn of his daughter eagerly. Doña Milena gently nudged him with her elbow but he had already seen her row rise and join the line waiting at the foot of the stage.

"Verdad Pacheco." Clemente, Milena, Ifiginia, Carlos, and Domingo jumped to their feet and clapped and called her name. "Gracias a Dios," Carlos shouted. The people around him laughed. When the graduates tossed their hats into the air, Clemente whispered, "Gracias a Dios."

VERDAD Y ESPERANZA

When Verdad returned home, several people noticed a change in her. It was perhaps that she had gotten older, grown a little more sophisticated, or maybe it was because now she had a degree. She seemed content.

Ifiginia, who had realized her dream and become engaged to Tito Bravo, a rich fútbol player from Ciudad Victoria, was sure she knew what was going on with Verdad. Ifiginia was relentless as they lay in the shade of the cabana by the pool.

"You are in love! Admit it! ¡Tienes un novio! You have

a boyfriend."

Verdad blushed. "I cannot tell you how nice it is not to be running to classes, to worry about tests and papers. And to hear Spanish all the time. I was so glad to see Papi."

"Do not change the subject. Tell me."

"There is nothing to tell," Verdad said.

"Does he know? You know, about . . ."

"¡Claro que no! Of course not!"

"¡Aja! Aha! So you admit it. There is someone." Ifiginia smacked Verdad on the leg.

"Oh, stop it. There is nothing going on with anybody. What is wrong with you?"

"I just want you to be happy. You have worked so long and so hard. Now it is time for you to find a man!"

Verdad turned the page of her magazine. "I am happy,

Ifiginia. The library will open soon, I have lots of things to keep me busy, and I am at home again."

Ifiginia did not believe her.

Armed with shovels, axes, trowels, brooms, and paintbrushes, the people of Esperanza had been busy building the new library. It stood a few blocks away from la Iglesia. It had displaced several rundown casitas but don Carlos had relocated those residents. Some people suggested that the library, la biblioteca, be named for him. But he declined that honor.

"It is not my library; it is for the people of Esperanza. Todos, everyone," he explained.

While the men put the finishing touches on the pink stone building, Verdad worked to fill the shelves with books. She hung a poster telling about story hour, la hora de cuentos, and arranged small chairs around a low table for the children she hoped would come to the library. Everything smelled new and fresh, from the carpeting, to the wooden shelves, to the books.

This afternoon she had scheduled an open house for the

people of Esperanza. A library was a new concept for many of them and reading was not a priority in many households; it was something one usually did only to get through school. She had gone door to door, leaving notices about the open house. With every person she spoke with, she made sure to emphasize that the open house was free and there would be refreshments. Milena Varela had her maid make dozens and dozens of churros, the fried sticks of pastry rolled in cinnamon sugar while still hot, biscochitos made with anise, vanilla, sherry, and cinnamon, and the chili powder and cocoa powder galletas de chocolate. Pitchers of limonada waited. A vase of flowers from the Varela jardín adorned the table with the cookies.

Verdad had a stack of blank library cards waiting to be filled out. She had asked Ifiginia to help her sign up people at the open house. She had great expectations on this sunny day.

The mariachi band played as everyone went into the library. They trickled into the new space and at first, politely sampled the cookies. The more children who came, the faster the cookies disappeared. Doña Milena seemed to have a never-ending supply and she and her maid kept the trays filled. The visitors milled around the shelves, pulling out this book and that book, flipping through the pages. Padre Mateo gave Verdad a hug and told her how proud he was of her accomplishment. They both knew what hard work and sacrifice it had taken to get to this day.

Verdad cleared her throat and in a loud, steady voice, welcomed the visitors and asked don Carlos to stand next to her. She seemed composed and looked very sophisticated in her dark blue suit with the white shirt underneath.

"Today is a very important day for the people of Esperanza. Today we open our library! This library is a place where everyone in Esperanza can come to find enjoyment through books. This library is for adults and children alike.

"Books are amazing things. They hold more than anything else in the world. They give us knowledge of the world, of other people, and of ourselves. They teach us, giving us lessons, showing us morals, showing us life.

"Books paint pictures in your head. Books help you to escape to the wonderful places that authors create. Books can take you to a world of your own.

"Sometimes people have trouble reading and I want you to feel that this library is a place where you can find help.

"None of this, this beautiful building, these shelves filled with books, would have been possible without the incredibly generous help of don Carlos."

The people gathered in the library were now spilling out the door; people stood in every possible spot. They applauded for don Carlos.

Verdad continued. "Tengo una sorpresa para ti. I have a surprise for you, don Carlos."

With that, Domingo Dos Ojos stepped out of the crowd and went to the shelves of books. He pulled out a slim volume and took his place next to don Carlos and Verdad. He opened the book. He pocketed his sunglasses, looked out at the people, and cleared his throat. He looked at don Carlos and smiled. He began to read, slowly and hesitantly.

"Era un viejo que pescaba solo en un bote en el Gulf Stream y hacía ochenta y cuatro días que no cogía un pez. En los primeros cuarenta días había tenido consigo a un muchacho. Pero después de cuarenta días sin haber pescado los padres del muchacho le habían dicho que el viejo estaba definitiva y rematadamente salao, lo cual era la peor forma de la mala suerte, y por orden de sus padres el muchacho había salido en otro bote que cogió tres buenos peces la primera semana . . ."

(He was an old man who fished alone in a skiff in the Gulf Stream and he had gone eighty-four days now without taking a fish. In the first forty days a boy had been with him. But after forty days without a fish the boy's parents had told him that the old man was now definitely and finally salao, which is the worst form of unlucky and the boy had gone at their orders in another boat which caught three good fish the first week.)

Don Carlos interrupted. "Impossible! You cannot read; you never could! You memorized this. That is all. Anyone can do it."

Some of the people jammed into the library gasped.

"No, don Carlos. I can read. Verdad taught me."

Even more people gasped; no one ever argued with or contradicted don Carlos.

"No, Domingo, I know better."

With a broad smile, Domingo continued to read.

> "Entristecía al muchacho ver al viejo regresar todos los días con su bote vacío, y siempre bajaba a ayudarle a cargar los rollos de sedal o el bichero y el arpón y la vela arrollada al mástil. La vela estaba remendada con sacos de harina y, arrollada, parecía una bandera en permanente derrota.
> El viejo era flaco y desgarbado, con arrugas profundas . . ."

> (It made the boy sad to see the old man come in each day with his skiff empty and he always went down to help him carry either the coiled lines or the gaff and harpoon and the sail that was furled around the mast. The sail was patched with flour sacks and, furled; it looked like the flag of permanent defeat.
> The old man was thin and gaunt with deep wrinkles . . .)

Don Carlos grabbed the book out of his big hands. He rifled through the pages and jabbed his finger at one.

"Read this."

Domingo took the book from him and another time, began to read. Again, slowly.

"El muchacho salió. Habían comido sin luz en la mesa y el viejo se quitó los pantalones y se fue a la cama a oscuras. Enrollo los pantalones para hacer una almohada, poniendo el periódico dentro de ellos, se envolvió en la frazada y durmió sobre los otros periódicos viejos que . . ."

The boy went out. They had eaten with no light on the table and the old man took off his trousers and went to bed in the dark. He rolled his trousers up to make a pillow putting the newspaper inside them. He rolled himself in the blanket and slept on the other old newspapers that . . .)

Don Carlos interrupted again. He grabbed the book and turned to a page near the end. He shoved the book at him.

Domingo was enjoying himself.

"Muchos pescadores estaban en torno al bote mirando lo que traía amarrado al costado, y uno estaba metido en el agua, con los pantalones remangados, midiendo el esqueleto con un tramo de sedal. El muchacho no bajó a la orilla. Ya había estado allí y uno de los pescadores cuidaba el bote en su lugar.
–¿Cómo está el viejo? –gritó uno de los pescadores."

(Many fishermen were around the skiff looking at what was lashed beside it and one was in the water, his trousers rolled up, measuring the skeleton with a length of line. The boy did not go down. He had been there before and one of the fishermen was looking after the skiff for him.

"How is he?" one of the fishermen shouted.)*

Domingo turned to don Carlos in triumph. It was the first time his friend and employer had ever been unable to speak. One of the people in the crowd began to clap; a few more joined in. Soon, everyone, even the children, were clapping. Verdad waited for them to quiet.

"Until very recently, Domingo could not read more than a few words. He has worked very hard. He has read this entire book, and more! Reading opens doors to whole new worlds. I hope you too will come and visit the library often, and open your own door to new worlds. Gracias."

Domingo turned to replace the book on the shelf. Don Carlos palmed his shoulder.

"Pues, mi amigo, well, my friend, you can read! I am proud of you! And you say Verdad taught you this? I have made a very wise investment in sending her to school." Carlos looked deeply into the eyes of Dos Ojos.

"And I think that she has taught you other things, no? Things that pertain to the heart."

Domingo tried not to smile. He slipped on his sunglasses.

"Sí, don Carlos. But, I have always honored your advice to protect her and not let anyone, not anyone, harm her. Lo juro, I swear."

"I believe you. So, what are we going to do about this, these matters del corazón, of the heart?"

"I think it is time I go to speak with don Clemente." Domingo looked over to the desk where Verdad and Ifiginia had a line of people anxious to get a library card. Clemente stood to the side of the line and watched the process.

"But, not now. Not here," Domingo said.

"Claro, no aquí. Of course, not here." Carlos set off to find Milena. He took her by the elbow, excused himself to the woman she was talking with, and after moving a discreet distance away, whispered in the ear of his wife.

Domingo saw her look over at him with a look of astonishment that turned into an enormous smile. Her eyes filled with tears.

Carlos, Milena, and Domingo were all thinking the same thing: Domingo had better talk to don Clemente soon.

*The Old Man and the Sea, Ernest Hemingway

SEGUNDO Y VERDAD

The last person in the long line of people who signed up for a library card and all that it represented was Segundo. When Ifiginia saw him step up to the desk, she reached for Verdad.

"I can take care of him. You have things to do."

"No," Verdad said. "It is no problem. I need to do this." She felt her heart pounding and took a deep breath.

"Buenos tardes. Welcome to the new library. Would you like to get your own library card?" She took in the curly-haired child, her child, and struggled to smile. He was dressed neatly and his hands were clean. He stood up tall, all eight years of him, and smiled at her.

"Sí, por favor."

Verdad thought, He is polite as well.

"¿Dónde está tu madre? Where is your mother? I know you are very grown up but I still need your mother to sign your card, too."

"She is waiting outside. She said there were too many people in here, that she needed some fresh air." He smiled again.

What a charmer, she thought.

"How is this—we will fill out the card and then, can you take this outside to her and ask her to sign it? You can bring it back." Verdad was thankful that she would not have to meet Lotus face to face. She heard Ifiginia let out a sigh of relief. "Tell me your name, por favor. ¿Cómo te llamas?"

Ifiginia elbowed her.

"Segundo García." He slowly began to spell his name. "S-E-G-U-N-D-O-G . . ."

"I have it. Gracias." Verdad went through the ceremony of asking for and filling in his address, date of birth, and slid the card over to him.

"Take this to Lotus, er, your mother, and ask her to sign it. Bring it right back to me, okay?"

When Segundo brought the card back to Verdad, she explained that she would keep one half of it in the library. She gave him the other half to take home.

"Try to remember to bring this with you any time you visit the library. But, if you forget, we will always have this card here." She sorted through the alphabetized index cards in a long green metal box and filed the half that Lotus had signed under the letter "G".

Segundo skipped out the door and Verdad saw him clasp the hand of La Extraña, the Strange One. They began to walk away from the library, Segundo matching his pace to the awkward gait of the woman. Verdad saw that she had more difficulty walking than she remembered her having. Her hair had streaks of silver in it. Everything about Lotus seemed to be aging. A raven appeared from seemingly nowhere and landed on the shoulder of the boy. That did not surprise Verdad.

CLEMENTE Y DOMINGO

The big man stood outside the door of the Pacheco casita. He removed his sunglasses, put them in one of the pockets of his white guayabera. He smoothed the vertical rows of tiny pleats, alforzas, over his chest, straightened the hem, and counted to ten. His breathing was shallow and rapid. He was sure his heart would pop out of his chest.

He carried a bouquet of flowers from the garden of doña Milena in one hand and in the other, a gift of cigars and brandy for Clemente. As he tried to negotiate the task of knocking on the door and holding onto the gifts, the door swung open and there stood Verdad. Behind her sat her father, the curve of his shoulders evident even when he was seated. Verdad grinned at Domingo and pulled him inside.

"Señor Pacheco, Verdad, thank you for inviting me into your home," he began. Clemente waved his hand through the air.

"You know me. Do not be so formal."

"Sí, sí. Don Clemente, these are for you." The big man handed the cigars and brandy to him. "I hope you will enjoy them."

Clemente motioned for Domingo to be seated. Domingo turned to Verdad and shoved the flowers at her. "For you. Flores."

She laughed and thanked him. "Let me find something to put them in," and disappeared. Domingo could hear her rustling in la cocina. Domingo thought he might as well get it over with.

"Don Clemente, as you know Verdad and I have spent a great deal of company together these last few years. I have always shown her the greatest respect." He paused and waited for some response. Clemente nodded.

"We have become very close. As a matter of fact, we have fallen in love and I am here to ask you for the hand of your daughter in marriage." There--it was out. Still Verdad had not returned to the room.

Don Clemente leaned his head back against his own chair and closed his eyes. He spoke softly.

"You are much older than my daughter. And, you are a sicorio,a hitman, for don Carlos, correct? I do not want my daughter involved in that. She deserves a better life."

Domingo thought he heard a gasp come from la cocina.

"Comprendo. I understand, I truly do. But in the time I was staying with Verdad in Texas, the time she went to school and even after, up to now, I have been not so involved with that part of the business of don Carlos."

213

"What else could you do to provide for my daughter? Like me, you have no real skills. I want her to have more than she has, than I have been able to provide for her. I want her to be able to hold her head up high when she walks through Esperanza."

The eyes of don Clemente remained closed. Domingo wondered if he was uncomfortable seeing his different colored eyes, or if he were afraid to meet his eyes, to speak these words to him with his eyes open.

"Claro. Of course. Verdad and I have been talking about this. I have spoken with don Carlos—not to ask for her hand, no, no—but to ask him if he would let me leave that part of the Varela family businesses and do something less, pues, well, unsavory. He has agreed. I am going to be the manager of la lavandería and el cine. Don Carlos has always paid me handsomely and, with the income Verdad will earn from the library, we will be very comfortable."

Don Clemente remained silent.

"I hope you understand, though, that I will always be faithful to don Carlos and his family, don Clemente. If he needs me, I must be there for him."

Don Clemente opened his eyes and regarded the man standing before him. He saw the condition of his starched shirt, his guayabera, soaked through with perspiration. He saw the pleading in his strangely-colored eyes and he knew just how serious he was. And proud. Verdad returned from the kitchen and placed a pitcher brimming with the flowers Domingo had brought on the table next to him. She took the hand of Domingo.

"Papi, por favor. We love one another. Domingo is a good man. He is gentle and he is always considerate of me. Please. We must get married."

Don Clemente started up out of his chair.

"No, no, not in that way! ¡Papi! No, we love each other so much that we cannot stand to be apart."

Clemente heard the begging in her voice. She was a beautiful woman, just as her mother had been. And, just as María Teresa, she would not stop until she got her way.

"All right. Get married. Tienes mi bendición. You have my blessing."

Domingo swept Verdad up into the air and spun her around the tiny room. He then got down on one knee. Before he could say anything further, she said, "Un honor para mi ser tu esposa. I would be honored to be your wife."

He rose and he bowed to Clemente and he shook his hand.

"Wait," Clemente said. "What is your real name? I cannot let my daughter go around being called Señora Dos Ojos!"

They all laughed. "Mi apellido, my last name, is Yebara. Don Clemente, I will take good care of her. You will not be sorry, te prometo. I promise.

Clemente Pacheco believed Domingo Dos Ojos Yebara.

VERDAD, DOMINGO, Y PADRE MATEO

It was pointless for Verdad to try and talk to Ifiginia about this. Her best friend was so wrapped up in the plans for la boda, her wedding— el vestido de novia--the dress, los anillos--the rings, the flowers, the band, the dress, the fan, la torta—the cake, the dress, the shoes, the dress —that Verdad could not get a word in edgewise. Besides, Ifiginia no longer cared about chastity. Her fiancé and she had been having sex since they became engaged. She rhapsodized about it so much that Verdad wanted to throw up.

She could not talk to doña Milena, either. Doña Milena never knew about her mistake with Silvio and the baby, who was eight years old now. Verdad was afraid it would break the hearts of her and don Carlos if she revealed her secret.

And forget las monjas. She already knew what they would say and she could not stand the thought of a lecture on her indiscretion, even if it had been quite some time ago.

So, that left Padre Mateo. A priest was supposed to be able to counsel couples on these things, to have sage advice about the most intimate of moments a couple would share—their wedding night. And, even though she knew little about that important night, she did know that it would set the tone for them as a married couple for the rest of their lives.

She met with him in his office one afternoon. Padre Mateo leaned back in his chair, steepled his fingers, and smiled at Verdad.

"So, how go the wedding plans?" he asked.

"Padre, Domingo probably thinks I am a virgen, a virgin. We have not spoken specifically of it but we have never done anything."

This was not something Padre Mateo had considered when he thought of the union of Verdad and Dos Ojos. The age difference, his job with don Carlos all these years, Domingo working in town in whatever capacity—yes, but the wedding night? No.

"It is obvious that Domingo adores you, Verdad. I do not think I have seen anyone so loyal and so in love."

Verdad blushed and nodded her head.

"Can you and he talk about other things, without embarrassment or without it leading to an argument?"

"Yes, Padre Mateo. We talk about so much and he is so kind and understanding. It is just that he is old-fashioned, and I think he expects me to come to him, you know, whole."

Padre Mateo replied. "Personally, I do not think that a man has a right to ask a girl he wants to marry whether she had previously fallen from virtue, as they say here, and that the girl has no obligation of admitting anything about her past to her fiance. In Los Estados Unidos many girls have had sexual relations before they get married. But, here, in Esperanza, in Mexico, I do know that things can be different. Often, people think that if a man wants to know what kind of girl he is marrying he should be allowed to ask her about her past, and that she should honestly tell him. After all, it is important to a man to know that he is marrying a good girl.

"But, on the other hand, you have a right to know if you are marrying a good man. Would you want to know about any of his possible involvements?"

Verdad replied. "No, I do not think so. We have already had our blood tests and everything is okay. We are both healthy in every way. Most men have some knowledge about women before they marry. I think it is almost expected." She was surprised at how easy it was to talk with el padre about this most

221

intimate subject. Perhaps it was because she knew about his time in Los Angeles, his novia—girlfriend, and their daughter.

Padre Mateo thought about this. "You and Domingo should come to talk with me together. There are things the priest has to discuss with engaged couples and I will figure out a way to broach this subject." He saw the look of fear on her face. "Do not worry, I can do it in such a way that we never have to tell him directly. It will be fine."

A few days later, Verdad and Domingo met with Padre Mateo in his study. Padre Mateo was touched to see how nervous they both were. He knew why Verdad was nervous but had no idea why Domingo was. She had to remind the big man to take off his glasses. Padre Mateo knew he hid behind them, that they kept everyone from seeing what was in his mind and in his heart. He could only guess how difficult this discussion was without them.

"We are meeting here today and, if you would like, in the next few days to be sure you start your marriage off on the right note. I know you have talked about many things but I will bring up some things you might not have considered. It is so important to communicate with one another throughout your married lives. It is absolutely vital."

"We are having only a civil ceremony, Padre Mateo. But, we would like you to attend. It will be you, my father, and the Varela family," Verdad told him.

He expected as much, knowing the expense of la boda could be enormous.

He talked with the couple about finances, how they planned to run their household, their faith, and finally, about children.

"I suppose that you will want to have children, no?" he asked. He could not help but look down at the mermaid tattoo on his forearm. He saw Domingo follow his glance.

Domingo looked very uncomfortable. He was sweating. He reached into his shirt pocket for his glasses, changed his mind, and reached over to Verdad to take her hand.

"Sí, Padre Mateo, I would like to have as many children as possible! As many as Verdad will put up with!" He tried to chuckle at his little joke but the sound came out like a gurgle.

"Many people have some misconceptions, if you will, about children and the intimacies of marriage. Often, one comes to this point in their relationship with certain expectations, expectations that are not always reasonable. While I believe that complete honesty throughout your marriage is crucial, there are times when, quizas, maybe, your expectations are a bit unreal. The important thing is that you love one another and trust one another, no matter what."

Domingo was silent. Verdad looked at Padre Mateo with gratitude.

"So, do you have any questions? Anything either of you wish to say?"

Both Verdad and Domingo said, "No, Padre", and after Padre Mateo reminded them to have their witnesses in place for the ceremony, the session seemed to be over. Padre Mateo rose from his chair and came around the desk. He reached out his hand to Domingo.

"You are marrying a fine woman, Domingo. I wish you both all the happiness en el mundo, in the world."

He gave Verdad a peck on the cheek. The session had been relatively painless and he was glad Verdad had not had to suffer any embarrassment.

A short while later, there was a knock on the door frame and when Padre Mateo looked up, he saw Domingo.

"Padre, may I speak privately with you?"

"Por supuesto, of course, Domingo." Padre Mateo closed the door and they sat down again.

Domingo did not remove his sunglasses this time and seemed to be in agony.

"Despite what many people would expect of me, because of the life I have lead, because of the kinds of people don Carlos does business with, people would be surprised to know I have never been with a woman. I have no idea, other than the things school boys laugh about, what to do, how to do this. I love Verdad more than life. But, I do not want to disappoint her. I do not want to hurt her. I know that you have taken a vow of celibacy but I have also heard that you lived with a woman up north, that you had a child. I thought, perhaps, you could tell me . . ."

Padre Mateo cleared his throat. This was totally unexpected.

"Yes, I have taken that vow. And, yes, I did have a child. It is a long story for another time.

"Verdad loves you, Domingo. You two must be gentle with one another, always listen to one another. Verdad is nervous about this subject, also. I think you will work things out if you forget all about those schoolyard tales and just rely on your love for her."

The face of the man sitting across from him was blank. Padre Mateo was not sure if he understood.

"Keep your expectations simple, Domingo. Be realistic with Verdad. Every marriage is different and every beginning to a marriage is different. If you love one another, without judgment, your love will continue to grow."

Domingo had tears in his eyes when they again shook hands. The meeting was over.

Padre Mateo sat back in his chair and this time, he took a deep breath. He was surprised but he was also very relieved. The inexperience of the big man would make their wedding night less awkward.

How different this meeting had been than the one with Ifiginia and her fiancé, Tito. Yes, the meeting was over and he was very glad.

THE WEDDINGS OF IFIGINIA Y VERDAD

Verdad loved Ifiginia but she did not know how much more she could stand to hear about her wedding. She had her own wedding to plan, albeit much simpler and smaller. Tito and Ifiginia seemed to fight constantly and Verdad wondered if they would actually get married. Because of the wealth of don Carlos, Ifiginia and Tito decided to forego the tradition of asking their padrinos, their godparents, for financial help. Don Carlos paid for everything. El vestido de novia, her wedding dress, came all the way from New York City. Ifiginia found the one she just had to have in a bridal magazine and nothing else would do. White silk, lavish with crocheted lace with a light blue slip underneath, it was flown in to Matamoros and a local seamstress made the alterations. The same seamstress made a copy of the dress for the flower girl. The flower girl and ring bearer were dressed as identical, miniature versions of Ifiginia and Tito. Ifiginia followed the tradition of having three ribbons sewn into her lingerie: The first, yellow, symbolizing the blessing of plentiful food; the second blue, to call forth good financial fortune; and the third, a red ribbon to bring the blessing of a passionate marriage.

Ifiginia wore a long, lace trimmed mantilla, a veil, which came to a point over her shining dark hair. She carried the fan that her mother, Milena, had carried at her wedding down the aisle instead of a bouquet of flowers. Tito wore a traditional matador outfit of slim-fitting black pants and a bolero jacket.

The ceremony at la Oficina del Registro Civil, carried out by the justice of the peace, proceeded without much fuss. The important wedding, to Ifiginia and Milena, was the religious one. But no couple could have a church wedding and be legally married without the civil ceremony first.

At the church, the pews were decorated with blue satin bows and with carnations dyed to match. Blue was the color Ifiginia had chosen for her wedding. Doña Milena said a traditional prayer to bless her daughter and her husband-to-be with a prosperous new life together.

Verdad was la madrina de ramo, the maid of honor, and carried white lilies for la Virgen. Doña Milena had bought her a Flamenco-style dress with ruffles at the hem, perfectly suited to her figure. It was a pale shade of blue, like a summer sky. Verdad also carried el lazo, the lasso, made of a large loop of rosary beads. This was looped around the shoulders of Ifiginia and Tito, his first. The loop was symbolic of their binding love and that they would share the responsibility of marriage for the rest of their lives. Ifiginia had searched far and wide for just the right lazo and in Ciudad Victoria, found a design called "Ladder to Heaven Elegance Crystal Lazo" made with diamond cut crystals and gold accents.

Tito and Ifiginia recited the traditional prayers in which they asked for help in being good spouses, good parents, and that their love be as strong in old age as it was now.

At the end of the ceremony, el lazo was removed by Padre Mateo who then gave it to Ifiginia as a memento of her becoming the mistress of the heart and home of the groom.

A Bravo brother carried the arras, the 13 coins, and handed them to Tito after the exchange of los anillos, the rings. Tito gave them to Ifiginia to show his acceptance of his responsibility to support her. She then gave them to Verdad to hold for the rest of the ceremony.

Tito kissed the cross. Ifiginia kissed the cross. This part of the ceremony respresented their swearing of faithfulness to one another. When Padre Mateo pronounced them el marido y la mujer, man and wife, the couple kissed with great passion. The guests in the church began to applaud and to laugh. Padre Mateo then introduced them, "Los Bravos."

The bride and groom walked down the aisle as a mariachi band, dressed all in blue satin with matching blue sombreros, played the recessional. And as Tito and Ifiginia left church, the guests tossed red beads at them for luck. So festive, so traditional!

Again, the Leopold Bus Line was employed to carry the guests. Ifiginia and Verdad had decorated the inside with elaborate white papel picado banners, paper banners decorated with cut-out birds, wedding bands, champagne glasses, flowers and hearts. On this occasion, it was Leopold who drove.

At the reception held in the Varela courtyard, there was a huge feast of spicy rice, beans, tortilla dishes using chicken and beef. Don Carlos himself made both red and white sangría for the guests, the chilled beverage made of wine mixed with brandy, sugar, fruit juice and soda water. After, there was a traditional Mexican torta, a cake with nuts, dried fruit, and rum. All of the guests joined hands and formed a heart around the newly married couple when they danced together for the first time. Verdad watched her best friend, her sister, awash in love and excitement. Ifiginia seemed to float from guest to guest, Tito in tow. His smile was as broad as hers.

His family hired a palanquin, a horse drawn cart, to carry the couple the short distance from the reception to their new casa on the Varela land. The matching white horses were festooned with blue satin ribbons. Tito and Ifiginia were leaving the next day for Padre Island, Texas, for their honeymoon. It was a place Ifiginia had read about in her bridal magazines that she chose for the shopping and the nightclubs.

Two weeks later, Verdad and Domingo were wed. In contrast, for her ceremony at la Oficina del Registro Civil, the Civil Registrar Office, Verdad wore a slim-fitting ivory dress. Over it she wore the embroidered ivory lace bolero jacket her mother, María Teresa, had worn when she married Clemente. It had been tucked away all these years, wrapped in muslin, and looked as new as the day Maria Teresa had worn it. Domingo wore a crisp white guayabera and drawstring pants. They were

233

much better suited to his body. The ubiquitous sunglasses were in a pocket. Verdad carried the fan Ifiginia had carried, the one that belonged to doña Milena.

The justice of the peace of Esperanza performed their ceremony with the customary list of 11 items that explain the purpose of marriage and each of their roles within the marriage. He began with the traditional statement that marriage is a moral state and the foundation of family life. Both Verdad and Domingo listened intently to the little man with lenses so thick his eyes looked enormous.

He focused on Domingo and reminded him that he was to protect and nurture his relationship with Verdad.

He then reminded Verdad to show Domingo tenderness and consolation and to provide advice to him.

Following each statement, Domingo and Verdad replied," Sí, accepto, Yes, I accept".

He reminded them that each spouse is expected to offer respect, confidence, and fidelity. The eighth and ninth statements reminded them that both parties should work to control their faults and support each other instead of insulting each other.

He concluded with statements about the blessing of children and the responsibility that husband and wife have to set an example for their children.

Again, they replied, "Sí, accepto".

When the justice of the peace announced them man and wife, Padre Mateo blessed their union. The kiss of the newlyweds was quite chaste.

The Varela family provided a reception at their home for the small group, again with spicy rice and beans. Again, don Carlos made the sangría. The wedding cake was just like the one Ifiginia and Tito had, just smaller.

Clemente wept openly during the wedding ceremony and again at the dinner in the courtyard under the stars at the Varela house. He could not help but remember his wedding, his beautiful bride, María Teresa. How he longed for her to see their daughter on this day.

Domingo had no family of his own in attendance. He was ashamed of them and he did not want to spoil this special day with fights and drunken displays.

After the intimate dinner and the torta, don Carlos and Tito carried a traditional wedding chest to the courtyard, and presented it to Verdad and Domingo. It was handmade of wood, decorated with tin, and had a place in the seat that opened for storage. Inside were brightly wrapped gifts that doña Milena and Ifiginia had bought for their apartment behind the library. Usually, the wedding chest held gifts for the family of the bride but these were for the newlyweds. At one point, as the newlyweds were opening the gifts and thanking the Varelas for them, a pale blue pebble, el guijarro azul, dropped from the sky. It landed at the feet of Verdad.

"What is this?"

"Where did it come from?"

"Why is it here?"

"Surely, it is a sign, a token of luck for your marriage."

Everyone laughed nervously at its startling appearance. Domingo placed the pebble in the wedding trunk. As he and his bride said their good-byes in preparation to leave, it was forgotten.

Clemente, now receiving a handsome amount of extra money in his weekly pay envelope for his help with the library, had hired a limousine to take them to Bagdad Beach. It was once prosperous as a port during the Civil War in los Estados Unidos and used for smuggling cotton. Now, it was an isolated fishing settlement and just perfect for their honeymoon. As they drove away, Verdad looked out the back window and saw everyone watching them drive off. Los gemelos, the Varela twins, chased after the limo. Don Carlos and doña Milena smiled and waved. Ifiginia and Tito, holding hands, turned to each other to kiss. Clemente, standing next to a beaming Padre Mateo, wiped his eyes and tried to smile at them.

There was another guest, this one not invited. Cuervo was hidden in the branches of a tree in the Varela courtyard. He, too, watched them drive away.

SEGUNDO

At nine years of age, Segundo was now old enough to begin to wonder about his father. He wondered why he did not have one. He knew enough about the goings on of families to know there was usually a man, a woman, then children. He had seen enough cows and horses and dogs to know how a baby was made. He could not imagine his mother ever having done that, even to get him.

"¡Bastardo!" He heard that often from some of the other children at school. One boy even told him his mother was a puta,

239

a whore, and that is why no man would step forward and claim him as his son. He fought with that boy and before they could do any serious damage to one another, las monjas, the nuns, separated them. They too heard the taunts, the questions about his origin. When the children began their cruel goading of Segundo, they stopped them short and told them he was a gift from Heaven. Yet, for some people of Esperanza, he puzzled them. While they knew it went against the Catholic church to believe in curanderas, spells, and potions, there was always a niggling doubt about where he came from.

Segundo excelled at school. He seemed to learn everything quickly and thoroughly, with little effort. He loved to read and visited the library often. His favorite books were about explorers, Spanish conquistadores. Verdad set aside every book she could find for him.

He pretended he was a conquistador, sitting tall and proud atop a black caballo, a horse, named Diablo. Instead of searching for oro, gold, for the queen, he had searched for other tesoros, treasures, to give to Lotus. In his imaginings, he would

240

ride into their little dirt yard, Cuervo on his shoulder, followed by many men on horses (but no horse would be as noble as his), carrying the riches he had found. He would leap from his horse and kneel at the feet of his mother.

"Mama Lotus, muy estimada, most esteemed, here are all the fortunes of the world. I have discovered them for you and you alone."

And Lotus would be so happy. He would take her to a wise man and magically, her foot would be fixed and she would be just like everyone else. No more pain, no more limping. She could dance throughout every day. They would live in a grand house and never want for anything. Cuervo would get a majestic bed, one lined with sparkling gems.

News of his discoveries would spread like a raging fire throughout all of Mexico and it would reach the man who was his father.

In his daydreams, his father was tall and handsome, strong and wise. The man would come to Esperanza and ask where to find Segundo, the boy who was so brave and daring. This hombre, his father, would ride a pure white horse named Tornado. After he swooped down and hugged Lotus and Segundo, Segundo and he would mount their steeds and ride off in search of other adventures.

These daydreams occupied much of his waking hours. Lotus would watch him in their small dusty yard, fighting imaginary enemies with a stick, his imaginary sword, sitting astraddle the porch railing, calling to his imaginary horse. Cuervo was ever present during these adventures, balanced on his shoulder or safely perched somewhere nearby.

Ah, the imagination of a child, she sighed. His imagination seemed to be more active than most. That was good, she thought. It would carry him far and always give him hope. Even though they did not have much, he had these dreams.

One day, Segundo asked Lotus, "Where did I come from?"

"From heaven, of course, mi angel. From heaven."

242

"No, Mama Lotus. Where did I come from?"

"Cuervo found you in his nest and flew with you in his claws. He hovered above this very house and I went outside to see what he was doing. Whoosh! He dropped you into my arms."

Cuervo tilted his head and listened to Lotus intently when he heard his name. On the shoulder of the boy, he began to bob up and down. "Cuervo, Cuervo, Cuervo," he screeched.

Lotus and Segundo laughed. Segundo told her to watch. As a signal to fly, he flung his arm toward the horizon. Cuervo lifted from his shoulder and took flight. When he was but a speck in the sky, Segundo sliced the air with a shrill whistle. Cuervo came corkscrewing back to his shoulder.

The questions were forgotten for that moment but Lotus knew there would be more. She also knew funny stories about the bird would not suffice.

One day she ran into Padre Mateo in el Mercado. He inquired about her health and about Segundo.

243

"Oh, that child! What a fertile imagination he has. He always has so much fun with his make believe. But, something has been troubling me, Padre."

She took him by the arm and steered him away from the other people in the market. "The other children are sometimes mean to him and say he is un bastardo."

Padre Mateo shook his head. "I was afraid of that. Children are so cruel. They learn it from their elders, though."

"Yes," Lotus replied. "It has to come from somewhere. Do you have any suggestions as to what I should tell him? I mean, he is starting to talk about his father. He has woven a very elaborate tapestry in his little head and I do not want him to be hurt when he learns the truth. I cannot tell him that someone abandoned him and left him on the bus. That would be even more cruel for him to find that out."

"Let me think on this, doña Lotus. I will come up with something," Padre Mateo answered.

The next Sunday, Padre Mateo began his homily in this way: "When God created man, he made him in the likeness of God. Genesis 5:1

"For the Lord does not see as man sees; for man looks at the outward appearance, but the Lord looks at the heart. 1 Samuel 16:7.

"God accepts everyone, whether they are outcasts or sinners. 'So the last will be first, and the first will be last'. Matthew 20:16."

And he paused. He paused for a minute. He paused for two minutes. He looked out at the congregation and said not another word. His eyes passed over every person in the church. The people began to whisper to one another, to shift uncomfortably in their seats. Many looked away. At the end of five minutes, Padre Mateo spoke again.

"God accepts us as we are, as long as we come with sincere hearts and try our best to do what is right, with His help.

245

We should also make an effort to reach out and continually show our love by accepting and including others who may feel rejected.

"In the world of today, we are often quick to turn away those who are different from ourselves or who we have stereotyped. In so doing, we risk losing the potential that person can offer to us. God created us and loves us more than we can imagine. Teach your children and learn yourselves to accept one another."

Domingo Dos Ojos thought he was talking about him; Verdad thought he was talking about her; don Carlos thought he was talking about him. Lotus García knew what he was talking about but she could not but help thinking he was also talking about her.

It was the shortest homily given by Padre Mateo ever.

LA NIÑA

Ifiginia became pregnant almost immediately. Milena even wondered if she had been pregnant when she and Tito married but never brought up the subject. It did not matter now; all that mattered was the baby.

According to Ifiginia, she had the worst morning sickness, the biggest swollen ankles, the worst symptoms EVER of anyone in Esperanza, in all of México. She lay in bed until noon every day; she did not want to stress the baby. She was very careful with her diet and ate exactly what her doctor in

Matamoros told her to eat. From the books that Verdad ordered for her, she became an expert on nutrition, on the stages of pregnancy, on the upcoming delivery, on the first days of life, first weeks, first months. Of course. she would breastfeed. She slathered herself in cocoa butter to keep her skin from developing stretch marks. And, the debate over the names began. Tito and Ifiginia would NOT name this baby from the list of the most popular baby names that year. Or the year before, or the year before that. This baby would have a traditional Spanish name, one that none of their friends had used for their babies.

When she found out in her 21st week, through an ultrasound, that they were having a girl, the quest for the perfect name narrowed a little.

She gained very little at first but in her seventh month, her abdomen and her breasts ballooned. She had difficulty walking more than a few feet, sitting in a chair, breathing, eating, dressing herself, undressing, bathing, doing anything, so the most Ifiginia did in a day was to peek once every morning into the nursery next to the master bedroom as it was decorated and readied for this child, and to sit up in bed and read baby books. She orchestrated the decorating of the nursery from her self-imposed exile in bed and kept the maid running with messages, fabric swatches that came in the mail, pictures from magazines, and her sketches. Tito indulged her every whim; you would think he was the first man on the planet to have a baby on the way.

Milena and Carlos shopped nearly every day for the baby, bringing practically a warehouse of car seats and strollers for Ifiginia to inspect and to select from, buying and returning more clothes than any one baby could wear in a year, rushing to Matamoros to find just the right pacifier, the softest blanket made only from the finest cotton, ordering the newest baby monitor from Los Estados Unidos. This baby would want for nothing.

Ifiginia grew restless in her confinement and insisted that Tito take her to the library to see Verdad one day. She struggled into a maternity dress, the largest one in her closet, drew on flip-flops since no other shoes would fit any more, and waddled to the car. He pulled up right in front of the library, in front of the

"No Parking" sign and blocked the wheelchair ramp. He raced around to the passenger side and extracted, carefully, a very uncomfortable Ifiginia. When he had deposited her on a bench near the check-out desk, he ran back to the car and raced away to find his wife peach ice cream. It had to be peach.

Verdad looked at her inflated friend and shook her head.

"Are you sure there is only one baby in there, not a whole litter?" She laughed until she saw the tears well up in the eyes of her friend.

"I am the biggest, fattest mujer, woman, in all of México right now," Ifiginia panted. "This is the worst thing I have ever experienced. I do not know how women do this over and over and over. Why they do it. Once is more than enough." She rubbed her belly. Verdad saw the outline of her navel through the maternity dress.

"Well, at least you have a nice pedicure," Verdad said.

"Tito did it for me! He is surprisingly good at it," she replied.

Verdad again shook her head. Ifiginia looked her friend up and down.

"And you, any luck?" Ifiginia asked.

"No, I am not pregnant yet but, it is not for lack of trying. Domingo is growing disappointed and is blaming himself. I have told him not to feel that way, yet, I cannot help but wonder. I mean, you know, I . . ." and Verdad stopped.

"I do, and I am sure it will happen. Just when you least expect it. I have heard so often about people giving up all hope and then, ¡de pronto! Suddenly! They get pregnant."

"Why does everyone say 'they'? It is the woman who is pregnant, not the man," Verdad said.

"You will see when it is your turn. Now that you are married, it will be as if you and Domingo are both experiencing it all."

Segundo came into the library, politely greeted Verdad and Ifiginia, and scurried over to the "New Books" cart. He gave

Ifiginia a funny look as he went by. Verdad noticed him peeking at her belly as he scanned the new titles. Verdad signaled to Ifiginia to look at the boy. They burst out laughing when they saw the amazement on his face. He blushed.

"I think you just gave him nightmares!"

Ifiginia delivered right on her due date and María Fernanda Milena was born with the normal amount of effort and an abnormal amount of noise on the part of Ifiginia. Domingo and Verdad waited for a week to visit the new family at home. Ifiginia lay in repose, the baby in an elaborate bassinette beside her bed. The hair of the new mother was freshly coiffed, her nails manicured with a soft pink polish, and her pink satin and lace bed jacket added to the air of a pampered princess in her royal chambers. She sported a sparkling tennis bracelet, a gift from Tito, the diamonds glinting as she moved her hands. The new father stood proudly at the head of the bed.

A nurse lifted the tiny baby and presented her to Verdad. The nurse discreetly stepped away and all but disappeared.

Verdad held Fernanda and marveled at everything about her, from her tiny fingernails, the long eyelashes to her round bottom that fit so perfectly in her hand. The eyes of the two women met; Ifiginia knew that Verdad was thinking of her own baby.

Verdad tried to hand Fernanda to Domingo who raised his hands in protest and backed away. Don Carlos laughed at the fear Domingo exhibited of the tiny baby and said, "You had better get used to this! You will soon enough have one of your own!" Domingo was silent. Don Carlos took the baby, dressed from head to toe in mint green and lavender, the colors of the nursery, and swaddled in a matching blanket, and stepped toward his friend. "Here, amigo mío. I would like you to hold my first grandchild."

The look of pride and love in the eyes of his friend told Domingo that he could not refuse his request to hold the child. Domingo stiffly held his arms in a cradle and Carlos deposited the baby there. He let don Carlos present the infant. Fernanda was almost invisible in his arms. Domingo stared down in wonder at her. He smelled the top of her head. She made a tiny noise and moved inside the blanket. Domingo looked up at Verdad and gave her an enormous smile.

THE BLUE PEBBLE

Every month when Verdad discovered she was not pregnant, she grieved a little more. She got daily reports from Ifiginia on what Fernanda was doing. She had missed out on the infancy of her secret son and never had the joy of seeing him accomplish the seemingly tiny but so important events.

In the evening, she went home to their apartment to start la cena, their dinner. Even with her husband present, the emptiness she felt was sometimes almost more than she could bear.

Domingo and she consulted with nearly every doctor

255

from Esperanza to Matamoros and back. They spent three days in Brownsville, Texas, visiting fertility specialists. No one could find a problem with either of them.

When she met with the doctors on her own, she told them about Segundo and begged them not to tell Domingo. They made copious notes in their records; they honored her request. Domingo provided the sperm samples required at each appointment with an air of resigned embarrassment.

One doctor suggested it was all in her head, that she should just forget about it and she would get pregnant.

"There is nothing wrong with my head!" she huffed as they sat in line at the border crossing. "That man does not know what he is talking about."

Secretly, she wondered if God were punishing her. She believed that the longer she kept Segundo a secret from Domingo, the longer it would take her to become pregnant. If she never told him, she risked never becoming pregnant. She went to Padre Mateo.

"What do I do? I cannot tell him about Segundo, now, after all of this time. He never questioned a thing on our wedding night. We were both so nervous. I think God is punishing me. For getting pregnant in the first place and now for not being honest with my husband."

Padre Mateo tried to reassure her that God was not punishing her. "Perhaps there is a reason God is having you wait for this baby you want so much. Be patient. It will happen."

Verdad still despaired. "I do not smoke, I do not drink, I do everything I am supposed to. I eat the right foods. Domingo has even lost weight in the last year and he is taking vitamins."

"Perhaps there is something you have not considered. Doctors do not have all of the answers all of the time in matters such as this. Have you thought of seeking help from someone with, shall we say, less parochial methods? There are other people to see, alternative practices of medicine out there." He waved his hand toward the window. "Not even so much out there." He sat back in his chair and let this idea sink in.

Slowly, Verdad grasped what he was saying. She shook her head, no, and said, "I cannot do that. Padre, think about what you are asking me."

"It is your decision. It was just a suggestion, something to ponder."

Verdad did ponder what he had suggested. He had never come right out and told her to go to Lotus García but what else could he have meant? Besides, why would a priest send her to a curandera? She read every book and magazine she could get into her hands about becoming pregnant. She had gone to nearly every doctor in the phone book; she had taken the advice of each, sometimes doing just the opposite of what another had said. Their love-making had become a chore, a burden. The growing sadness she saw in Domingo was almost more than she could face. She became withdrawn and silent. This was her fault. But, she had avoided all contact with Lotus for the past nine years.

Finally, she closed the library early one day and got on the Leopold Bus Line and had Leopold drop her off at the García house. She saw the questions in his eyes but she did not confide in him. All she said was, "It is something of a private nature. Everything else is fine."

She walked up the steps to el porche, the porch, where she had visited so many times in her dreams. The floor was swept clean, a pot of marigolds bloomed by the door, and the large front window was clean and polished. It all looked just the same as in the journeys she took in the hours of darkness.

She reached up and pulled on the rope that hung from a bell at the door. She expected a loud clanging but instead, heard a soft chime. From inside the little house, she heard Lotus approach. ONE thump, ONE thump, ONE thump. Lotus opened the door and her face showed her surprise to see Verdad standing in front of her. The two women looked at one another, each hesitant to speak first.

Finally, Verdad said, "Doña Lotus, I am so very sorry to intrude upon you. I wondered if I could speak with you about a private matter."

Lotus almost swooned. She was afraid this day would come but she did not expect it to arrive without any kind of warning. Clearly, Verdad had come about Segundo.

"I have been waiting for you, doña Verdad. I knew you would come to see me one day but I did not know when. Please come in."

Verdad was puzzled by her seeming foreknowledge but attributed it to her special abilities. Inside, they sat at the kitchen table, the one Verdad had seen Segundo sit at. Lotus offered her something to drink.

"Gracias, no. It is just that, well, I am having a problem and I do not know who else to turn to."

Lotus knew it must be a very grave problem for her to come there and could think only of Segundo, that she would lose him just as she lost Harold, her first child so many years ago. Before Verdad spoke again, she blurted out, "I know I did something wrong on the day I found him on the bus. I never told anyone where I got him. I never went to la Oficina del Registro

Civil with him. I am sorry. Now you have come to take him back." She suppressed a sob with the last statement.

"¡Ay Dios mío! No! Never! He is your son. I know that. I would never do that to him, never take him away from the only mother he has ever known. I would never do that to you. I know how happy he is with you. He is such a good boy. It is because of you he is so healthy and smart. I gave up my right to any claim on him the day I boarded the Leopold Bus Line and got off without him. No, I would never take him from you."

Lotus inhaled sharply, swallowed her fear, and smiled at Verdad. She began to return to normal and reached over to the woman and covered her young, smooth hand with her own gnarled and spotted one.

She studied her eyes. Lotus had a natural knack as a focused listener and a keen observer of facial expressions and body language. She was gifted in the art of sizing up the person before her and she saw the pain in Verdad. "What can I do for you, m'hija, my daughter?"

Now it was Verdad who choked back a sob.

"My husband, Domingo, and I are trying to have a baby."

Lotus smiled at the mention of Domingo Dos Ojos. She knew of their union but still could not reconcile them being wed.

"We have seen every doctor there is to see and tried everything they suggest. We have endured test after test and still, no one can find any reason we cannot conceive. Padre Mateo suggested that I look for help from, pues, from some other source."

"Padre Mateo sent you to me?"

"Well, not exactly. We were talking and he said I should explore other options."

"Entiendo, I see. Does your husband know you are here?"

"No, I have told no one. And, I have another problem with that. I have not told Domingo that I was pregnant before, that I had Segundo. Such a proud man, he would be so terribly upset. And, if don Carlos found out, especially that it involved Silvio Salazar, we would find the head of Silvio in a ditch. As much of un idiota as he is, even he does not deserve that."

Lotus chuckled and with some difficulty, got up from her chair. "No, we do not want that. Wait here. I may have something that will help you." She went to another room in the little house. ONE thump, ONE thump, ONE thump. Verdad looked around the room as she waited.

On the windowsill of the big window, she saw a small bowl filled with los guijarros azules, blue pebbles. How odd. Could it be a coincidence? She went to the bowl and picked up one of them.

Lotus returned and saw Verdad holding the pebble. "These were passed down to me by my mother, and they were passed down to her from her mother. They came from very far away. You were gifted with one of these on your wedding day, no? What did you do with it?"

"I think it is in the wedding trunk. How did you know? Did you . . .wait, it fell from the sky." Understanding came to her in the next second. As one, she and Lotus said, "Cuervo."

Lotus continued. "It was a wedding gift from Cuervo. I saw him steal one from this very bowl. I have to keep a constant vigil over him. He steals just about anything and everything." She handed Verdad a small bottle filled with a clear liquid.

"When you go home, take out la piedra, that stone. Place it under your bed, under the very middle of it, between you and your husband. Then, tonight, ask Domingo to rub a few drops of this oil onto your belly. Tell him to do it slowly, not to rush. Tell him to also rub some on himself, on his manhood. In the morning, when he has left, retrieve the pebble and rub a drop, just one drop, into it. But, do not let anyone know about the pebble. It is just for the two of us to know about."

"And Cuervo!"

"¡Sí, sí! Cuervo is a very wise bird. He communicates many things to me. Just by the way he flies, I know when it will rain. Most people think he is a bird that represents death but el cuervo, the raven, also is a bird of birth. He is as black as the night but remember, the black of the night gives birth, gives light, to a new day.

"Segundo will be home from school soon, so you should leave. We will meet again. One day we must decide how to tell him about you, about us." Lotus clumped along beside Verdad and showed her to the door.

Verdad turned to her. "I want to do something to thank you. May I pay you?"

"You already have, m'hija. Trust me."

That night, with the blue stone positioned under the bed, Verdad handed the bottle of oil to Domingo and asked him to please rub a few drops of it onto her belly.

"Con agrado, with pleasure." The instant the unguent touched her, her skin began to feel warm. Domingo slowly soothed the balm into her skin and he could also feel its heat in his fingers. Verdad took his hand and placed it on his pene, his penis. She moved his hand up and down, letting the oil soak into his skin. He looked at her in amazement.

"Nunca, never have I felt anything this hot. What is it? Is it safe?"

Verdad laughed at her husband. "It is a little something I picked up. Yes, it is safe. Just enjoy." Domingo dribbled a few more drops onto her belly and worked his hand lower and lower. She gasped in pleasure.

Their love-making that night reached a new intensity.

In the morning, Domingo let his wife sleep and he showered and dressed as quietly as he could. He looked down at her and shook his head. She was always surprising him.

After he left, Verdad crawled under the bed and found the pebble. It had somehow become almost buried in the carpet and she had a moment of near panic when she thought it was lost.

She sat on the edge of the bed and dripped oil from the bottle Lotus had given her onto the pebble. As she massaged the oil into the pebble, it became warm. The depth of its colors intensified and it was no longer just a pale blue pebble. Verdad looked closely at the stone and in it she could see the swirling colors of the sky and and beyond into space, and every shade of blue in the sea. As she looked at the now shining blue pebble, she felt cool and refreshed. She lay back on the pillows and drifted to sleep; she seemed to be drifting on a cloud of calmness. She floated with the wonderful weightlessness of water.

El guijarro azul floated with her, clasped loosely in her left hand as she drifted. Her breath was slow and even. She could not open her eyes, but in her mind she saw a streak of blue that faded from very dark, almost black, to almost no color. She felt as if she had been drugged but she was not. She had entered the sleep of peace and acceptance.

Domingo returned home to find her still asleep.

"Verdad, what is wrong? Are you sick? You have been asleep all day. You never opened the library."

"I do not know why but I was so tired. I just had to sleep. I could not keep my eyes open." She sat up in bed and looked around the room. "I had the most wonderful dreams."

"All right, mi bella durmiente, my Sleeping Beauty, I will get you something to eat."

When she heard Domingo in the kitchen, she opened her hand. It was empty. There was no guijarro azul. She patted the bed linens but it was not there. Neither was it under the bed.

She stopped looking and lay back once again on the bed. It would turn up. She did not have to worry about it.

When Domingo brought her dinner to her, he found her in a deep sleep. He took her plate back to the kitchen and placed it in the refrigerator.

AFTER THE SLEEP

After her deep sleep, Verdad was different. She seemed to be in another world, away from any cares. Even Ifiginia did not perturb her.

She worked just as steadily at the library, came home to clean and cook as always, but it was as if she floated in an aura of calm. Even don Carlos noticed it.

"So, Domingo, what is your secret? What encanto, magic spell, have you cast over Verdad these days?"

"I have done nothing, don Carlos, nothing! Since the day

269

I came home and found her asleep like una princesa en un cuento de hadas, a princess in a fairy tale, she has been like this. She seems to be somewhere else all of the time. Maybe she is reading too manyof the books of the children at the library!" Domingo was just as puzzled as everyone else.

"Well, whatever you did, you should bottle it and sell it. I know quite a few esposos, husbands, who would like to have some for their wives!"

Verdad had always been tall and thin, almost too thin. Almost overnight, her body seemed to be fuller, ripened, but not at all heavy. Her skin glowed and her hair glistened in the sunlight as well as the moonlight. At night, Domingo would awaken and look at her and think he saw a faint indigo glow surrounding her entire body. If he blinked and looked again, it was gone.

Lotus watched Verdad from a distance and knew why she looked and behaved as she did. She said nothing to anyone but merely waited. But, she made sure she visited la Oficina del Registro Civil and with the assistance of Padre Mateo, she legally adopted the boy.

Padre Mateo was among the first to guess the reason for the change in Verdad. He had seen the ripening in her before and this time, he was happy for her. He, too, said nothing.

Domingo came home one evening after collecting the receipts at el cine y la lavandería to find Verdad standing in front of the open refrigerator. From a huge jar, she fished out slices of chile peppers and ate them with great delight.

"Verdad, querida, love, what are you doing? You know that too many chiles will upset your stomach."

"They used to, Domingo, but I cannot seem to get enough of them lately. They are all I think about. These are not that hot and they do not bother me."

"Well, take it easy. You are not used to this many." Domingo started to walk away and stopped. He spun around, ran to Verdad, and danced with her all around the apartment.

"You silly man, what are you doing?!!"

"¡Estás embarazada! You are pregnant! I suspected as much. You have been walking around as if you are in a dream and now, this, eating enough chiles to feed el Ejercito Mexicano, the Mexican Army. ¡Dios mío! A baby! We are going to have a baby!"

Verdad was stunned. It had never occurred to her that she could be pregnant. She felt almost the same as she always had, just a little more tired some days. True, her clothes were starting to feel snug but she blamed that on todos los postres, all of the desserts, she made for Domingo. He had an enormous sweet tooth and she found she enjoyed the treats almost as much as he did.

She ran to the phone and insisted on an appointment to see her doctor the next morning before she was due at the library. That night as she and Domingo ate dinner, every time she looked up, he was grinning at her. She tried to warn him not to get his hopes up but she could not help but grin back at him. If you had asked either of them, they would have replied that they did not sleep that night for more than a few minutes, if at all.

Domingo accompanied Verdad to the doctor. He asked if he could go into the examining room with her but Verdad and the nurse gave him an emphatic "no" in response. He sat in a chair in the waiting area. He jiggled his foot. He paced. He started at the ceiling. He surreptitiously looked at the other women sitting with him. He knew not all of them were pregnant but he tried to compare them to Verdad, to her luminosity of late. None seemed so radiant.

The doctor walked out with Verdad to the waiting area, both of them wearing smiles. "Congratulations, Señor Yebara, you are going to be a father!" Several of the people around them began to clap.

"¿Cuando? ¿Cuando? When? When?"

"In about siete mesas, seven months." The doctor laughed when he saw the expression on the face of Domingo.

"The time will pass quickly, do not worry! The baby will be here before you are ready."

For both Verdad and Domingo, seven months might as well be seven years.

VERDAD

Verdad tried to be sensible about her pregnancy. She saw the doctor regularly, took her vitamins, walked as much as she could, and got plenty of rest. She hired a young girl to help her out at the library and avoided the heavy crates of books that still arrived weekly for the new library. When Domingo attempted to pamper her, she put an immediate stop to it.

"No estoy enferma. I am not ill. Women have been having babies for thousands of years. I do not want to be treated any differently."

Domingo agreed yet he kept a constant eye on her.

Unlike her friend, Verdad gained only a modest amount of weight and was able to wear her regular clothes for many months. Even at the very end of her pregnancy, when she felt the baby was growing by the second, she stayed slim.

"You tall girls. ¡Bah!" Ifiginia said every time they saw each other.

Her baby, Fernanda, was nearly a year old. Everything she had outgrown, or in all honesty, never had a chance to wear, was packed into cartons for the Yebara baby. Ifiginia was sure Fernanda and the baby of her friend would be as close as the two women had been.

"And, if I have un niño, a boy . . .?" Verdad liked to tease her.

"Then he will just have to wear pink!"

Milena Varela and Ifiginia Bravo threw a baby shower for Verdad. Old classmates who still lived in Esperanza and even the most distant relatives were invited. Padre Mateo, along with Carlos and Domingo, refused to attend. They had been present at the shower for Ifiginia, along with Tito and all of his teammates. It was quite embarrassing for the men to endure the stories of labor and delivery. When Clemente heard the other men were not going to the shower for Verdad, he knew it would be safe to decline as well.

Verdad agreed to the shower as long as it was not over the top, as the one for Ifiginia had been with a mariachi band, a roasted pig, lavender and green balloons, a cake that almost outdid her wedding cake, and elaborate favors, brought in from Dallas, Texas, to give to her guests. Verdad asked that her shower be kept intimate and simple. But, as with everything Ifiginia had her hand in, this shower was not. Verdad was nearly overwhelmed when she walked into the church where the shower was to be held.

A pink and blue papel picado, a cut paper banner, festooned the church hall. Every woman there was handed a blown-up balloon to put under their dress or blouse to make them look pregnant. A purple and orange rocking horse piñata hung from the ceiling and its twin sat in the center of a table laden with food that each woman had brought: limonada, taquitos and guacamole, mini-quesadillas, and hundreds of galletas, cookies. On its own table was a pastel de chocolate, a chocolate cake, sitting atop a lime green cloth. A mountain of brightly wrapped gifts filled and surrounded a crib.

The games began. The festive mood was heightened by a boisterous game of musical chairs. Afterwards, doña Milena passed rolls of toilet paper around the hall and each person took a length that they estimated would be enough to go around the belly of Verdad. Everyone took lengths that were much too long, some on purpose which produced much laughter.

When it was time for the piñata, each woman was blindfolded, spun three times, then handed a stick decorated with streamers. Everyone ringed the piñata but stood far enough away not to get hit. As each woman swung the stick and attempted to make contact with the rocking horse and to break it, Ifiginia raised and lowered the piñata. The women sang,

Dale, dale, dale,
no perdas el tino,
porque si lo pierdes,
pierdes el camino.
Esta piñata es de muchas mañas,
sólo contiene naranjas y cañas.

Hit, hit, hit.
Do not lose your aim,
because if you lose,
you lose the road.
Piñata is much manna,
only contains oranges and sugar cane.

Some shouted directions: "¡Más arriba! More upwards! ¡Abajo! Lower! ¡Enfrente! In front!" The sight of the women with balloons under their clothes, blindfolded, as they swung at the piñata added a note of absurdity to the celebration.

The rocking horse piñata was broken open by one of the aunts of Verdad, Tia Carmina. Candy mixed with pacifiers and baby booties flew everywhere.

No one went home empty-handed; doña Milena handed a rose to each and every guest as they departed. As per tradition, the gifts were not opened at the shower itself. Domingo would have to take down the crib and carry everything home. He and Verdad would then open the gifts at home.

Verdad worked at the library until the day she delivered. Anyone who came into the library was taken aback to see her still there.

"You should be at home, resting, preparing for the arrival of the little one." She lost count of how many times she heard that or something like it. Everyone had some little piece of advice for her:

"If your belly is pointy, the baby will be a boy, and if it spreads out to the sides, the baby will be a girl."

"If your face looks rounder, the baby will be a girl, and if you gain weight on your rear end, the baby will be a boy."

"Tie a hair to your wedding band and suspend it above your belly. If it goes around in circles, the baby will be a girl. If it sways from side to side, the baby will be a boy."

"If you lift your hands above your head, your baby could be strangled by the umbilical cord."

280

"If you see something ugly when you are pregnant, your baby will be ugly, too."

"Babies who do not listen to music during pregnancy end up being deaf."

"If you watch a lunar eclipse during your pregnancy, your baby will have a cleft lip." Verdad heard this one the most.

"If you have heartburn, your baby will be very hairy."

Verdad was always careful to thank the concerned person politely when they gave her their piece of wisdom but when they left, she could not help but laugh.

Segundo came into the library just as often as ever; Verdad even felt he was coming in more frequently. He stared a great deal at her belly but never said anything. One day Segundo stood next to her desk and fiddled with the things on it.

"Segundo, what do you want?" she asked. She could tell he was hesitant to speak.

"Can I ask you something?"

"Por supuesto, Segundo, of course."

"I just want to know," he blurted out, "did Mama Lotus have a big stomach, did hers get big, as big as yours or even as big as doña Ifiginia before I was born? One of the boys a la escuela, at school, said girls who swallow semillas de sandia, watermelon seeds, get fat like that. His sister got fat and she had to go away; that is what his father told him. Did Mama Lotus eat watermelons? Did you?"

Verdad shook her head at the schoolyard stories. Some things would never change. But, she knew she had to take this conversation seriously.

"No, Segundo, I did not swallow watermelon seeds. I am having a baby. But, this is definitely something you should take up with doña Lotus. Aquí, did I tell you I have a new book for you? It just came in and I saved it for you." She pushed the book about Hernán Cortés across the desk to him.

His eyes grew round and he exclaimed, "I know who he is. Hernán Cortés was a Spanish adventurer and conquistador who overthrew the Aztec empire and claimed México for Spain. He killed Montezuma."

Segundo never failed to astonish Verdad. She sent him to a big comfortable chair nearby to read the new book. At least, for now, his query was abandoned. She made a note to find books on Mexican heroes, not just Spanish conquerors.

SANTIAGO CLEMENTE YEBARA

Baby Santiago was born with a blue pebble in his left hand. The hospital and the doctors and nurses all pressured the new parents to have it examined, tested, and if necessary, biopsied. Verdad very politely refused. Its origin was of no mystery to her. It simply explained what happened to the pebble Lotus told her to place under her bed the night Santiago was conceived. That it reappeared at his birth made perfect sense to Verdad.

What was of a greater concern to her and to Domingo

were his eyes. It was hard to say what color they were at his birth. Over the next few days, the colors shifted, as if little Santiago could not decide which he liked best. In a second, they changed with his emotions. When he cried or became angry they would flash dark dark dark, the darkest of colors. As he calmed, one, then the other, seemed to glow amber. Domingo and Verdad hoped they would both be one color, for his sake. Verdad hoped they would be black. She could think of few animals with amber eyes that were very appealing. All of the ones she brought to mind were animals such as tree frogs and snakes. Domingo reminded her that owls, goats, and cats had yellow eyes. That made her think of lions and tigers and panthers, then of wolves--all predators and animals to be feared.

It did not matter. Santiago was healthy and he was finally here.

Ifiginia came to the hospital with Fernanda, the tiny pink cyclone, who ran up and down the halls and squealed until a nurse took her by the hand and found crayons and paper to occupy her. Ifiginia and Domingo wheeled Verdad to the nursery and looked in on the other babies. As they looked at Santiago, compared his size to the other babies, don Carlos and doña Milena approached them; don Carlos carried something behind his back.

They greeted one another with un abrazo, an embrace, and patted each other gently on the back. Don Carlos and Domingo shook hands. Doña Milena and Verdad kissed each other on the cheek.

Don Carlos announced, "¡Mami Verdad! ¡Papi Domingo! ¡Felicitaciones! Here is a present for Santiago—it is what all of the best-dressed babies are wearing these days." His eyes twinkled.

Verdad and Domingo thanked him and doña Milena. Inwardly, Verdad groaned. She did not want to start with that kind of thing.

She and Domingo opened the tastefully wrapped package and inside, found una gorra de beisbol, a baseball cap with a tiny black pony tail attached, just like that of Domingo, and a pair of child-sized, blue blocker aviator sunglasses.

The card read, "For Top Gun Dos!"

When Verdad and Santiago were released from the hospital, one of the nurses pushed them in a wheelchair to the entrance to await Domingo. She moved them away from the other people waiting outside. Verdad saw her look all around. Then the nurse presented her with a screw-top glass vial with el guijarro azul, the blue pebble, cushioned in a bed of cotton.

"I am not supposed to have this, señora Yebara but, I think it is most important that you have it. I have seen many things in all my years working in the maternity ward, some very strange and most, very wonderful, even miraculous. Pero, but, I have NEVER seen a baby with a pebble in its hand when it was born. I know it is frowned upon by the Church to talk of these things, but there must be a reason your child was born with this special gift, perhaps he possesses the power of other worlds. Nurture that gift and be sure it is used only for good."

Verdad thanked the woman and tucked the vial into her purse. When she had settled Santiago in the crib set up in their bedroom, she tucked it away behind a book. She wondered just a little about the blue pebble; she would have to watch Santiago and see if the words of the woman were true.

The next few weeks were filled with visits from friends and of course, don Clemente. He came by every evening after working, clutching a bag with something for them all to eat. While Verdad and Domingo enjoyed their meal, he walked from room to room, speaking softly to his grandson.

Mira la luna
Comiendo su tuna;
Echando las cáscaras
En la laguna.

Aquel caracol
que va por el sol
en cada ramita
llevaba una flor
que viva la gala
que viva el amor

que viva la concha
de aquel caracol.

Watch the Moon
Eating tuna*;
Throwing the shells
In the lagoon.

That snail
It is on the Sun
on each sprig
wearing a flower
¡que viva la gala
¡que viva love
¡que viva la concha
that snail.

*prickly pear

The nonsense words seemed to have a mesmerizing effect and with his amber eyes, he would look intently into the eyes of his grandfather, of Clemente, as if he were trying to understand.

"Look how smart mi nieto, my grandson, is, Verdad! He is listening to every word," Clemente pronounced.

One rainy day Lotus García and Segundo rode the Leopold Bus Line and came to visit. Santiago was four weeks old. Segundo clutched something wrapped in many layers of el periodico, the newspaper, and he proudly handed it to Verdad.

"I made this for your baby. Mama Lotus had to help me a little but I did most of it."

As the new mother carefully unwrapped the soggy paper, slowly removing one layer at a time, Segundo stood next to her and breathed into her hair in his excitement. She saw doña Lotus look around the apartment, then nod once. A wet, pathetic-looking Cuervo waited outside.

Inside the many layers was el Ojo de Dios, Eye of God . Segundo had made a fairly complex weaving with yarn of pale blue, aqua, and indigo, across two sticks. Verdad had seen them in the market, ones usually bought by tourists, but none were as beautiful as this one.

Lotus García told her, "El Ojo de Dios represents the power to see and understand things unknown, the unknowable, the Great Mystery."

"The four points represent earth, water, air, and fire. Mama Lotus taught me that," Segundo added. "I made this one to protect Santiago."

"We will hang it above his bed," Verdad replied. She knew that would disturb many people, including her husband and father, but she also knew it carried great spiritual significance. She had waited for this child for so long. She wanted him to be protected.

The day came for the baptism of Santiago, el Bautismo. It would be a dual ceremony with Fernanda, who was now over a year old. Ifiginia had insisted that they wait until the Yebara baby was born before Fernanda was baptized. That Sunday was even more special because the people of La Iglesia de la Santa Cruz were giving thanks that the rain had been abundant this year. There was corn in the doorway of the church, an age-old custom when crops were good. As Verdad and Domingo stepped into the shelter of the old building and shook out their umbrellas, she glimpsed ancient, pre-Columbian history blending with the modern.

Ifiginia and Tito had asked Verdad and Domingo to be the godparents of Fernanda, el padrino y la madrina. In turn, Verdad and Domingo had asked Ifiginia and Tito to be the godparents of Santiago. It was the very strongest bond the friends could have. If anything happened to the other parents, los compadres, the godparents, would act as second parents to the child.

As tradition dictated, the family of Tito provided the white christening gown, el ropón, for Fernanda, this one being handed down for many generations. It was a very long embroidered, handmade dress with a hat to cover her head before and after the water ceremony. Verdad and Domingo gave the baby gifts of a Bible and of a silver medal of the Virgen of Guadalupe with a gold edge. When Verdad presented Ifiginia with the medal, they both had to fight back tears. Ifiginia squeezed her hand.

Santiago also wore el ropón, his being an embroidered white shirt and pants with a long skirt on top, along with a hat. Ifiginia and Tito gave him his own Bible and a simple but elegant cross to hang in his room.

Padre Mateo lit a baptismal candle for each child, signifying the child was enlightened by Christ. He entrusted each candle to the parents and godparents and charged them with keeping the light burning. Santiago slept during the whole ceremony and Fernanda yowled when her head was anointed with water. She tried to push the hands of Padre Mateo away.

Over a breakfast in the Varela dining room, the families congratulated one another on their beautiful children and grandchildren. It continued to rain.

THE PICNIC

Under one small, black paraguas, umbrella, Leopold and Padre Mateo walked through the market one day. The rain had been coming for so long, people began to make jokes about seeing an ark. This amount of rain was quite unusual for Esperanza. In the library, the pages of the books stuck together and Verdad asked everyone who came in not to try to pull them apart. Fires were built in homes in the middle of the day to dry out clothing and bedding. Dogs that used to freely trot through the pueblo now hid under porches and in barns. Bread would not rise; babies slept all day and were awake all night. Armadillos were confused by the darkness and came out during the day to hunt for ants and termites. More than the usual numbers became road kill, so confused by their day time wanderings that when a car approached, instead of shuffling off into the brush, many were seen to jump into the air, thus encountering many fenders.

"Padre, I stop my bus every time I see one of these creatures on the road. If it is still alive, I try to hurry it along. If it is dead, I pick it up and put it in a barrel I lashed onto the undercarriage of the bus. Lately, I am stopping more for armadillos than I am for people!"

The two men chuckled and slogged through the puddles. The hem of the cassock Padre Mateo wore was ever muddy these days.

"You know, Padre, you have been with us for more than ten years now. It is closer to fifteen."

"I have? How do you know?" Padre Mateo could not believe that much time had passed.

"I keep track of these things. It has been ten years since Silvio moved to Matamoros; his daughter, Alma, is nearly ten years old." He brushed the rain off of his shoulder that the umbrella did not stop.

Without saying it aloud, both men acknowledged that Segundo was almost ten years old, as well.

"The people of Esperanza want to celebrate the time you have been with us. You are very important to us. You have accomplished many things since you have arrived."

Padre Mateo shook his head. "No, Leopold, the people of Esperanza have accomplished many things. I have just been a conduit of the Lord."

"Pues, we still want to celebrate. We are planning a picnic in your honor. You do not have to do a thing but attend. We are handling the rest. No arguments."

Padre Mateo knew with almost certainty that the women were handling the rest.

"Gracias, Leopold. I will be there."

The party was planned for the next Sunday afternoon. It would be held on the property of Leopold and Graciela, in a meadow behind the barn where the bus lived. If it rained, they would move the bus outdoors and use the space in the barn.

This was the same property, the same casa, where Leopold had grown up. It had been passed down to him and he would pass it down to his first son, Onofre, the son who had become an attorney.

The morning of the fiesta for Padre Mateo was slightly overcast but finally, there was a hint of blue in the sky. As the hours unfurled and the people of Esperanza left La Iglesia de la Santa Cruz after mass, the temperature rose, and the clouds floated off to the east. Leopold drove the Leopold Bus Line back and forth from la plaza to his home, transporting the congregation and their contributions to the party. Even Lotus García and her son were in attendance.

Brightly colored blankets polka-dotted the meadow. Each was covered with food and drinks. Padre Mateo visited each little island in the grass and sat for a few minutes, thanking the people for their faith in him, and tasting a bite here, a bite there. That was one of the benefits of being the priest for the pueblo; he never wanted for sustenance.

Don Carlos had hired the mariachi band to stroll through the meadow and keep things lively. He also provided the pigs that were being roasted in a pit at the edge of the field. Children played tag and ran between the blankets. No one objected; this was a fiesta!

The stream behind the house where Leopold used to swim with Graciela when they were children, was swollen with the rain and no one, human nor animal, was permitted to go there. It was running too rapidly.

Ifiginia organized Pass the Apple, enlisting nearly everyone at the party. Men and women grimaced and laughed as they passed la manzana from chin to chin. Even the mariachi singers joined.

Tito hung a huge piñata, shaped like a star with seven points that represented the deadly sins, from an old tree, and he danced it up and down on its rope. Everyone was given a chance but it was a very old nun who finally shattered the papier mache star and sent candy and coins flying. No one had ever seen a smile so huge on her face.

Padre Mateo, always a passionate man, was quite moved by the crowd and the festivities. More than once, he had to wipe tears from his face. As the afternoon wore on, he paused to survey his flock. Mud-spattered children sprawled on the ground, mothers scolded the children for getting mud on the blankets, neighbors who had not spoken in a long time chatted freely, and lovers strolled with their arms around one each other. Many, no, most of the men were engaged in a very boisterous drinking game. Dogs that had finally come out from their hiding places scampered through the crowd, cleaning up scraps of food. The heart of Padre Mateo was full.

He strolled to the edge of the meadow. The water in the stream was noisy as it rushed by, occasionally lathering up over its banks. He stood alone and went into a brown study, pondering his present life, and slipping back into memories of his life before he became a priest. The words to a song he used to sing with his daughter, Marisol, came back to him:

> Row, row, row your boat
> Gently down the stream.
> Merrily, merrily, merrily, merrily,
> life is but a dream.

He traced the outline of the mermaid tattoo on his forearm.

With a shrill cry of alarm, Cuervo darted by, a sooty black streak. Over and over he circled and cried. Everyone was accustomed to his antics, and, at first, Padre Mateo paid him no mind.

The insistence of the bird penetrated the reverie of the priest, and when he roused himself, he saw a tiny pink object in the water. It was the Bravo child, Fernanda, and before he could think it through, Padre Mateo waded into the arroyo. The water was turbulent and it was cold; he made the sign of the cross. He thrashed deeper and deeper and yet came no closer to the child. The froth of her frilly petticoats helped to keep her afloat. He pushed forward, slipping on the muddy stream bed, stumbling on rocks, being slammed by tree limbs and other debris. He inched closer to the child, her eyes closed, her face pale. Still Cuervo screamed and a few people began to run to the stream.

Padre Mateo went under the water and he floundered. The water terrified him. He came up coughing and swearing. The little girl was closer and, over and over he snatched at her, at her hair, at her dress, at her bare foot, anything. She spun around and around, just out of his reach. In one motion, Padre Mateo ducked under the water and pushed off from the rocky bottom. He reached out and snagged the child and pushed her up, up, up out of the water. He too pushed up his head from the roiling mess. How would he get both of them back? He was tired from swimming, from fighting the current. So tired. The mermaid on his arm glistened; her tail seemed to pulsate, as if she were swimming. Merrily, merrily, merrily, merrily. He found the strength to move forward with the child.

Segundo ran back and forth on the edge of the flooded arroyo, calling out for Padre Mateo. When he saw him struggling to hold the limp child and to begin the battle back to safety, Segundo leaped into the stream. He was swept along to Padre Mateo and he latched onto his cassock. The three whirled through the water, finally arriving at a spot where the water was slightly less wild and just a bit shallower, and they inched their way to the bank, Segundo kicking furiously until he managed to get a foothold in the mud.

Padre Mateo shoved Fernanda onto the muddy shore and beached himself beside her. Segundo climbed out of the stream and stood over them, dripping and gasping for air. Several people, including Tito, grabbed for Fernanda and began to revive her. Ifiginia fainted. Verdad and Milena tended to her. Padre Mateo lay on his back on the shore, catching his breath, and thanked God for saving the baby.

Someone threw blankets over him and Segundo and as they helped them, Fernanda coughed and spewed, then let loose with a mighty and angry bawling.

Leopold ran up to Padre Mateo and enfolded him. He pulled Segundo into the embrace.

"Padre Mateo, you are a hero! You saved Fernanda. If it had not been for you being right at that very spot at that very moment, who knows how this would have ended. And, Segundo, you saved Padre Mateo!" He hugged him so tightly that Segundo could not speak.

Padre Mateo shook his head. "No, Leopold. I thank you for your kind words but it is not I who saved her. It was Segundo and Cuervo. And, the Lord. Always, our Lord. He sent Cuervo to tell me that Fernanda was in danger."

As soon as everyone saw that the baby, Padre Mateo, and Segundo were safe, they began to pack up their things. While the people of Esperanza were overjoyed that there had been no tragedy, the picnic was over. A much quieter crowd left the meadow than the one that had been assembled only a short while ago.

LOTUS GARCÍA

Quite a few people lay awake that night.

Ifiginia and Tito tucked their baby in between them in their bed and kept vigil over her. Great fear and then, enormous relief welled up in both of them over and over during the long night.

Don Carlos and doña Milena knelt and thanked God for saving their granddaughter.

Domingo, as well as many other fathers, stared at the ceiling and second-guessed the events of the day: what if that had been their child in the water?

Padre Mateo relived every wet moment of the rescue, from the unrelenting clamor of the bird to the bravery of Segundo.

Graciela reassured Leopold that he was not at fault but he could not help but feel a great sense of responsibility. The picnic had, after all, been on his property. He was also filled with amazement for the way his grandson had conducted himself.

Verdad was full of pride for the fearlessness Segundo showed. She so wished she could share her feelings with someone.

Lotus García lay on her narrow bed and thanked every deity she could think of for Cuervo, Segundo, and the way the day turned out. She finally knew why Cuervo had come to them.

Over the next days, all the talk was about the rescue. Fernanda was more precious than ever, Padre Mateo more loved, Segundo more appreciated by his classmates and everyone in

Esperanza, and Cuervo risked growing too fat to fly from all of the morsels people offered him.

Lotus and Segundo waited in their yard for the Leopold Bus Line to arrive and take them to the market. As it approached, Lotus looked at her casita. It was neat and clean; it sported a fresh coat of paint, flowers in pots, vegetables in the garden. The front window reflected the bright sun. She saw manzanas, apples, growing on the once scrawny tree that had appeared one morning long ago.

Her dark-eyed, curly haired son stood at her side, Cuervo perched on his shoulder. Segundo was as tall as she now. She had everything she could ever wish for.

The bus stopped for them and as they boarded, whistles and cheers greeted them. Lotus thumped to her seat and Segundo waved to everybody. They were both embarrassed with the attention but also just a little pleased.

They arrived at the market and went about their errands. Padre Mateo strolled among the stalls, chatting. The mariachis were setting up, getting ready to entertain the crowd. When their shopping and trading was finished, Segundo and Lotus sat by the fountain, in the shade of a tree, and enjoyed sweet potato emapanadas, filled pastries. Once again, Segundo told Lotus that he was going to sing in a mariachi band and dress in a silver-studded charro outfit with a wide-brimmed hat. He bragged that beautiful women would swoon over his romantic songs. Lotus shook her head and laughed.

Leopold, the owner of Leopold Bus Line, danced alone to the mariachi band. He wore his blue bus driver shirt with his name emblazoned over his heart, his cap tilted back on his head, his teeth flashing in a wide smile. He saw Lotus and Segundo sitting under the shade of a tree and motioned them over. Lotus shook her head no and grinned. Leopold waved to them a second, then a third time. Segundo bounced up and down in front of her, his excited face begging her to give him permission.

"Go, Segundo, go. Dance with that crazy man."

Segundo darted through the crowd until he reached the bus driver. He took the outstretched hands of Leopold and they stomped and twirled to the music.

A tall, thin woman stepped out from the crowd and moved close to Leopold and Segundo. It was Verdad, the young woman from the bus so many years ago. Verdad wore a necklace with a small blue stone hanging from it. In the crowd behind swayed her husband, Domingo, sunglasses in place, holding their baby, Santiago. His huge hands enveloped the child. Leopold held out a hand to Verdad and she took it and one of the hands of the boy. Overhead, high in a tree, a black raven bobbed up and down and whistled.

Lotus saw all of this. She watched as Leopold, Verdad, and Segundo glided to the marriage of instruments: the plaintive resonance of the violins, the thumping bass of the guitars, and the blaring of the trumpets. Verdad smiled down at Segundo, then looked to Lotus. She beckoned to her with her head. *Come, come join us.*

Lotus waved her hand in dismissal, but just as that day so long ago, she found herself inexplicably drawn. She rose and straightened her skirt. Leopold, Verdad, and Segundo danced toward her. Verdad held out her hand. Lotus took it and that of Segundo. She joined her body to their graceful movements, and she, Lotus García, plied and pirouetted, tapped and twirled, stomped and slid, floated and fox-trotted, grapevined and glided to the guitars and violins and trumpets.

PALOMA TURQUESA

Una Americana with flaming red hair arrived in

Esperanza late one afternoon in the cab of a PeMex gasolina

truck. Paloma Turquesa, whose true name will be revealed

shortly, had been traveling at a precipitous rate of speed from

Matamoros, enjoying the quaint casitas and fincas, farms, when

her black Mercedes convertible hit a tope, one of the treacherous

speed bumps. They are treacherous only if you do not know how

slowly you must approach and navigate over them. Her wrecked

suspension compelled her to abandon her little, but very

expensive, black car on the side of the dusty road leading into

Esperanza and to hitch a ride in the PeMex truck. Eusebio, the handsome driver of said truck, the man who sported long shaggy sideburns, could not believe his luck.

"I had no idea what that sign back there meant. You know, the one with the two black bumps that look like, well, you know." The pelirroja, the redhead, grinned at her driver.

Eusebio threw back his black maned head and roared. "¡Sí,yo sé!   El tope worked, did it not? Most visitors find out the hard way. It made you slow down, even stop aquí. Now you must spend time in lovely Esperanza."

Esperanza had not been in her travel plans. She had hoped to make it to Vera Cruz, further south and on the coast, without incident. She had heard it was comparatively safe there and she relished the idea of living near the sea. But,why not Esperanza? Maybe the sleepy little town would welcome her. She was looking for a new place to live, some place to inspire her art, get her out of cold winters and away from the commercial crowds of places like Santa Fe, New Mexico, or Sedona, Arizona. No more trendy artist colonies.

Eusebio had tried to tell her his name but she just could not grasp how to pronounce it, especially after he spelled it for her. "Try 'Shebo'," he offered. It is what mi familia calls me. Me llamo Shebo Medina."

Shebo had trouble with her name as well: Her apellido, her surname, of Tarkowski, was nearly impossible for him. Paloma Turquesa is who she became on the dusty, bumpy ride into Esperanza. A new name for her new life as a rich widow, la viuda rica. It worked for her.

Shebo glanced at the woman out of the corner of his eye as they drove along. He had never seen a pelirroja, a redhead, up close before. He often saw the putas in Matamoros with their dyed and sprayed hair and they never looked very appealing. This one, though, surely she was a real redhead. Her skin was fair, lightly freckled, and her blue-green eyes were clear and bright. Everything about her looked authentic, even her eyelashes. He could not help but wonder if the rest of her was.

Pamela and Shebo drew a lot of attention as the big tanker rumbled to a stop at the lone gas station of Esperanza. Shebo hopped out of the cab and scrambled around to the other side to help his passenger. The owner of the station, Taciano, stood in one of the open bays and watched the stranger hop down just as agilely as Shebo had. Taciano waited until Shebo had brought the woman into the office out of the sun before he made a move to greet them. Paloma had to squeeze past him in the doorway. Shebo fished in the red cooler with melted ice for the coldest bottle of Jarritos soda pop. He handed it to the woman.

Taciano asked, "¿Qué tal, Shebo?", never taking his eyes off of her. He was a short, bandy-legged man.. He had on faded black jeans and a yellow shirt that barely covered his torso; on the back was the PeMex logo in bold black letters. His rotund belly made Paloma think of someone who had swallowed a bowling ball. He made her uncomfortable. There was something just a shade too intimate in the way his black eyes bored into her.

"Muy bien, amigo. Quiero presentarte a mi amiga nueva, Paloma Turquesa. I want to introduce you to my new friend."

Taciano swept his cap from his head and bowed. Several large flakes of skin floated to the ground from his bald scalp. She had to refrain from making a face.

"Es un placer. It is a pleasure." And that was about all she would ever hear the small man with the scraggly beard say directly to her. Taciano Zaragoza was definitely a man of few words yet, he noticed everything.

As Shebo told Taciano where to find the Mercedes, Paloma took in what she could see of the little pueblo of Esperanza and admired how clean and orderly it was laid out. She heard the women calling to each other in the market, saw their bright goods in the stalls, and excused herself from the two men. She walked along the hot unpaved street, seemingly unaware of the stares she drew from everyone who saw her. It felt good to be out in the open, out of her car and the PeMex truck, and she wore the sun beating down on her like a second skin.

"¡Cuidado, señora, el sol! Careful. The sun will burn you in no time." A tiny woman with leathery skin pointed to her own face and then reached out to the face of the gringa. "Aquí, here," and she handed Paloma a chal, a shawl, made of fine aqua wool. She showed her how to drape it over her head and bare shoulders to keep as much of her protected as possible.

Paloma rummaged through the large bag that hung from her shoulder. She found a twenty dollar bill and tried to hand it to the woman.

"¡No, no! ¡Es un regalito! A gift!" The little woman whirled and hurried back to her stand. Hands clasped in front of her belly, she turned away as Paloma went by and spit in the dust.

"Now I have insulted her," Paloma realized. Rather than add insult to injury, she resisted stopping at her stall and buying something. She noted where the woman and her woven items were located for another visit. She might make a good subject to paint some day.

Shebo caught up with Paloma. He had seen the interaction between the two women and realized she needed some help.

"She is a feisty one. Se llama Serafia. Her name is Serafia. Just give her some time. She will be more friendly eventually. So, where do you plan to stay? I would offer you my home but it would not look right. I mean, you, a beautiful woman, staying in my house. As much as I would like that . . ." and again, he threw back his head. His laughter boomed. Several people turned to look at them. Serafia shook her head and busied herself with refolding her shawls.

"Well, I have no idea, actually. I had not thought that far. Is there a hotel or a bed and breakfast?"

"¿Aquí? Here? No. But, there is Padre Mateo. Let us ask him if you can stay with las monjas, the nuns, at least for one night."

Paloma saw the tall, handsome priest talking with a well-built and well-dressed man.   Shebo introduced her to first Padre Mateo and then to the other man. Carlos Varela was immediately taken with her and never moved his eyes from her. When Carlos learned that she needed a place to stay, he jumped in to offer his guest house.

"Mi esposa, Milena, would love to have you come and stay with us. Our daughter, her husband, and our granddaughter live on our land and they will be thrilled, tambien, also, to meet you. An Americana! Y una pelirroja bella, a beautiful redhead! They will be thrilled."

"Well, if it is not too much trouble, I would love that." What am I doing, she wondered? Oh, what the heck. How bad could this guy be? He was standing there talking to the village priest.

Padre Mateo watched the exchange between Carlos and Paloma. A barely perceptible tingle shot through him but he tucked the moment away for later scrutiny.

"Padre Mateo, please come and eat with us tonight. Shebo, you, too! Milena always has an overabundance of food and she will be thrilled with the opportunity to entertain. I know she is often lonely out there."

Although refusing don Carlos made him nervous, Shebo made his apologies, saying his familia was waiting for him, that he had not seen them for tres semanas, three weeks. That was the truth but also, in reality, sitting at the dinner table of don Carlos was the last thing he wanted to do. He would not be thrilled.

When she heard of the plans, Milena insisted that Verdad and Domingo be invited. They could drive Padre Mateo and the new woman to their hacienda. Ifiginia would be happy to see her friend and the maid would watch the little ones, los niñitos, while everyone visited. Milena welcomed the opportunity to practice speaking with someone other than Verdad, whose English was a bit clumsy, and to spend time with una Americana.

When Domingo and Verdad and Santiago arrived, Shebo loaded luggage into the trunk and said Buenos Noches to all. Verdad insisted that the woman sit up front with her husband so she could see all of the sights on the road as they drove along. Domingo steered the big black car in silence, his head never turning, and Paloma supposed he never took his eyes off of the road. She could not be sure, though, because she could not see his eyes for his sunglasses.

Verdad sat in the middle of the back seat, Padre Mateo next to the window. Verdad wore a long, white skirt and a flowered top, Padre Mateo his usual black cassock. Her knee touched his. The way the light played on them, it was a study in black and white, like the keys of a piano. Paloma saw the easy comfort with which they chatted, and from their conversation, learned about the new library, a bit about some of the people of the town, and about the solid little boy, Santiago, belted into his car seat. He too was silent as they drove along and looked out the side window. He wore sunglasses that matched those of his father, just smaller.

319

Domingo spoke into the intercom when they arrived at the Varela compound. The gate swung open and they slowly drove up to the house. Golden light from the last rays of the afternoon sun shone on the large house, making it glow. An attractive, dark-haired woman who looked to be the same age as Paloma, maybe a bit younger, stood in the shade of the arched entry and waited for them.

"Padre Mateo, Domingo, Verdad, y Santiago. Bienvenidos." They each gave their hostess un abrazo, a hug, as they entered the house. Her eyes swept the newcomer from head to toe and she stepped forward to kiss her on the cheek. "I am Milena Varela. Welcome to our home. We are very pleased that you have decided to honor us with your presence," she said formally.

Paloma complimented her on her English and thanked her for inviting her. Milena hooked her arm through hers and together they walked into the house. Padre Mateo thought, "Uf, at least that went smoothly." He had worried that Milena would not take to the Americana.

Milena showed Pamela to her rooms in the guest house and told her to join them when she felt refreshed. She told her to take her time, even take a short nap. "Carlos is on the phone with one of his business associates. Who knows how long he will be."

Pamela set about making herself at home in the guest house next to the pool. It was furnished simply and tastefully, just as the main house had been from what she had seen. She hung her clothes in the closet, tucked a few things into a dresser, and finally, sat on the edge of the crisply dressed bed. The coverlet had a large embroidered "V" at the bottom and the pillow cases were also monogramed, white on white. She slid her feet out of her sandals, enjoying the cool tile on the bottom of her feet. She lay back. She heard water gently lapping in the pool outside, a few birds calling to one another, and almost instantly, she fell asleep.

It was growing dark when she awoke and she felt rested. She had not slept well in recent weeks; perhaps it was the import of finding a new home. Embarking on this journey was a very unusual experience for Pamela Tarkowski. She had always let her husband attend to their financial needs, make travel arrangements, and if she were being honest with herself, control her life. That had all been fine with her. She had her art and she enjoyed the freedom and ability to spend hours and hours lost in its creation. While she had had a modicum of success with selling some of her pieces in the shows her husband arranged for her, she was not all that interested in selling her pieces. It felt as if she were handing over one of her own children when she parted with a painting; she had birthed it and did not like to think that she was putting a price on its beauty.

She still worked in oils, despite warnings about the fumes, the chemicals, and the time it took for them to dry. She could manage the colors more easily. The colors were more luminous and blended well. Acrylics dried too fast and she did not like to work quickly. She enjoyed seeing what arose from the colors. The smell of turpentine was familiar and comforting to her; its aroma cloaked her like perfume some days.

Now, Paloma needed to get ready for dinner with her new acquaintances. She hoped they would become friends. She had a feeling this was a place that would become important to her and perhaps she could make it her home.

After she dressed in a pair of worn but clean jeans and a white blouse, she plaited her long hair into a single braid, slid small earrings with raw pieces of turquoise in them, and arranged the aqua shawl that Serafia had given her in the market. Paloma checked herself in the mirror over the dresser. Hanging over the frame, seeming to watch her, was a small pinkish brown snake with a silver sheen. She started and a scream came out before she could stop herself. She backed away from the mirror. The hard shiny scales of its belly reflected in the glass.

There was a knock on the door and the voice of a child called out in halting English. "Señora? Lady? Mrs.? Are you in there? Mama told me to tell you it is time for la cena, for dinner."

Paloma jerked open the door and asked the boy standing there, "What do you know about snakes?"

He shrugged his shoulders.

Paloma made a hissing sound and moved her hand in what she hoped was a sinuous snake-like way. She pointed to the dresser.

"Culebra? Snake?" The boy ran into the room to look. "Muy padre! Very cool!" He grabbed the snake behind the head and it writhed and wriggled its tail. He let it twine its tail around his wrist and forearm, then took off with it and from her doorway, Paloma saw him toss it over the wall around the pool and into the flowering bushes that grew there.

"Gracias, er, Marco? Rafael?" The boy waved and ran toward the main house.

She walked along a lighted path to the main house and with every cautious step looked for snakes. *Okay, okay, you are in Mexico. Snakes live in Mexico. Just keep your eyes open.* She took quite a few deep breaths on her short walk.

Milena appeared from the back of the house and gave Paloma un abrazo. Paloma was beginning to feel as if she were an old friend. "I hear you have met one of our ferocious and wild beasts! Very good! I hope you were not too scared."

"What ferocious beast?" Carlos asked.

"There was a snake in my room. One of your sons got rid of it for me."

While Carlos could speak English, he was not as fluent as his wife or daughter. Milena translated for him.

"A snake? What did it look like?" He looked worried.

She described the snake, using her hands to indicate its size. She also described how it wriggled when picked up.

"That is probably a blind snake, no worries. They are actually good. They live underground and eat termites and ants. We do not see them all the time, mostly after a rain. Please do not give it another thought. It was more scared of you. They cannot see much, just changes in the light." Carlos closed his eyes and stuck his hands out in front of him, imitating a blind man. Milena slapped at his hands and directed them into the dining room.

Everyone was already seated when they entered. Carlos pulled out her chair, then that of his wife. The men stood as the women sat. She saw that Domingo had removed his sunglasses, as well as those of his son. Both pairs were tucked into his shirt pocket. She tried not to stare at their eyes.

After Padre Mateo had given thanks for the meal and friends, old and new, the food was passed.

Ah, this was real Mexican food, not like the kind Paloma was used to from the chain restaurants in the States: Omelettes with black beans, freshly made salsa, and onions served with spicy Patatas Bravas, fresh fruit, and chilled white wine.

She was seated next to Padre Mateo and watched everything he did. Paloma felt very foreign and out of place but she guessed she would commit no etiquette sins if she followed his lead. She saw that he, as well as everyone else, kept their hands on the table at all times. He waited for Milena to start before he began eating so she did, too. He left a bit of the omelette and a few pieces of fruit on his plate. She did the same. When he was finished, he placed his fork, prongs down and the knife across the plate with the handles facing to the right. As she positioned her utensils, she asked Milena how to make the sauce for the potatoes.

"It is muy <u>fácil</u> very easy. I just sauté onion and a little garlic. When the onion is soft, I toss it with paprika, a splash of hot sauce, and some fresh thyme from the garden. It may not be gourmet but I have always added ketchup and mayonnaise. Everybody has their own version but this is the one mi familia likes best."

It sounded easy but Pamela knew it would be a different story if she tried to recreate it. It was always more than just tossing in some ingredients.

When Santiago and Fernanda had eaten a few bites of fruit and the omelette and started to play with the remainder, the maid came to take them and the twins off to play.

"So, Paloma Turquesa," Padre Mateo began, "tell us how you came to find Esperanza."

"Well, my name is, me llamo Pamela Tarkowski but Shebo, Eusebio, had trouble saying my name and came up with a new one."

Carlos raised his glass. "I like the new name. It suits you. Perhaps, if you stay in Esperanza, you will adopt it. To Paloma Turquesa." She thanked him and took a sip of her wine.

"I would like to find a place to live and to work, and I am enchanted with this place. Except for the snakes! Everyone has been so friendly, well, almost everyone." She remembered how Serafia had spit in the dust. "I am an artist and I am looking for a loft, a barn, or something to use for my studio. I do not really care where I live, or what kind of house I have, just as long as the studio has the right light and lots of room. I sometimes paint big. Really big."

Again, Milena translated.

Carlos said, "Ah, a pintora. Como Frida Kahlo. Like Frida Kahlo."

Milena then asked, "What kind of things do you paint?"

"I paint mostly portraits."

Milena translated, "Retratista".

"Not your typical, formal portrait. I try to capture the real essence of a person. It usually takes me a long time to complete a portrait because I like to spend a lot of time with each subject, so I get to know them."

"Quizas, perhaps, you could hang one or two of your portraits in the library. We have much blank wall space yet," Verdad offered. "How big are they?"

Pamela smiled at the younger woman. She was grateful for her support. "Not everything I paint is all that huge. It would be a great opportunity for the people of Esperanza to see what I do.

"What kind of stone is in your necklace, Verdad? I have never seen one that color. Turquesa? Turquoise? Is that your birthstone?"

Ifiginia snorted into her wine glass.

Verdad shot her a look before she turned to the newcomer. She said, "It is a long story but yes, in a way, it is my birthstone, la piedra de nacimiento. I shall tell you all about it another time."

"Well, all we have to do now is find you a place to live, sí?" Carlos said.

"That is assuming I decide to stay here. And, what about my car? I really need to get it taken care of. I do not feel comfortable leaving it on the side of the road out in the middle of nowhere. Can I trust the man at the gas station?"

Carlos and Domingo laughed heartily.

"I would not worry about your car, señora. Everyone knows this is where Carlos Varela lives. I doubt that anyone would dare to bother it." Domingo and Carlos exchanged looks. "If anything, they washed and waxed it for you!"

"You know you have already decided to stay in Esperanza. We would not let you go now even if you tried!" Carlos said.

Milena nodded. "Believe me. You are here to stay." This was said without a smile.

The sun ducked behind a cloud. A shadow seemed to pass over everyone in the room and the body of la gringa suddenly felt chilled. She pulled her chal, her shawl, around her shoulders.

Padre Mateo saw her involuntary shiver and said, "Let her decide on her own, amigos mios. Naturalmente, of course, you want a beautiful and talented artist gracing the town but it is her decision in the end.

Milena stood to begin clearing the table. "I would not be so sure about that." This time she smiled.

MILENA Y CARLOS VARELA

Carlos first saw Milena as a 14 year old; he was 18. She was selling raspados in Matamoros. The snow cone-like treat with fruit flavorings was one of his favorite things to eat.

She leaned over a block of ice and scraped it with a knife. She slid the ice into a cup and continued until there was enough for one serving. The process was slow and it gave Carlos the opportunity to watch the pretty girl. When she asked him, "¿Qué sabor quiere?", he told her, ""Fresa, por favor. Strawberry, please." He did not say it out loud but the color of her lips reminded him of the fruit. He shook his head at this thought.

She is not much more than a child, Carlos!

He stood near her cart as he enjoyed el raspado. He asked about her familia; she said she had none. He asked where she lived, "¿Dónde vives?" She hesitated and then told him she slept in a rented room with six other street vendors, all girls and women. "It is hard to keep anything of your own in a place like that." When he asked her about school, she laughed and said, "I have not had time for school for a long time."

He said good-bye and went on his way. He was just starting out in the business of selling las drogas and he had appointments to keep for his boss, el jefe. But, the thought of the pretty young girl living in squalor and selling shaved ice to strangers bothered him. It was not right. He knew from what he had seen and heard how young girls without families and proper homes could end up. He thought about his own sisters and shuddered at the thought of what could befall them.

He returned to his home and continued to move up in the drug business. Carlos was never ostentatious and knew how to keep transactions confidential. El jefe trusted him and gave him additional responsibility. In a few years, Carlos was in control of his own tiny pasillo, corridor, with people working for him. His ability to remain emotionally unattached and to step back when business matters became volatile served him well. Squabbles rarely turned into betrayals in his operation. He was never without his friend, Domingo Dos Ojos. Those who tried to steal from him were dealt with rapidly and decisively.

Almost daily, he stopped at the stand to buy a raspado, leaving overly generous tips, las propinas, for the young girl. He learned her name was Milena. Sometimes he brought her small presents, regalitos. She always thanked him politely for anything he brought but seldom showed much emotion. He wondered if it was because she expected that whatever he gave her would vanish not long after she took it back to the room she slept in.

One day Carlos said, "I like you, Milena, and I would like to help you."

"Oh, I am sure you would. Many men wish to help me." She turned back to flaking the ice and he saw the sneer on her face. By now, she was 17 and had learned much about men. He had seen her grow up, turning from a pretty girl into a stunning woman.

"No, I am serious. And, I have the most honorable of intentions."

This was hilarious to her. She knew his reputation, how he earned the money he left for las propinas, the big tips, and she could not put honorable anywhere near his name.

"Let me show you," he begged. "I will give you a place to live and you will not have to work on the street. You will not have to work at all."

"And, how will I repay you for your generosity, ey?"

Carlos had an answer ready. "Be my wife." This time he left no tip and he did not wait for el raspado. With Domingo behind the wheel of a new black SUV, he drove off.

PALOMA Y LAS CULEBRAS

After dinner, Ifiginia and Verdad walked Pamela back to the guest house.

"The groundskeeper watches closely for snake nests but occasionally, like today, they will find a way in. Just be alert. You have to watch out for el serpiente de cascabel, the rattlesnake, at night. Just stay on the walkways and you will be able to see them." Ifiginia knew she was frightening la gringa with her warning, but she could not help smiling to herself. When they arrived at the guest house, Ifiginia made a great show of searching behind the doors and under the bed for snakes.

"I think you are safe. Quizas you should leave the light on en el baño, just so you can see if you have to get up during the night," she said.

"Oh, stop it," Verdad said. "Sí, hay muchas culebras aquí, many snakes here, but they tend to stay away from humans. And, not all of them are poisonous. I will have to introduce you to Lotus García, our version of a folk healer. She can tell you much more about snakes."

"Is she a curandera?" Pamela asked. "I have read about them and I would be very interested to talk with her."

"Just do not tell everyone you meet that you believe in that stuff," Ifiginia warned. "A lot of people think las curanderas are evil, that they practice la magia negra, dark magic. Some people call her la bruja, a witch, and say she will steal your soul." Again, Ifiginia could not help herself.

"Bastante! Enough! Let nuestra amiga nueva, our new friend, get some sleep, though I am not sure how she will be able to accomplish that with all this talk of witches and snakes. Sleep well, Paloma." Verdad gave Pamela a kiss on her cheek and grabbed the hand of Ifiginia to pull her out the door.

Pamela, or Paloma, as everyone in Esperanza now called her, found a parcel of ground just outside of el pueblo, blessed with a grove of Mexican plum trees. It had a structure on it that could be turned into her home and studio. She continued to stay in the Varela guest house until the broken floorboards were replaced and a new floor of hand-molded Saltillo tile in rich terra cotta tones was installed, the meager plumbing was updated, and sections of the building had been partitioned into a kitchen with a multi-colored talavera tile counter, a large bedroom with French doors that opened out into a patio with a hot tub, and a bath with a glass block shower. She also required an adobe fireplace in the corner of the studio. It would help to heat the expansive space. Carlos acted as the general contractor and oversaw every step of the renovations. His name seemed to procure materials and labor much more rapidly than Pamela had thought possible. Her studio/casita still occasionally smelled of the mules and the hay they ate that had been housed in it but she welcomed the smells. Those odors mixed with the aromas of turpentine and oil paints.

When it was all completed, she had an intimate dinner party and invited her new friends to see her studio. She let it be known that she was ready to paint and wanted the people of Esperanza to pose for her. While some people were reluctant with the idea of Pamela painting their portrait, Ifiginia was anxious to be her first subject. Ifiginia was just developing a lovely roundness with her second pregnancy and Pamela immediately envisioned her as a Madonna.

Ifiginia had arrived at the studio early in the morning before Pamela was finished with her desayuno, her breakfast. That could have been the first time Ifiginia was ever early for anything. Pamela got her charcoal pencils and brushes and tubes of paint lined up. She asked that Ifiginia wait until the portrait was done before she looked at it.

"I am so excited to be the first to be painted. Who else are you going to paint? Mi madre y mi padre? My mother and father? Of course, you will have to paint Verdad y Domingo. Y mi esposo, my husband Tito. Tito and I cannot decide where we will hang my portrait. I want to put it in the living room, or the entry way, but Tito wants it in the bedroom. No one will see it in there except us. I think it should be some place out in the open." Ifiginia nattered on and on. She reminded Pamela of the bright, cheerful parakeets she heard chattering in the plum grove.

"Well, let us just see if you like how I represent you. You must realize I have my own style and I do not often end up with formal, true-to-life portraits," Pamela replied.

"I know, I know, but I think whatever you do will be just fine. I am so excited to have my portrait painted. Will it look like an Andy Warhol picture? You know, with all of those colors. I love the colors he used for Elizabeth Taylor. Will my portrait look anything like that?"

"Ifiginia, I think it might be better for you, since you are pregnant, if I work from photographs of you. I do not want to tire you. It is hard work sitting in the same pose for a long period of time. I know pregnant women get swollen feet and I surely do not want you to go through that."

Ifiginia groaned at the memory of how swollen her body had become when she was pregnant with Fernanda but she protested. "No, no, I want to be here while you paint. I asked my doctor if it was safe to be around the fumes and he said as long as there was good circulation, and there is, the baby and I would be okay. Please let me stay."

Pamela thought for a moment. "How about this? Why not lie down and that way you can keep your feet up and I will not feel so worried about you being uncomfortable." She dragged over an old fainting couch she had reupholstered in a midnight blue velvet. It had an ornately carved wooden frame and legs. The padded, rising back suggested the body of a woman.

"Oh, so sexy. Tito will like this!"

Ifiginia arranged herself on the fainting couch, fanned her

dark hair around her shoulders, and struck a pose. Pamela tried not to laugh at how awkward she looked.

"Honey, just relax. Get yourself comfortable and just be yourself."

It took a few false starts but finally, Ifiginia looked more natural. Pamela began. The idea of reclining had been a good one. Ifiginia became quiet and soon, her eyes closed and she dozed off. Perfect, Pamela thought. She drew many sketches, focusing on her face and her ripening abdomen.

Ifiginia came every day to the studio, usually early, and the two women often ate desayuno, breakfast, together. Ifiginia gabbled about anything and everything. Pamela could not help but like her. She learned a great deal about the people of Esperanza from these conversations. All except for the Varela family; that was one area Ifiginia did not discuss.

On the last day that Pamela needed Ifiginia, she prepared a special breakfast for them of Chorizo con Huevos, spicy sausage with eggs, mashed avocadoes, and salsa.

343

"I hope this does not give you heartburn," Pamela said as she placed the thick ceramic plate with the steaming food in front of Ifiginia. She passed her a bowl filled with plums from her trees, and filled her glass with freshly squeezed orange juice.

Ifiginia played with a tortilla and did not seem to have her usual hearty appetite. When asked what was wrong, if she were ill, she replied, "Oh, Paloma, you take such good care of me. I admire you so much. Here you are, in a new country, all alone, you do everything for yourself, and you are so talented. I wish I could be more like you."

"You would be surprised if you knew how hard it is for me sometimes. I miss my husband. I miss the U.S., I miss my friends, but I also love it here. This is the opportunity I had been looking for nearly all of my life, at least most of my married life. I am living my dream."

"What happened to your esposo, your husband? How did he die?" Ifiginia did not tiptoe around the subject.

"Rob had a heart attack. It was very surprising because he was still young, 60, and in very good health. He worked out all the time, ran, skied, swam. He never let anything white pass his lips – salt, sugar, starch. He stopped drinking years ago, too, and he never smoked. I guess it was something that was going to happen, no matter how careful he was." She saw Ifiginia frown.

"I know 60 might not sound very young to you, but, believe me, Rob lived more like he was 40. And we had no warnings."

"No, 60 is young. Mi padre, Carlos, is not even 60 yet and I do not want to even think of something like that happening to him. He has so many things he wants to do yet. Mi madre would be deprovista, bereft, without him. Pobre Roberto. Poor Robert. Pobre Paloma. "

"It is okay. He was a private investment banker. We had a great marriage and he left me very wealthy. Very wealthy. We traveled, had a beautiful house, just about everything I could want. But, I had to first be Mrs. Tarkowski, the wife of Robert

Tarkowski. Always. Now, even though I miss him terribly, he has given me the possibility to start fresh. I have more money than I could ever spend.

"My work is changing since I arrived in Esperanza. I used to paint whatever I felt like—landscapes, portraits, still lifes. Nothing was very original. Rob called it my little hobby. It used to make me angry when he said that. He usually brought it up when we had a dinner party with his business associates. It was as if he had to put me down.

"I want my work to have value, to tell the viewer a story. Maybe here I will find my muse; the beauty of this place seems to be trying to seep into my work. There is a feeling I have here that I have never experienced anywhere else. It is almost supernatural."

Ifiginia looked at her and said nothing. Pamela could tell she did not quite grasp what Pamela was talking about. "Finish eating. I want to complete this painting today and let you get back to Tito and Fernanda."

Although only a few weeks had passed, the body of the young woman had changed considerably. Most changed was her face which had grown softer and rounder. Pamela did not want to have to change the portrait.

As her model got settled and she uncovered her canvas, a movement by the fireplace caught her eye. Pamela turned to look at the brown snake with yellow stripes on its sides and back. "Holy shit! Ifiginia, a snake! Culebra!"

Both women ran into the kitchen area, behind the counter. Ifiginia called her father and within minutes, Carlos drove up. Carlos laughed as he swung open the studio door. "Another snake, Paloma? Dónde está? Where is it?"

Pamela pointed to the fireplace where the brown snake lay on the hearth.

"That? It is not dangerous. It is a garter snake. He was probably cold last night and came in to get warm by the fireplace." He winked as he said this. "He will not hurt you if you leave him alone. Get me a broom." The snake flicked his tongue, tasting the air and its odors.

Pamela said. "He better not have been in here all night! Just shoot it, or something." The thought of the snake being in the house all night turned her stomach. She stretched out the broom to him over the counter.

Carlos laughed as he took it and slowly approached el serpiente, the snake. He did not want to startle it and have it slither off somewhere where he could not get to it. He held out the straw end of the broom and let the snake curl onto it. From the doorway, he turned and pretended to shake it at the two women. He left the broom outside in the dirt, knowing the snake would move away when it felt safe. "You are lucky, Paloma," he said. He eats all kinds of things and will keep a yard free of spiders and lizards."

"I would much rather get a cat. Thank you, don Carlos. Now, go home, so we can get some work done."

Carlos bowed and left, saying something about Paloma being a snake charmer.

"Tu estás lleno de mierda. You are full of shit," Paloma called out as the door closed.

Ifiginia tried not to look surprised at the easy familiarity with which Paloma Turquesa spoke to him.

That night, Pamela stood in front of the painting of Ifiginia and shook her head. It just was not right. It did not capture the essence she wanted to portray of the young woman. Anyone with a modicum of talent could have painted this, she thought. I am just going to have to let it sit and see if I can figure out what to do with it.

TITO BRAVO

Of course, she was obligated to ask Tito to pose next. Ifiginia would not even let her entertain the thought of asking anyone else.

Tito intrigued Pamela. His muscular athleticism was evident in his every movement. At first she thought she would paint a portrait to complement the one of Ifiginia, like a matched set. But, after observing Tito for a few short minutes, she realized that this painting must be totally different.

He sat very still for her and she examined his face: High

cheekbones, a broad forehead, strong nose, wide set eyes, thin lips. Very handsome and confident of his good looks. Sometimes, when he turned his head a certain way, his left eye seemed to move ever so slightly too close to the other eye, giving him a predatory mien. No wonder he was such a formidable fútbol player.

After a few preliminary sketches, she decided that in order to capture his essence, she had to paint him nude. But, how was she going to get him to disrobe without major embarrassment? And, what would Ifiginia say? And, don Carlos?

"Tito, you are muy guapo, very handsome. I hope you do not mind me saying that."

Tito grinned. She knew he had heard that often.

"Also, you have an amazing body." Again, she got that grin back from him.

"That to me is your essence and what I want to capture in this portrait. What would you say if I focused on your legs and,

351

um, your, how do you say, nalgas? Buttocks? Would that be uncomfortable for you?"

Before she could finish her sentence, Tito disrobed. Unabashed, he stood in front of her, even turning from one side to the other for her inspection.

"No problema, doña Paloma. I have no problem with nudity."

"But what about your wife? Your father-in-law? I do not want this to cause any trouble for you." God, but he was self-assured. He had no tan lines and she had to concentrate to keep her eyes on his face.

"I expected you to ask me this. Is that not the whole point of painting a portrait? To capture their very personaje, their persona? Their identity? I am una atleta, an athlete. This is my job today. Sometime later in my life, I will be someone else. But, for now, it is my responsibility, my obligation to be a competitor."

"Shall we start?" While she was happy that he had acquiesced so easily, Pamela was only too aware that she would have to talk to Ifiginia and perhaps even to doña Milena and don Carlos before this went any farther.

That evening, Pamela visited the Varelas. They were watching their granddaughter and Pamela was grateful for the distraction. Carlos was in the pool with the little one, pushing her on a raft. She had on a bathing suit with a flotation ring built into the waist of the top, as well as inflatable swimmies on her arms. Pamela watched the proud grandfather. She was impressed with his body. In his early 50's, he still had the physique of a much younger man. Though he was short, he had a powerful body with no fat, a slim waist, and a strong upper body. A thick gold chain with a cross graced his neck and chest. He was fairly hairy but not so much that it was unattractive. In the water, he looked like a sleek otter. How I would like to paint him, she thought.

The underwater lights gave the water a dreamlike look, the rippling water bending the light, distorting the images of the mosaic tiles on the bottom. The warm breeze made the leaves on the trees sway and chatter, as if they were gossiping to one another. So serene.

She turned to Milena who was keeping a watchful eye on the pool.

"Milena, Carlos, I have a situation I must tell you about. It concerns Tito."

Carlos laughed loudly. "He is muy gallito, cocky, no?"

"You mean you already know? That I am painting him nude?"

"Ifiginia could not wait to tell us. She thinks it is the ultimate compliment. She is extremely proud that she is married to a fútbol player," Milena said. She kept her eyes on the pair in the pool.

"So it will not be a problem? I was so worried that you would find it inappropriate."

Milena turned to her and smiled. "Not at all, Paloma. As long as things stay on the, how do you say, up and up? No problema."

Pamela lay back on the pool chaise and felt the evening envelop her. The velvety night sky, festooned with a million stars, looked like the cloak of Merlin.

"This is paradise. I am so glad my car broke down here!"

"No es oro todo lo que reluce," Milena said. "It is not all gold that glitters."

Pamela did not know how to respond.

Pamela continued to sketch and paint and soon had a growing list of many names of people who were eager to be models. She wanted to approach Lotus but hesitated. When she saw her in the marketplace with her son, she was intrigued but something about the woman kept her from asking. She was not sure if it was because she believed she was a curandera, or something else.

Esperanza was growing. Slowly, one new house, one new business at a time. Telephones were finally becoming common place items. Each improvement made life easier for the people of the pueblo, but also cost them something, whether in ways to spend their limited incomes, or in the traditions they had long held close. Some people feared the growth. Others embraced it.

One day, as she sat in the cool shade by the fountain in the plaza, she watched the old woman, Serafia, at her stall. Pamela marveled at her weather-beaten skin, wondering how long it had taken the sun to damage it. The skin on her face and neck was thickened and and had many folds, while her forearms and the back of her hands seemed to have thin skin with fine wrinkles. She sported many bruises and in places, her skin seemed to have torn.

Pamela pulled her sketchpad from her shoulder bag and began to draw Serafia. Despite her harsh and battered appearance, Pamela saw a trace of the young woman she had once been in the bones of her face. She saw kind eyes, an innocence and goodness in her, and that is who she drew, a younger woman with smoother skin, bright eyes, and dark hair. Not the craggy old woman, la vieja.

Serafia saw Paloma looking at her. Paloma was a familiar figure in Esperanza by now. When she drew out her sketch pad, she tried to be unobtrusive but some people still became uncomfortable. Serafia turned away, then her curiosity got the better of her. She moved around to the front of the stall and straightened her wares. She looked at Paloma again who smiled at her and the woman lowered her head. Pamela felt she had to try to broach the cultural divides that existed between them, one caused by geography, one caused by misunderstanding. Pamela finished her sketch and walked over to Serafia. The little woman drew herself up and faced her with a look of wariness and defiance.

"Aquí," Pamela said. "Un regalito. A little gift." She held out the paper and watched as the old woman looked at the drawing. Serafia looked up at Pamela with a look of confusion and of amazement. She took a step back. Pamela gently moved the drawing a little closer to her.

"Para usted. For you. Un regalito." The weather-beaten face broke into a wide grin, one that was missing several teeth.

"Gracias, señora."

"Paloma. Me llamo Paloma."

Serafia jabbed a wrinkled, bent finger at the drawing. "Aquí. Su nombre. Your name."

Pamela added her name to the drawing.

"Sí,sí, doña Paloma," Serafia said.

When Pamela drove up to her studio, something was waiting for her at the front door. A four foot snake skin, la piel de culebra, this one with a v-shaped head, lay on the threshold, like an anonymous threatening message. She stepped over it and carried her purchases into the house. She looked around the casa and saw no snakes but the presence of the outer coat of the venomous snake, meaning it had outgrown its old skin, gave her pause. She went back outside and inspected the skin. It was in one piece, showing the entire length of the snake and the pattern of its scales. She wished she knew what kind it was. The skin looked like a sock turned inside out. Snakes were becoming a regular occurrence at the studio. Was she, as Carlos had said, una encantadora de serpientes, a snake charmer? Did she somehow summon them? Lotus García would know. Pamela would have to break down and pay her a visit.

PALOMA Y LOTUS

Pamela asked Ifiginia to go with her to see Lotus. She knew the older woman did not speak English and she did not trust her skills with Spanish. She also did not want to tackle the first meeting with Lotus alone. Ifiginia suggested that Verdad accompany her instead, knowing that Verdad would welcome the opportunity to see Lotus and possibly Segundo.

Pamela picked up Verdad at the library in the late afternoon on her way out of town. The snakeskin lay in the back of her new SUV.

Verdad and Pamela chatted easily on the dusty, bumpy ride.

"Did you know we are supposed to get cable in Esperanza?" Verdad asked her. "And, cell phones. I do not know how long it will take but good things are coming to us."

Pamela said she did not know about that and secretly, she wondered how good it would be for Esperanza.

Verdad drew in a deep breath and complimented her on her new car. "El aire acondicionado, the air conditioning is a blessing, ¿ no?"

"Oh, yes. I cannot imagine being without it here. I thought it would take a long time to get this car once I ordered it but with the help of don Carlos, it was here very quickly."

"Claro! Of course. Don Carlos makes everything happen muy rapido." Verdad smiled.

"I did not want to get a black car. There is so much dust.

But, the dealer seemed to be very anxious for me to get this color."

"Pues, well, all of the cars of don Carlos are black. Since you used his name, they must have thought you and he have some kind of connection." She laughed. "You know, that you are una buena amiga. Muy buena!"

"What? But, that is not true! He and Milena are very good to me; they have both been so helpful since I arrived. There is nothing going on between Carlos and me!"

Verdad saw that the neck and face of the other woman were covered with red blotches. Was it anger or embarrassment?

"Oh, you know how people are. If there is not something to talk about, they make it up." Verdad worried that she had offended Pamela.

"Well, I am going to have to be much more careful, I guess." Pamela concentrated on the road. The two were silent the rest of the trip to the García casa.

Pamela did not know what she actually expected to see when they pulled up, but the casita where Lotus and Segundo, and Cuervo, lived was very normal. It was like all of the others in the area, just better cared for. The garden was neat and weed-free, a healthy apple tree held ripening fruit, and a bicycle stood against the front railing. The big front window was well-tended and streak free, the front porch swept clean.

As Pamela approached with Verdad, the front door opened. Lotus thumped out and smiled at them. "Bienvenidos! Welcome! Please come inside. I have just made limonada."

Pamela offered her a basket filled with plums from her trees and Lotus thanked her. Lotus lead them to the kitchen to a small wooden table covered with bright yellow oil cloth. A drinking glass held wildflowers from the fields around the house. Pamela heard her struggling to catch her breath. Lotus saw Pamela looking at her. She waved her hand in front of her face, as if to dismiss her effort.

"Segundo brings me flowers nearly every day. He is such

a good boy." She looked at Verdad and both women smiled. Pamela noted how similar they looked; they could be related.

She pulled out a black sketchbook and asked Lotus if she minded. Lotus shook her head.

"No, no, it is good. Pero, but why you would want to draw this old, crooked woman is a mystery!"

Lotus was not at all as Pamela expected; she was warm, welcoming, and seemed comfortable with strangers. Why did everyone call her "La Extraña", the Strange One?

"So, tell me why you are here, Paloma Turquesa. Sí,sí, I know your name. Everyone in Esperanza knows your name! You are very famous here. I do not think we have ever had someone from Los Estados Unidos living among us. May I? ¿Por favor?" Lotus gently lifted a tendril of her red hair. She rubbed it between her fingers, then sniffed it. Without warning, she yanked out a single hair.

"Oh, I did not expect that!" Pamela laughed. Lotus

pocketed the hair in her apron. Pamela was beginning to understand her nickname.

"Doña Lotus, I have a problem. Everyone has said you are the person to consult about it. It is not really a problem. It is just that I have a great many . . ." She waited for Verdad to translate.

Before Verdad could finish, Lotus interrupted. "Serpientes. Snakes. Yo sé. Yo sé. I have wondered where they are all going and one day I followed one of them and it lead me directly to your house. I could smell sus primos, its cousins, all around your barn. Something draws them. Is it you?"

Without waiting for an answer, Lotus continued. Verdad managed to keep up the translation. "Some people think of the snake as the devil; others see it as a healer. It has no eyelids so it uses its eyes to see into hearts and souls of others. Because of this, it represents wisdom." She paused to let Verdad catch up.

Pamela stood up. "I brought a snake skin that I found at my door. Would you look at it and tell me what kind it is?"

The three women trooped out to the car. When Pamela lifted the back, Lotus was right at her elbow.

"Ah, that. It is some kind of serpiente de cascabel, rattlesnake. We have many kinds in México. You must always be alert when you are outdoors. They lie in the sun and soak up its warmth and you could stumble across one without any warning. He likes to hunt at night." The woman held up the snake and squinted at it. "See here? That is the tail, where its rattles are. Campanitas. Little bells.

"When la serpiente is ready to shed the skin, his eyes become cloudy. He looks as if he is in a trance. He sheds the skin because he has outgrown the old; he achieves a higher wisdom that comes with the passing of time. Just as we all do. As he begins to shed, his eyes begin to clear, as if he can see the world anew. Las serpientes have the ability to move between life and death and back again."

Pamela was impressed with her knowledge and familiarity with snakes. But she was still troubled.

"Why are they coming to me? What makes them want to even come into the house? I thought snakes were afraid of humans."

Lotus looked at Pamela for a few long moments. "Las serpientes are guardians. They are said to guard los tesoros, treasures. Think about it, doña Palmoa. You may not know why they are coming to you now but in time, you will. But, be careful. Not every snake will be your protector."

Cuervo circled high overhead, his shrill cry punctuating the last statement.

"Bueno, Segundo and Cuervo are coming. I want you to meet them." They trooped back to the house, this time with Lotus in the lead.

Cuervo stayed on the porch on his perch when Segundo came in. The boy washed his hands at the kitchen sink before being introduced to Pamela.

"Segundo, I am very glad to meet you finally. I have heard many good things about you."

"El gusto es mío. The pleasure is mine." He bowed slightly to her and then shook her hand. Everyone laughed. He gave Verdad a hug.

"You have such nice manners."

"Gracias, señora. Will you paint Cuervo?" Outside, the bird bobbed up and down on his perch. "Con permiso," Segundo said. He sliced a piece of one of the plums that Pamela had brought and took it to his friend. He laid it on the porch railing and Cuervo hopped down from his perch. He spread out his wings and tilted his head toward the boy. Segundo rubbed the neck of the large bird as if he were a dog. "¡Come! Eat!" Only then did Cuervo nibble at the fruit.

"I have never seen people with such a way with animals!" Pamela said. "Verdad, can you charm animals, tambien, also?"

Verdad shook her head. "No, these are very special people, doña Paloma."

She examined Segundo with the eye of an artist. "It is remarkable how much Segundo looks like you, Verdad. But, I also see a lot of doña Lotus in him." Pamela saw Lotus and Verdad exchange a glance.

"Did I say something wrong?"

Lotus answered. "No, no, doña Paloma. I suppose in such a small pueblo, we are all related in some way."

After a few more minutes of conversation, Verdad and Pamela got ready to leave. She left the snake skin with Lotus.

Cuervo finished his piece of fruit and flew into the yard. He rolled in the dirt, taking a dust bath to rid himself of insects, Segundo explained.

"You know so much about animals," Pamela said to Segundo as they watched the bird. Segundo looked away but before he did, Pamela saw the trace of a smile on his face.

In the midst of the acrobatics, Cuervo hopped under the SUV and struck at something. Pamela did not have to wait long to find out what it was; Cuervo flew back onto the porch and dropped a black and yellow snake at her feet. Still alive, it wriggled away and disappeared in the grass at the edge of the yard.

"Did you see where he was, doña Paloma? Under your car." Lotus looked intently at her.

"Oh, I saw, all right. That is closer than I like," she answered.

"That kind of snake is harmless. It is a rat snake. A tiger rat snake. We call them that because of their markings. They are actually quite beautiful. He eats just about anything, frogs and toads,even ratones if he grows large enough. This one can vibrate his tail like a rattlesnake but he does not have a rattle. He just acts like it. Sometimes he will puff up his head to look bigger. But that is about as dangerous as he gets..Did you see that Cuervo brought him to you as a gift?"

"Beautiful or not, I want nothing to do with it!" Pamela replied.

"I also have a gift for you. Give me your hand." She

offered Pamela a blue stone, placed it in her open palm, then securely closed her fingers around it.

"It will help. Keep it close to your heart, Paloma. Trust me."

On the drive home, Verdad talked a bit about Lotus. "She was very talkative today. Some days you cannot get her to say a word. She must have felt comfortable with you, doña Paloma."

Pamela agreed. "Thank you for taking me to her. I felt as if she has much to teach me, things I need to know. I am not quite sure what everything means, though. And, I suppose I should be pleased that Cuervo gave me a gift of the tiger snake." The thought of finding more snakes at her home disturbed her.

She examined the stone she still clutched in her hand. It was very similar to the one Verdad wore around her neck.

"What do you think she meant when she said this would help me?"

Verdad fingered the stone on her necklace. "I was having trouble conceiving and I went to Lotus for help." She blushed. "I cannot go into all of the details. Some of them are too personal and the others, pues, you would think I was loca, crazy. But, in less than a year, Santiago was born. I know you probably think she is just a strange old woman. She is that but she is more. I do not know if she has powers or not. The church says we are not supposed to believe in those things. But, so many things seem to happen because of Lotus García, things without explanation. If she says to keep it close to your heart, I would do so."

"What could it hurt?" Paloma laughed at the thought of the stone holding special powers. Yet, at the same time, she envisioned little Santiago.

At home she found a velvet pouch in her jewelry box, deep blue in color, the color of midnight, and put the stone in it. She took a heavy silver chain and hung the pouch from it, like a medicine bag. She tucked it under her shirt where it fell between her breasts.

TRUTH

When la Americana had left, Segundo and Cuervo went inside the casita and found Lotus cleaning up.

"Mama Lotus, what did doña Paloma mean when she said I look like doña Verdad? I have heard other people say such things."

Lotus knew the time had come. She also knew she had to be very gentle in the telling. While Segundo was very smart and sometimes wise beyond his years, this could be painful.

"Mi vida, my life, you know I love you so very much,

373

more than anything en el mundo, in the world."

"¡Claro! Of course. You tell me all the time!"

Lotus was glad he was so sure of himself. He might not be after this conversation. She stood at the sink and washed the glasses her guests had used.

"Once upon a time, a young girl had a baby, un niño, just like you. She loved him very much but she did not have un esposo, a husband, and she was unable to care for him. She had to make sure he had a good life, and that whoever took care of him could give him everything he needed—food, clothes, books, and a place to sleep. And, most importantly, love. Above all else, he had to know he was loved." She turned around to look at him.

"Sí, Padre Mateo often comes to our classroom and tells us that we must love our neighbor, but also ourselves." Segundo fooled with the ends of the apron Lotus wore.

"Padre Mateo is a very wise man, Segundo. You should listen to him. Anyway, one day the girl who had the little boy found someone to take care of him and the little boy went to live with another woman."

Segundo asked, "Did she have other children? Did he get brothers and sisters?"

"No, no. She herself had never been married so she did not have children but she loved all children very much. She took good care of the little boy and he grew tall and became very brave." Her heart had begun to thump madly; it felt as if it wanted to turn over in her chest.

"I am brave, Mama Lotus."

"¡Sí, por cierto! Indeed!"

"So, this boy came to live with someone who was not su madre, his mother, but he was happy. Did he get to see his real mother sometimes? Did he know who she was?" he asked.

"He did get to see her but at first, he did not know she was his mother."

"Did he see her in the plaza?"

375

"I am sure he did," Lotus answered.

" En la Iglesia? In church?"

"Of course," she answered.

"En la biblioteca? In the library?"

Lotus gazed into his eyes, the dark eyes that were so much like her eyes, so much like those of Verdad, so deep and wise. He gazed back at her with a pleading in his eyes.

"Sí, he would most often see her in la biblioteca. They became good friends."

"So, Verdad knows his real mother?"

"Segundo, Verdad is his real mother." She watched for a reaction. Instead of pain or fear or tears, Segundo gave her a big smile.

"I know, Mama Lotus. I am that little boy and Verdad is my mother. I have always known it. Cuervo told me. But, I love you, Mama Lotus. You too are my mother."

Lotus hugged him to her. She did not doubt that somehow Cuervo had told him about his birth mother.

"Some people do not think it is wise for someone to have a baby without a husband. You know that, ¿correcto? Correct? So, this is something that you should not talk about with anyone but Verdad and me. Do you understand?"

"What about Padre Mateo? He says we can come to him and tell him anything and it will be safe with him."

"Sí, Padre Mateo tambien." She was finding it very hard to catch her breath.

"May I be excused? I have a new book that doña Verdad chose for me and I am very excited to start it. Oh, wait! Is it still correct to call her doña Verdad? Should I call her something else?"

"No, I think doña Verdad is just fine. That is how you have always known her. Perhaps one day when you two are alone, you can tell her that you know she is your mother. I think it would please her that you know."

"Claro. Of course." And, he sprinted off to the porch with a library book, Cuervo in tow.

Lotus turned back to her sink. The conversation had not been as difficult as she had imagined it might be yet, it was one of the hardest things she had ever done. To tell her son, the child she loved so mightily, that someone else was his real mother. Her heart had calmed a little, yet it still thumped erratically in her chest. She was suddenly very tired. She untied her apron and draped it over the front of the sink. She turned to go into her bedroom to lie down until it was time to start dinner. Lotus found it hard to breathe. She combed through the bowl of blue stones until she found one that felt right in her hand. She looked out the big front window at Segundo sprawled out on the floor of the porch. The black bird sat on his perch overhead and groomed himself. He halted his search for lice. Cuervo turned his noble, sleek head and looked directly into her eyes.

THE SLEEPING STONE

Pamela told Tito that she did not need him to pose any more. She felt she had captured him and just needed to put finishing touches on the portrait.

She needed to rework the portrait of Ifiginia, as well, but she was anxious to move on to other people. She had a series of portraits in mind: Domingo and Verdad, Carlos and Milena, Lotus and Segundo.

The first night Pamela had kept the blue stone close to her heart, she dreamed of mystical animals. All of the animals she dreamed of occupied the four-legged or winged bodies that carried them through their lives but they also possessed the faces of humans, the people of Esperanza. In her waking hours, the images of the dreams haunted her and she found herself searching any person she saw for the animals that came to her at night. The animal images that inhabited her dreams crept into her real world. Night after night, vivid dreams awakened her and she could not go back to sleep. She worked in her studio, feverishly trying to capture what she had seen. The more tired she became, it seemed the less able she was to sleep. And, the more tired she became, the more she painted. She was more productive now than she had ever been when Rob was alive. But, her nerves were raw and she often went for days without seeing anyone. She had to set the alarm clock to go off to remind her to eat. Some days, even the act of eating was too intrusive and she feared if she spent too much time away from her subjects, they would vanish. She was on a journey and at the end of the journey she would learn something of great import.

She began her portrait of Lotus. In it, Lotus was recognizable as the woman people encountered by day but

Pamela also saw her as wolf. This wolf was both fierce and loving. As she painted, Pamela portrayed Lotus as a human wearing the fur of a wolf, but still recognizable as the strange woman. In her kind and wise eyes, Lotus gazed out from the painting as the matriarch of ancestral spirits, as divine midwife. The wolf in the picture possessed a great stillness that spoke of healing and creation.

As she painted and exhaustion threatened to rule her body, she wondered if the dreaming stone, as she thought of it, was at the root of her fantastic imaginings. Never before had she felt such a frenzy to create. Perhaps it was just the suggestion of its magical qualities that had captured her.

It took many days but, Pamela, finished, or so she thought, the painting of Lotus. She had to sleep. She slipped the necklace with the pouch holding the blue stone from around her neck. She let the blue stone tumble out and she held it in her hand. It was a different color, deeper, more intense, than when she had first seen it. Or, was it? Perhaps she had remembered its color incorrectly. It seemed to have grown, as well. Impossible.

A stone was a stone. She returned the stone to the pouch and hung the necklace on the portrait of Lotus. She dragged herself into bed and fell into its embrace, hoping to find sleep.

She found sleep, but now sleep did not bring the images that so inspired her. She slept around the clock, missing the next day, and the day after that. She did not hear the ringing of the telephone. She did not hear Ifiginia knocking on her door. She did not hear Tito calling her name from outside her bedroom doors.

She plummeted down into a black void that was sleep. She did not have the ability to rise up from it, even if she had wanted to. She needed sleep just as much as she needed the air. But, sleep was also her enemy. It seized her and would not let go. It seduced her into going deeper, deeper, and deeper still into its depths. It shackled her in its dark caverns and imprisoned her within its mysteries.

Instead of seeing the fantastic illusions she put on canvas, she dreamed of being in a place that was dark, wracked with rubble and ruin, full of strange people going nowhere. She became one of those people, unable to find her way home. She knew home was just over the next hill. She could see a golden light on the horizon. She knew how to get there but the more she tried, the further away it moved. She asked the strange people for help, for direction, and they turned away from her. Buildings and highways sprang up between her and the place she needed to go. More decay, more disorder. Wind buffeted her, blew against her as she tried to find her way.

She tried to claw her way up to consciousness, out of this desolate place. Someone was calling her and she had to answer. Yet, she could not. She did not like this place; it felt meanacing, and she had no control. The force of the wind grew stronger. It battered her and was loud all around her. A spot of soot appeared and blurred her vision. She wiped at her eyes, in her dream and while she lay on the bed. The soot grew bigger, grew nearer until it formed into a great black bird. It was Cuervo. He had something to tell her.

"The end is the beginning."

Above the wind, she heard bells, like the carillons of cathedrals, lyrical and pleasant-sounding but she could not recognize the melody. It felt as if the sound were traveling over a great distance. It grew stronger and closer, and Pamela felt herself rising, moving nearer to being conscious again. Yet, she struggled. Sleep wanted her, it tried to possess her.

A soothing moistness, like drops of dew on the grass in the early morning, brushed her face, stroked her skin. She tried to open her eyes but still, she remained behind a veil. The bells called to her again and again. She knew she must awaken. Oh, but sleep was so enchanting. Tan encantador.

Pamela willed her eyes to open, willed the dark images to depart, and she found herself in her bed with doña Milena bending over her. Doña Milena dabbed her face and neck, her wrists, and her ankles with a scented cloth. Behind her, Carlos stood, his face full of concern.

"So, you have returned, mi amiga," Milena said. It was such an effort for Pamela to speak. She smiled at them and pushed herself up on her elbows.

"Returned? From where?" Yet, she knew.

Milena helped her to fully sit up and to swing her legs over the side of the bed. Pamela felt the tile of the floor on the bottom of her feet. It was cool.

Carlos lifted her in his arms, like a child, and carried her from the room. He stopped in front of her easel and carefully set her down so that she could stand.

There was the portrait of Lotus. Instead of a wolf looking out at Pamela with its kind and wise eyes, it was a raven. She knew at once the raven was responsible for bringing the world into being and is sometimes considered to be the individual who brought light to the darkness. That was so much what Lotus had been and had done in her lifetime.

The necklace of the blue stone remained on the corner of the canvas. As she stared at the portrait that had all but consumed her, Pamela saw something more was different, something else that she did not remember placing on the canvas. A pale green snake with filmy unseeing eyes circled the neck of the raven, of Lotus: Ouroboros. It held its tail in its mouth,

creating a ring that would never end.

LOTUS Y EL GUIJARRO AZUL

While Paloma Turquesa was dreaming, Lotus was dreaming as well. El guijarro azul, the blue pebble she had chosen from the dish lay in her closed hand. It was cool and smooth.

In her sleep, she saw her mother. She smiled at Lotus and waved, but from a great distance. Lotus wanted to go to her and feel her embrace, smell her sweet scent that she remembered from childhood–cinnamon, cardamom, and oranges—but her mother remained just out of reach. Her mother turned from her and began to walk with women, women that Lotus almost recognized. She searched their faces and saw the familiar eyes and cheeks and smiles of these women, but who they were remained just out of reach. She felt as if she would remember their names any second. They passed through an arched doorway. Lotus followed.

She saw a wooden table with many people seated around it. The table seemed to stretch on forever. In the middle of the table were many candles. One was larger than the rest and from it, a sweet-scented smoke lifted and circled the ceiling. There were fragments of words, of letters in the smoke, and in them Lotus saw the names of the children she had cared for. When she had returned them to their parents, she had burned their names in her kitchen stove. Their names had floated over her head, much like this smoke.

Cuervo came to her and sat on her shoulder. Her gaze passed over and stopped on every person seated there. There were people who had left her life many years ago and whom she had not thought of in a long, long time. They all looked up at her and smiled.

Cuervo whispered in her ear. "Who are you? Tell me. Who are you?

"Who were you? Tell me. Who were you?

"Tomorrow, who will you be? Tell me.

"Is this a dream? Who are you? Tell me.

"Do you know what your true name is? Tell me. What is your true name?"

The questions rang in her head and sounded like a great bell tolling. It rang slowly, sonorously, and solemnly. It hummed in her breast and vibrated her very soul. She became afraid. She wanted to block the sound, send Cuervo on his way, and leave this place. But, she could not. Try as hard as she could, she could not get his voice out of her head. He remained on her shoulder.

At the table was an empty place. On one side sat her

abuela, her grandmother. On the other side sat her mother. They pointed to the empty seat. On the table in front of the empty place sat her treasured ancient canasta, the very basket made by one of these unnamed relatives, maybe by them all, the very one that carried Segundo when she found him. It was filled with countless blue stones. Lotus took a step toward the empty seat. The voice of the bird softened. The loud clangor of the bell lessened. She moved through the room, past the many people at the table, and approached her chair. Cuervo became silent. Very gingerly and with much reverence, she placed the blue stone she clutched in her hand into la canasta sitting at her place. Cuervo flew off. She took her seat between her mother and her grandmother. Across from her sat an old, old woman, one Lotus thought she knew but, as with the others, could not recall her name. The skin of the old was so thin, so transparent, that Lotus could make out the outline of her skull through it. The aged old woman held a piece of paper over the largest candle. On it was written a name. Her name.

Lotus watched the paper curl, turn brown, then ignite. The room smelled of marigolds.

"I am Lotus García."

She was no longer afraid.

AFTER LOTUS

It was job of Padre Mateo job to tell Segundo that Lotus had died. He dreaded any time he had to inform someone of the death of a loved one, but this time, it would be even more painful for all.

The first place Padre Mateo looked for Segundo was in the library. Verdad looked up at Padre Mateo as he entered. She started to greet him but then saw him look around the room, searching. She saw his pale face, the determined look on his face, and she suddenly, knew why he had come. She pointed to the window seat.

He found Segundo, sitting cross-legged on the seat, his head of black curls bent over a book. When the child saw the priest, his eyes lit up and he called out,

"¡Padre, Padre! Look! Doña Verdad found this book for me. It is all about México!"

"Silencio, niño, silencio." Padre Mateo sat next to Segundo on the seat. He looked at the page in the book illustrated with Aztec pyramids that Segundo had been studying.

"Is this hard for you to read? It is a very grown-up book." The priest was always surprised by his intelligence.

"No, pues, well, sí, some of it is but I ask doña Verdad about what I cannot understand. She is teaching me how to look up the words I do not know."

"Very good." Padre Mateo gently removed the book from his hands and closed it. He laid it on the window seat.

"Segundo, I have to talk to you about something. You can look at the book another day."

"Okay," the boy looked into the face of the priest. Tears welled up in the eyes of the child. "I know. It is about Mama Lotus. I heard the church bell this morning, just before the sun came up."

"The church bell? I did not ring the bell. You must have been dreaming."

"Perhaps, but the sound woke me. I got dressed and ate some fruit for el desayuno, breakfast. Then I watered all of the trees and flowers and came to the library. I tried to be very quiet so I would not wake up Mama Lotus. She is so very tired."

Tears began to spill from his eyes. "Did I do the right thing? Should I have gone to her? Tried to wake her up?"

"You did all of the right things, Segundo, ¡perfectamente! You are a good son. Doña Lotus has always been so proud of you."

Padre Mateo took a deep breath.

"Segundo, she has passed on. She is now with her mother, and the mother of that woman, and all of her relatives. She is at peace now."

Segundo drew himself up and nodded. "Okay." He looked out the window at the large black bird waiting for him outside.

"Where will I live?" Segundo seemed very accepting of her death.

"Well, for now, you can live with me. We must find you a proper home, though. Do you have any thoughts on this?" Padre Mateo had not had to consider for long what would happen to Segundo. He knew he would be well taken care of, no matter where he went to live.

"I would like to live with doña Verdad and don Domingo and Santiago. Doña Verdad is mi madre, my mother, too, you know."

Padre Mateo was at a loss for words. He knew the boy

was very intuitive and that doña Lotus had always been very straight-forward with him, but he did not know how much Segundo actually knew.

"I will ask her. Ahora mismo. Right now." Segundo ran to Verdad at the desk.

"Doña Verdad, Mama Lotus is dead and I need some place to live. May I come to live with you and don Domingo and Santiago? Oh, Cuervo would like to come, too."

Verdad opened her arms and embraced Segundo. "Por su puesto, of course, Segundo. You will come to live with us." She would tell Domingo later. She began to weep and looked up at Padre Mateo.

She whispered, "Gracias, Padre, muchas gracias. You have answered my prayers."

It would be several weeks before she and Domingo could legally adopt Segundo, but for now, he was taken care of.

THE FUNERAL

The body of Lotus García was prepared for burial by several of the older women of Esperanza, including Serafia. They undressed and washed her body. She was then dressed in the black skirt that she wore to church and a simple white blouse. The one piece of clothing she took such pride in, her black shawl with the embroidered red roses, was then draped about her shoulders. Her hands were folded on her chest. Serafia combed her once raven black hair with a scented oil and then plaited it into a single queue.

While all of this was happening, Verdad and Domingo

went to the funeraría to purchase a simple but fine wooden

coffin. Lotus was then placed inside the coffin which rested on

the old wooden table in the kitchen and covered with a white

sheet. Next to her body, Serafia placed the ancient canasta, the

old basket that once carried Segundo. Lotus would need it in the

next life and find comfort in its presence. Four lighted candles

formed a rectangle around her on the table. Segundo made a

cross from marigold petals on the floor in front of the table. He

also made a path outside the casita into the home with the petals.

For the next 24 hours, a velario, a prayer vigil, was maintained.

Never was her body left alone; visitors came to the humble casita

and brought covered dishes of food. Several of them, including

the Varela family, left money. The visitors sat with her body,

told stories about her, and even laughed aloud. Several of the

older men sat in a corner, drank liquor, and played dominos.

Segundo curled up on her bed and dozed throughout the night

and into the next day.

The coffin with the body of Lotus García was transported

to the church in a wooden cart. Segundo, Verdad, Domingo, las

Varelas, and los Bravos followed along in silence. Many of the

children that Lotus had tirelessly walked and told stories to were

in attendance; some were now adults.

Every seat in the church was filled; many people stood

along the walls. Even more lined the steps outside. At some

time in their lives, she had touched each and every one in some

way, and they had all come to say good-bye to La Extraña, the

Strange One. The coffin was carried into the church by Segundo,

Leopold, Domingo, Carlos, Clemente, and one of the sons of

Leopold, Ultimo. They waited with it at the door and Padre

Mateo walked to the back of the church to meet it. He blessed it

with holy water. They then proceeded to the altar.

Padre Mateo led the crowd in prayer. Knowing that

Lotus embraced many beliefs, and that some of the people who

attended her funeral had mixed feelings about a Catholic

ceremony for her, he kept the prayers short. He concluded by

telling them this: "While Lotus García lived alone for much of

her life, her final years were blessed with the presence and love of her son, Segundo Leopold García. Not even death can remove the love and care a family has for each other. Family is forever and love overcomes all. It is the responsibility of us all to help Segundo remember that his mother, Lotus García, is always watching over him and caring for him, as she did when she was living. It is the responsibility of Segundo to always remember her love and to cherish her even though she is no longer of this world."

Padre Mateo led the procession to the door of the church where the mariachis waited in a half circle to accept the procession. They sang a beautiful, sad melody, then turned, and lead the casket and the people through the town to the cemetery where Lotus García was buried.

FAMILY MATTERS

Segundo went to live at the Yebara casa with his new family. But, one question remained: What to do with the little house, la casita, Segundo had lived in with Lotus?

Domingo took on the task of helping to find out that doña Lotus owned the house outright. It had been passed down to her when her parents had died. It now belonged to Segundo. Should they sell it? Who would want to live there, with her reputation for being una curandera? Tear it down? Nunca, never. It would be too painful for Segundo. And, besides, la casita was a part of

Esperanza, just as Lotus had been. It needed to be taken care of and to remain.

On the morning of the day that Segundo was to be officially adopted by Verdad and Domingo, making him Segundo Leopold García y Yebara, Verdad took him back to the little house. They rode the Leopold Bus Line. No one looked twice at the procession of the tall, thin young woman, the dark-eyed boy, and the black raven on his arm to the seat always reserved for Lotus García.

When they arrived at la casita and made ready to disembark, Leopold looked at his grandson with pride. How he wished he could tell him they were part of the same family, the crazy mixed-up family his son had inadvertently created so long ago.

"Don Leopold, I am going to be adopted again today. Verdad and Domingo will be mis padres, my parents. Mami Verdad and I are going to get the rest of my things from la casita where I lived with Mama Lotus." As ever, Segundo was frank and earnest in the telling of the latest development in his life.

Leopold turned off the ignition of the bus. He stepped down behind Verdad and Segundo, and followed them into the little dirt yard of la casita. The few remaining passengers on the bus looked on, only slightly alarmed by the interruption of their journeys.

"Segundo, you are a very fine boy and anyone would be proud to have you as part of their family. I am very happy that doña Verdad will be your mother. Already, she loves you very much. She and don Domingo will take good care of you." With that, he stuck his hand in his pants pocket. He handed something to Segundo. It was a gold chain with a gold locket engraved on the back with a "V".

"This is La Virgen de Guadalupe. She is the Mother to us all. She will look over you and protect you, no matter where you go."

Verdad threw her arms around Leopold. "Don Leopold,

where did this come from? I had thought it was long gone. I lost it one day, on the bus, the day that . . ."

"I found it that day and have carried it with me every day since then. I have waited for the very perfect moment to give it to Segundo. What better day than this?" Leopold returned the embrace and drew Segundo in.

"We are all one big family, and, doña Verdad, I would be very honored if you would allow Segundo to call me 'abuelo', grandfather." Without waiting for a reply, don Leopold turned and boarded his bus. He had to take out his handkerchief and wipe his eyes before he could begin to drive again.

Segundo skipped ahead of Verdad and they entered la casita where he had lived with Lotus García. Cuervo sat on the perch on the front porch.

"It is different, now. It does not feel the same," Segundo said. He turned to Verdad with a look of despair. "She is no longer here."

"No, doña Lotus, Mama Lotus is no longer here, m'hijo, my son. You know that she died. You came to la Iglesia, the church, and then to el cementerio, the cemetery, to say good-bye."

"Yo sé, I know, but for some reason, I thought it would smell like her, or I would see something that reminded me of her."

"Everything here was hers and yours. What is it you are looking for?"

Segundo did not answer. He rifled through every drawer, under every cushion, in every corner. He went out to the shed and came back a few minutes later, empty-handed.

"They are gone. Los azules. Los guijarros azules, the blue pebbles."

Verdad helped him to look again but there was not one blue pebble to be found in la casita.

"¡Qué curioso! How strange! It does not appear as if anyone has been in the house. La puerta, the door, was locked when we arrived. Decide what you want to take home. Papi Domingo will be here soon with the car. We must go to la Oficina del Registro Civil. This is your big day!"

Domingo arrived with cardboard boxes for Segundo to put his clothes, his toys, and his books in. Together, they carried the boxes to the car. When Verdad had told Domingo that Segundo was going to be their son, that they would adopt him, he had fully agreed. He knew the pain and loneliness of growing up where he was not loved. He would never let that happen to anyone he knew if he could help it, especially this child. He put the key in the door of la casita, locked the door, and stood on the porch, watching his wife and Segundo settle in the car. He would now be twice blessed. Domingo backed the car out of the little yard, onto the dirt road that lead up to it.

"Espera un momento, por favor. Please wait for a moment." Segundo lowered the window and stuck out his arm. Cuervo could not be left behind.

"Que Dios me ayude," the big man muttered. May God help me.

Padre Mateo waited for them at the office of the registrar, along with don Clemente, Don Carlos, doña Milena, Ifiginia, and Santiago. When Verdad arrived, she opened her purse and pulled out a packet of papers.

"I have brought everything I could think of that you might need, señor: birth certificates, our marriage certificate, bank statement, letters of recommendation, a copy of . . ."

"That will not be necessary, señora. It has all been taken care of. All I need now is the signatures of you and of señor Yebara and the child is legally adopted."

Doña Milena embraced Segundo and his parents. "Vamos, vamos, dale! Come, okay! We will now celebrate with a feast like you have never seen!"

Domingo Dos Ojos caught the eye of don Carlos. They nodded to one another. Yes, it was all taken care of.

THE LEOPOLD BUS LINE

It seemed as if change came to Esperanza every day now. Cada día.

One day, as it rattled and rocked along the rutted bus route into town, the Leopold Bus Line gave up and refused to move another inch. Poor Leopold alit from the bus and creaked open the rusted hood over the engine. He tinkered. He oiled. He wiped. He added water. He begged. He swore. Se llevó el pañuelo a los ojos. He dabbed his eyes with his handkerchief. He told himself that it was perspiration that was making them tear. Finally, he conceded defeat and told his passengers that they would have to walk the rest of the long, dusty way into town.

As each person disembarked from the bus, they either said something in sympathy to Leopold or they silently embraced him. Some caressed the side of the old vehicle, stroking the flaking paint as if it were a living creature. This was a very sad day for the people of Esperanza.

When don Carlos heard about the ancient bus, he told Leopold he would take him to his automobile dealer in Matamoros. He knew he would be treated well and given a healthy discount.

"But, don Carlos. I do not want a car. I need a bus. How can I transport the people of Esperanza in a car?"

"Quizás, perhaps it is time for a change, Leopold," don Carlos suggested. "You may find something else in Matamoros that will serve your purposes."

Leopold was despondent. He could not leave the sad bus on the side of the road so he enlisted the help of his sons, all of them. One morning, en el sábado, on a Saturday, a very somber group gathered around Leopold Salazar de la Vega: Onofre, Hector, Santana, Fidel, Fortuno, Ultimo, Silvio, Basilio, y Lucero. No one, nadie, said a word. For the last time, Leopold climbed up into the faithful bus, adjusted his hat over his now silver curls, settled into the seat, and slipped the gears into neutral. As one, the proud sons of the proud man pushed, and slowly, the Leopold Bus Line made its last trip on the road into Esperanza. Several people joined them and helped them push. Soon there was no more room for the hands of anyone else on the sides of the old bus and the people who came out into their yards to watch reverently fell into place behind it. In silence, the procession made its way into Esperanza: Through the market, past the library, on to La Iglesia de la Santa Cruz where Padre Mateo made the sign of the cross over the bus, and beyond to the outskirts of town, to the automobile graveyard owned by Taciano Zaragoza who also owned the single gas station in Esperanza.

The Leopold Bus Line joined the rusting, silenced skeletons of vehicles that rested for all eternity in this hallowed junkyard.

A few days later, with a great laying on of the horn, The Leopold Express arrived in Esperanza. A brand new, white Chevrolet stretch van with tinted windows, air conditioning, removable floor mats, and a luggage rack on top, and even an AM/FM radio with something called a CD player rolled up to la Iglesia. Padre Mateo rang the church bell and a throng of people gathered. It took a long time for the crowd to quiet enough for him to begin.

"Today we seek the blessing of God as we gather with thankfulness to bless this vehicle and our use of it. We give thanks for the gift of this taxi for the purpose of convenience, recreation, and the livelihood of Leopold Salazar de la Vega."

The crowd responded, "Amén."

"Lord, help Leopold to use this gift thoughtfully, carefully, and never while under the influence of alcohol or any chemical substance that might impair his ability to safely drive

411

this vehicle. Give him a loving spirit as he drives, and take away from him all anger and impatience that might either put others or himself in danger. Amén."

Again, the crowd responded, "Amén."

Leopold stood with his hat in his hand as Padre Mateo walked all around the van and sprinkled it with holy water.

A great cheer went up and the mariachis began to play "Tijuana Taxi". They had practiced the song in secret after they had learned the taxi would soon arrive. Leopold rolled back the sliding doors. The taxi was built to comfortably hold seven passengers and the driver; however, more people than he imagined possible squeezed their way in. He slid behind the wheel and drove with great ceremony once around the plaza while the people who had jammed in with much elbowing and kneeing sat on the laps of each other, and those who could not fit inside ran along behind. Being the sentimental man that he was, Leopold se llevó el pañuelo a los ojos, he dabbed his eyes with his handkerchief. This was a very festive day for the people of Esperanza.

JUAN PABLO PANIAGUA

One of the newer residents of Esperanza watched the blessing of the taxi and the procession around the plaza with a feeling of homecoming. Juan Pablo Paniagua had been away from Mexico for quite some time, attending college, then medical school, followed by his various residencies in American hospitals. He had returned to Mexico with the hope of serving his people, of bringing better health care and nutrition to people in outlying communities. When the opening to run the clinic of Esperanza presented itself, el doctor Paniagua responded with great enthusiasm.

He had never forgotten the way his people embraced nearly any opportunity to have a fiesta. The blessing of the taxi was just one more reason. He watched the main characters of the event, saw who was el mandemas, the top dog, and who was el ultimo orejon del tarro, the bottom of the barrel.

The tiny clinic needed a major organizational overhaul and el doctor found the best way to handle it was to hire some of the local men and women to help. It took three days. He had the men take everything from the clinic and stack it on tarps en la calle, in the street. The women then dusted and scrubbed and sanitized the walls and floor and built-in cabinets. That was followed by a day of painting; fresh paint covered a lot of sins, he believed. He made an inventory of all of the medical supplies, noted what was needed, what was not needed, and then drew up a plan for the inside of the clinic. Everything would be labeled; nothing would be out of place. Nothing. Never. Nada. Nunca.

He interviewed the three people who still worked at the clinic, all local women, and asked them what they thought the people of Esperanza needed most. They told him all the same things: prenatal and postnatal care, dental care, nutritional information, sanitary instruction, first aid, immunizations. There was not one area that needed more attention than any of the others. It seemed to el doctor that Esperanza got by on some very outdated practices and a lot of hope. He believed he could change all of that.

He ordered uniforms for the women who worked in the clinic and handed them out with instructions that they must always be clean and pressed. He knew the more professional they looked, the more professional they became. In his interviews, he learned that none of the three had more than the equivalency of a high school education. And, none of them had had proper medical training. Everything they knew came from trial and error. He suspected that all three of them harbored many superstitions.

During this time, he held clinic hours en la biblioteca, the library. The worst malady he had to confront in those three days of reorganization and sanitizing was a splinter in the finger of one of las monjas, the nuns, which looked to be infected.

Things were moving along relatively smoothly for el doctor and the people of Esperanza. He established regular hours, began to schedule appointments in an effort to unclog the pack of people who seemed to think that Saturday afternoons and Monday mornings were the best times to seek medical help. Tuesday was immunization day: diphtheria, tetanus, and pertussis vaccines for infants, poliovirus, influenza, tuberculosis, smallpox vaccines for any and all. He knew many of the people resisted getting immunizations; if they did not show any symptoms, why endure the pain of the needle? Especially the babies.

Juan Pablo patiently explained the need for vaccines, asking each person how many people they had ever known who had polio or diphtheria in Esperanza. When that person replied, "Ningunos," none, he would then ask them what the greatest invention in the last 100 years was. The responses were many but all predictable: radio, television, automobiles, rockets, washing machines. El doctor would reply, "No, las vacunas, vaccines. Vaccines protect not only yourself but also others around you. Vaccines protect not only individuals but entire communities. If too many people in a community do not get vaccinations, diseases can reappear. Eventually, those diseases will kill us all."

If the person was still resistant about getting la vacuna or giving one to their baby, he would continue.

"It is like a boat with a leak in it. If we do not stop the leak, we will only be able to bail out the water but the water will never stop coming in. Soon, there will be too much water and the boat will capsize.

"If we do not stop diseases, even with one person at a time, we will soon be like that leaking boat, and all of Esperanza could capsize and drown."

Without knowing of the near tragedy with Fernanda, the

baby of Ifiginia and Tito, el doctor Paniagua touched a nerve in the community with his example of drowning.

Don Carlos and doña Milena accompanied Ifiginia when she took Fernanda to the clinic to get her vaccines. Poor little Fernanda. Never had she experienced anything more than being told "no" on a rare occasion and the shock of the needle produced such screaming that everyone in the clinic covered their ears. Even the still youthful-looking doctor. The grey hair that flecked his eyebrows and temples gave away his age. Milena thought he was just as handsome, if not more so than Padre Mateo.

El doctor tried to laugh at the wailing child but her cries made it nearly impossible for him to speak. Ifiginia said she would take her outside and Milena and Carlos could make an appointment for her next check-up. Her cries could be heard even through the thick walls but they soon turned into hiccupping and ragged gasping as she tried to catch her breath.

"¡Por dios! Que pulmones! The lungs on that child! She

is very healthy, no?" He finished his notes and turned to los abuelos, the grandparents.

"When will the two of you be coming in for sus vacunas, your vaccines? Soon? You need to have physicals, as well. When we reach a certain age, it is wise to look at our blood, heart, lungs, everything, just to be sure all is functioning well. One of the women at the desk can make appointments for you. Por supuesto, certainly, you do not want to have to sit and wait along with everyone else."

Doña Milena agreed and left the room to make all of their appointments. As don Carlos turned to follow her, el doctor Paniagua said, "Por favor, espere. Please, wait. I think you and I have something to talk about, señor Varela. Or, if I may be more familiar, don Carlos?"

"Con placer, with pleasure." Don Carlos smiled at the doctor.

"I have heard much about you, don Carlos. Much about all of the things you do to help the people of Esperanza."

Don Carlos dipped his head in acknowledgement. He said nothing.

"I know the library would not be here, that the many repairs to the church, and so much more, if not for your generosity." El doctor paused. He saw that don Carlos was looking closely at him, sizing him up.

"Thank you for your kind words. I do very little but I do what I can to help. I would like to help the clinic. I know it has many needs and that you have much to do to make it run smoothly. Quizas, perhaps, ¿una donación? a donation . . .?" Don Carlos reached into his pocket and pulled out a roll of bills. He thumbed through them, counting. "¿Cuanto? How much would help?"

El doctor held up his hand, indicating that don Carlos should stop.

"No acepto dinero de usted. I will not accept money from you. This is why I wanted to talk to you. I hope you understand. What you do, your way of earning that money, is contrary to everything I believe in." He smiled at don Carlos but felt anything but comfortable with the man.

It was a tense few moments while Don Carlos sized up e; doctor. He began to laugh.

"Tengo que decir que me sorprende. I have to say that I am surprised. But, I also must say that I respect your wishes. I respect you for standing firm in your beliefs. ¿Amigos? Friends?" Don Carlos once again extended his hand, this time in friendship.

El doctor heard don Carlos chuckle as he left the clinic.

Juan Pablo Paniagua sat for a long time at his desk. He rolled his shoulders and tried to relax. He had not been sure how it was going to go with don Carlos but knew that what he had spoken had to be said, and said early on.

A VISIT

Paloma Turquesa, originally named Pamela Tarkowski, felt more at home in Esperanza with every passing week. Most of the people waved hello or called out a greeting to her when she was in the pueblo. Occasionally, a much-appreciated basket of bread, una canasta con pan, still warm, appeared at her front door. She never knew who had left it, but always washed the well-used toalla, the towel, that covered the bread and left it in the empty basket with a note that said, "¡Gracias! ¡Por favor déjeme saber que usted es la aquí próxima vez! Thank you!

Please let me know you are here next time!" No one made a sound to let her know they were outside her door. She became used to occasional gifts and unannounced visits. Or, so she thought.

One day Pamela returned to her studio from a trip to el mercado, the market, to find her front door standing wide open. She knew she had locked it when she left; it was the only way she could keep the old door closed. She shoved the car into reverse and drove directly to the Varela compound. At the gate, she called into the speaker, "I need someone to help me. I think someone is inside my house." The gate swung open, taking its usual amount of time but now it was infuriatingly slow. She sped up to the la casa. Doña Milena stood in the doorway; don Carlos hurried to Pamela, opened the door, and motioned for her to get out.

"Quédese aquí, Paloma. No quiero que usted esté en peligro. Stay here, Paloma. I do not want you to be in danger."

Ignoring him, Pamela boosted herself over the console and into the passenger seat. "Conduces. You drive."

As they raced down the drive to the dirt road that connected their houses, don Carlos told her he had called Domingo and told him to meet them at her house.

Hearing this, Pamela could not help but wonder, Was this more than just a curious neighbor? Had someone really invaded her home? She became angry.

Domingo pulled up to her house seconds after they arrived. This time when don Carlos told her to stay in the car, she listened. She watched both men pull guns from the back of their belts. Domingo called out, "¿Quién está allí? Who is there?", but no one answered. They cautiously entered the house and disappeared from her view.

It felt like only a moment had flashed by when don Carlos came to the doorway and motioned to her to come in.

"Tienes que ver esto, Paloma. You have to see this, Paloma. I do not know who did it but, someone was definitely here."

Her sketchbook lay open on the floor. Many of its pages

had been ripped out and crumpled into balls, then discarded. A few had been shredded. Chairs were overturned, a vase lay shattered on the floor. The contents of her refrigerator had been tossed about. Broken egg shells lay shattered and smashed on the tile floor, their contents gone. The three looked into the bedroom. The canvases she had worked on since arriving in Esperanza had been laid out on her bed: Tito, nude; Lotus, transformed into the raven; Ifiginia in repose on the velvet fainting couch, the gentle swelling of her abdomen obvious. There was also the preliminary sketch of an old woman carrying sticks on her back; it was something Pamela had just begun to work on. A pungent odor filled the room. Every one of the canvases had been urinated on.

"¡Descreídos! Miscreants! I cannot believe anyone would defile your paintings. Especially the one of mi hija embarazada, my pregnant daughter. This is no schoolboy trick. This was done by someone muy malo, very bad, con una mente muy enferma, with a very sick mind." Domingo nodded in agreement. Both he and don Carlos continued to hold their guns in their hands, now pointing them at the floor.

The seriousness of the invasion began to hit Pamela. Someone had come into her home, uninvited. They had found her sketchbook, destroyed her work in it, and then defiled her paintings. And, why just these canvases? She had many other canvases in the house that she had worked on before she arrived in Esperanza. Stacked against the wall in a far corner of the studio, those seemed to remain untouched.

Domingo examined the still locked French doors of her bedroom and the heavy front door. He looked at don Carlos, inclined his head toward the door. It showed no signs of having been forced open. Domingo said, "Taciano."

"Taciano? What do you mean?" Pamela asked.

"Taciano is a cambiador de formas, a shape shifter,"don Carlos said.

"¿Un brujo? A witch?"

Don Carlos nodded. "He is muy malo and he uses la

magia negra, black magic, to execute his tricks. But now, he is no longer playing tricks."

Don Carlos slipped his gun into the waistband of his pants and took her by the arm. His grip was firm, almost too firm. "You are coming home with me. I will send someone to straighten this mess. You should not have to see it any more. No más. And, we are getting you un perro, a dog."

News of the break-in spread quickly. For a few days, Pamela became something of a celebrity. The old ladies in el mercado crossed themselves when they saw her coming. People who had never spoken with her before would call out, "¿Es todo bueno, doña Paloma? Is everything good?", then smile and nod when she answered, "Es bueno". La vieja, Serafia, pulled Pamela into her stall every morning and looked deeply into her eyes. "Okay?", the only English she seemed to know. "Okay!" Pamela would answer. Serafia would then thrust her hands away from her body, shooing Pamela away. As with everything she did, her concerns were expressed in a very brusque manner.

With his black shaggy coat, his massive head and paws,

and his thunderous bark, Pamela immediately named the big dog

that Carlos found for her "Oso" which meant "bear" in Spanish.

Carlos had chosen him because the owner said he was a trained

guard dog and Carlos was outraged that Pamela wanted to let

him live in her house with her.

"That is not at all acceptable, Paloma. He is meant to

patrol your property, chase off any intruders, protect you. You

cannot make a house pet out of him. It will ruin him."

Pamela pretended to agree with him but as soon as Carlos

left, she unhooked the big dog, a mix of German Shepherd and

Mastiff, from his stake-out chain and opened the door to him.

Oso padded around the house and sniffed everything. He made

her laugh when he marked the front door.

"No one will dare come in here now, right, Oso? Not

with you on the job." The big dog looked at her, trying to

understand her words. When she said his name, Oso, he cocked

his head and his stout tail thumped on the tile.

"What a good boy, you already know your name!" She

gave him a treat which don Carlos had warned her against doing. From that moment on, the only time he was out of her sight, and she out of his, was when she left to go to the market. The rest of the time, he lay nearby while she tried to repair the damaged canvases, on the floor outside of her bedroom while she slept, and sometimes just looking out one of the windows. Pamela believed he really knew his job was to watch over her and he knew that any danger would come from outside the house.

One night when she let Oso out for his last patrol and pee of the evening, Pamela heard something rustle in the underbrush around the plum trees. It made Pamela shiver. Oso stopped. He warily approached the stand of trees, the fur on his ruff standing straight up. She called to him. The dog moved further into the shadows, his black coat making him all but disappear in the night. Again, she called to him, and this time, he obeyed. He trotted back to her side, a low growl rumbling in his chest.

Pamela and Oso went inside and she locked the door. She left the outside light on. Oso went to a window and peered into the dark. Every so often he would growl and then turn to look at her. This continued for quite a while and she was afraid.

She telephoned don Carlos but there was no answer. Knowing he would have called Domingo Dos Ojos to accompany him, had he been home, she tried Domingo next.

"Domingo, lo siento mucho. I am very sorry. I know it is late but I think someone is outside the house. Oso will not stop growling. I do not know what to do."

Without replying, Domingo hung up the phone. Pamela knew he would be there very quickly.

She thought she heard the sound of an approaching car but saw no headlights. The sound stopped. Pamela huddled on the sofa; she was afraid to move. Oso, still in place at the window, was silent and they waited inside the house. Soon Domingo called out to her, telling her it was safe to open the door. When he stepped inside her house, she saw the knife in his hand and the blood on the front of his guayabera.

"What was it? Are you hurt?" Oso ran to the door and

sniffed Domingo, starting at his shoes. He stood on his hind legs, rested a foot on the shoulder of the big man, and moving all the way up to his face, sniffed and snorted until he was satisfied.

"Una culebra, a snake, doña Paloma. Muy peligroso. Very dangerous. I injured him and he is gone."

Without asking permission or giving an explanation, Domingo dragged a chair over to face the door. As he put his sunglasses in place, he said, "Buenos noches, doña Paloma", and she knew better than to argue with him. She went to her bedroom, leaving Oso outside of her door in his usual place. She wondered about the snake. What kind was so dangerous? And, why did Domingo insist on staying the night? As she fell asleep she decided that Domingo was doing what he would do for any member of the Varela family. It felt good to know she was in good company.

The next morning when she arose, the chair was still facing the door but Domingo was gone. Oso ran outside and excitedly sniffed the ground around the stand of trees. The dirt was kicked up and a few branches were broken but other than that, there were no further signs of a disturbance. Oso lifted his leg and left his mark on the area.

LESSONS

Padre Mateo and Verdad wandered through the market. Segundo and Santiago ran ahead and investigated the wares on display. Adding Segundo to their family had been easy. Santiago adored him and Segundo was patient and loving with his half-brother. Most of the time.

"Segundo is growing very tall," Padre Mateo said to Verdad.

"Yes, he has had a growth spurt and I can barely keep him in clothes! I feel as if I am constantly letting out the hems of his pants, or just buying new ones." Padre Mateo noted the pride in her voice.

"And, little Santiago . . . " They both laughed. Santiago was the image of his father with his stocky and sturdy body. Segundo often had to stop and wait for him to catch up.

They joined Pamela at the stall of Serafia admiring the embroidery on a long flowing red skirt. Despite her many years, Serafia had a steady hand and her needlework was exquisite. The old woman grinned at her, shaking her head. Pamela frowned. She was learning the fine art of haggling.

"Quince pesos, no. Ocho. Fifteen pesos, no. Eight." Pamela sounded frustrated, as well as looked it.

"Doce, ni más ni menos. No more, no less." Serafia yanked the skirt out of the hands of the other woman and began to fold it. She slid it under the bottom of the pile of skirts.

"Twelve? No. Diez. Ten. That is final," Pamela said as she pulled the skirt back out of the pile.

"Okay, okay. Diez."

A raven landed on the stall and began jabbing at the clothing.

"¡Váyase! Go away." Paloma flapped her hands at it. The old woman grabbed her hands to stop her.

"Es mi amiga. Es okay," she said.

Padre Mateo looked closely at the bird. It was not Cuervo. This bird was smaller and it looked away as he examined it. Yet, it stayed its ground.

"I believe we have a new resident in Esperanza," he said.

"Por lo visto," Verdad said. She and the priest exchanged looks. "So it seems."

Pamela, Verdad, and the priest moved on. Pamela bought them all limonadas and they sat in the shade by the fountain.

"I have been talking with Verdad, Padre, and I have an idea that might benefit the school. I would like to give art lessons to the children. Before you say anything, I know one of the nuns teaches art already. But, I would like to introduce them to new ideas, new media, and teach them a little about the schools of art."

"Sí, she has been with us for what seems like forever. She has never changed her lessons—apples, oranges, and grapes, occasionally a house here, a bit of perspective there. I have so many pictures of the church drawn by the students that I am running out of room in my file cabinet! I know how dull her class is. Pero, but, she is the art teacher." He shook his head. They all knew he could never get her to alter how she taught. It was prudent, it was mind-numbing, and the students hated it.

Pamela continued. "So, I thought I could offer a weekly art class for the younger students. En la biblioteca. At the library. We could start there and if we have enough students, perhaps move to the house Lotus and Segundo had lived in. We could combine music and drawing. I think the children would enjoy it."

"I will order books about some of the great Mexican artists of the world, starting with Diego Rivera and Frida Kahlo.

I studied about Ingrid Rosas in college. The children will like her abstract style. If the class is successful," Verdad added, "quizas, perhaps we could expand the lessons and try classes with adults."

He nodded. He liked the idea of turning the García casita into an art center. "We have many gifted people in Esperanza. Believe it or not, that man is very talented with a knife and carves incredible santos." He pointed at someone standing nearby, watching them.

"Ugh. Not Taciano. He is so dirty and so, so . . ." Pamela searched for a word.

"Inquietante," Verdad said. "Disturbing. I do not like to be around him. As a matter of fact, I have forbidden Santiago and Segundo from going into the gas station for sodas. There is something not right about him."

"You are wise to follow those feelings, Verdad. Do not let your sons go there alone." It pained him to say this but inside, he knew he was right.

"¿Quién, **Mama Verdad?**" Segundo pulled Santiago along by his wrist.

"**Para ya! Stop it! You are hurting me!**" The younger brother sounded as if he were going to cry.

"**Segundo, how many times have I told you to be gentle con tu hermano, with your brother?**" The question Segundo had asked went unanswered.

"**Paloma, er, Pamela, I think art lessons is a fine idea. You and Verdad can work out the details. I shall try to explain to the good sister.**"

Paloma **and Verdad and two boys said good-bye to him and continued in one direction, he in another. He caught sight, again, of the new raven. It did not seem strange that it was with the women and children, gliding along as they walked.**

PALOMA Y JUAN PABLO

On the way home from the market, Paloma stopped to purchase gasoline. A greasy-haired teen in a torn and filthy t-shirt came out to fill her tank. She saw Taciano standing in the doorway of the gas station, watching. She dug in her purse for money and when she looked up, he was still there. As she drove away, she looked in the rear view mirror. She saw him put a hand to his throat and touch a filthy white bandage. He sneered at her. "What a creep," she thought. What don Carlos had told her about him had seemed absurd at first. Slowly, she became unsure and the thought of un brujo stayed on her mind like the echo of a curse.

Her mood lightened when she thought of the guests coming to her house for brunch, the Varelas, the Bravos, the Yebaras, and el doctor. She had met doctor Paniagua at the clinic when she went in to get a booster for her tetanus vaccine. Verdad and Ifiginia had, not-so-subtly, told her that he was single—un viudo, a widower, that they thought he was very good-looking, and that she should see him outside of the clinic. They urged her to invite him to her house.

She told herself not to get excited by the visit; he was just someone she met in Esperanza. Yet, she found herself arranging and rearranging the flowers on the table, checking her hair in the mirror, straightening the pillows on the sofa.

Her old friends arrived all at once and there was a bustle of kissing and hugging in the doorway. Oso barked at them and wagged his tail; Carlos pointed to a corner of the room and ordered him to sit. Oso trotted away and did as he was told.

"I know, you do not have to say it. He should not be in the house." Paloma looked at Carlos with a little embarrassed smile.

"Paloma, if it makes you happy, then so be it. Just as long as you are protected," Carlos replied.

El doctor followed the crowd into the casita. He had brought a bottle of wine and as he presented it to Paloma, he kissed her on the cheek. "Thank you for having me."

Paloma saw Carlos frown, then turn away. What is that all about, she wondered.

Paloma had decided to try her version of a typical Mexican brunch for her guests: Hot chocolate with cinnamon and vanilla, beaten to a froth; a fresh fruit salad with walnuts, topped with a dressing made of whipping cream, powdered sugar, mashed avocados, pineapple juice, and candied ginger; scrambled eggs with salsa; and tender potatoes, fried with onions and strips of green chile. Carlos and Juan Pablo sat at the head and foot of the table. Domingo, as was his custom, sat with his back to the wall, facing the rest of the house and studio, so that he could see everyone at the table. He had removed his sunglasses and slid them into his shirt pocket.

The conversation was light and there was much laughter. Several times Paloma noticed that Carlos seemed to be very quiet, that he was watching Juan Pablo carefully. The two men were cordial but she sensed a bit of tension between them. She could not put her finger on what was going on between them.

"So, doctor Paniagua, what kind of name is that?" she asked.

He replied, "It means 'bread and water'. It refers to when the Royal Family of Spain had knights. Those that were favorites would be spoiled with riches."

Carlos interrupted. "I beg to differ but I have always heard that it referred to servants who had to work for their bread and water." He raised his cup to his lips, took a sip of the chocolate, and continued. "Not knights."

"It could be either, I am sure." Juan Pablo seemed to be

trying to keep the mood light. "I just know for certain that it means 'bread and water'. It is a fairly common name."

"Common, yes," don Carlos said. The two men stared each other down.

With that, Milena said, "I could not eat another bite. I am beyond full." Ifiginia and Verdad agreed and both of them rose to begin clearing the table. Pamela stopped them.

"Leave it, please, just leave everything. I would rather spend time having you relax, not working. It will only take me a few minutes later to put everything away. Besides, I am funny about people in my kitchen."

The rest of the afternoon passed without further tension. Ifiginia and Tito and Verdad and Domingo left together. They had left all of the children with the Varela maid and wanted to make sure all was well. Milena pulled Carlos up out of his seat and said, "Come, it is time to leave."

Paloma could see that Carlos was reluctant to leave but he went with her. Juan Pablo stood to shake hands and say good-bye, but it was clear he was not yet ready to leave. He went into la cocina and began opening drawers. "Do you have a corkscrew, Paloma? I am anxious to try this wine."

Carlos leaned over to give Paloma a kiss on the cheek. "Call me if you need anything, Paloma. Anything." He patted Oso on the head.

"Oso, you be a good dog and guard Paloma," he said. He had nothing else to say and no further reason to remain. Paloma closed the heavy door behind him. She heard the "krak" of a raven in the plum trees.

"That was interesting. He is an unusual man. He seems to have quite an interest in your well-being." Juan Pablo poured the wine into glasses he found in the cabinet.

"He is just taking care of me, he is always like that. I think he feels I need protection since I am alone here. He is like a big brother." She motioned to him to follow her back to the sofa.

"I would not say his interest is that of un hermano

mayor," he said as he got settled on the couch. El doctor Juan Pablo Paniagua put his arm around her shoulders. "Not at all."

PALOMA Y JUAN PABLO

It was of little surprise to most that Paloma and the doctor began to keep company. She often drove into Esperanza, parked her car at the clinic, and waited for him to finish with patients. Holding hands, they would walk to the fountain and watch the young couples stroll around the plaza. They were amused by the chaperones that followed the lovers. They both saw the new raven perched above them in the tree nearly every time they sat at the fountain.

"Thank goodness we are beyond the age of needing un

guardián de moral," Juan Pablo said as he nuzzled Paloma.

"Stop that! Even so, we cannot carry on in public." Paloma felt invigorated by his attentions and by the affection they shared in private but she knew many eyes watched everything they did, especially everything she did.

"Then let us find a place more private," Juan Pablo said.

As with most evenings, they headed for her house, the doctor following her little car out of Esperanza. This night, she had to stop for gasoline. He pulled in behind her car and jumped out to fill her tank. He saw Taciano watching from a darkened bay of the garage. While he returned the gas cap to its original seat and hung up the dripping nozzle of the hose, Paloma went to Taciano to give him money. Juan Pablo knew the reputation Taciano had and he kept a close eye on him. He saw the man take the money and hold onto her hand for just a beat. As she walked, actually ran, back to her car, he saw Taciano rub his hand over the front of his pants, over his groin.

"I do not want you coming here alone, Paloma. I know I cannot be with you every moment, but it is not safe," he said.

"He is so disgusting but what choice do I have? I do not like him any more than you do but I can handle myself." She felt herself bristle at the implication that she was helpless; she had been working hard to dispel that notion, in herself, as well as in her new friends. She brushed her hand, the one Taciano had held, on her backside, as if to wipe off his scent.

That night, as nearly every night since they had begun to see one another, Paloma and Juan Pablo had a small dinner then made love. Sometimes their hunger for each other could not wait and they made love as soon as they closed and locked the door to the studio. Paloma had hung curtains at all of the windows, as much as she hated to do so, so their passion could not be witnessed by anyone who happened to pass by.

After, lying on her bed in the semi-darkness of the bedroom, they always talked. They talked about their childhoods, their marriages, their time alone. Just as younger lovers did, they talked about their futures and sus sueños, their dreams. In a very short period of time, they had grown to love each other deeply. Paloma wondered if it happened so quickly because they were older, because they had a better idea of what they wanted in their lives now, they had been so lonely, because, because, because.

Most nights, Oso dozed outside of the bedroom door. When she let him out for the last time each night, he trotted around the house, sometimes investigating some scent he found fascinating, and sometimes even returning with the odor of some dead thing he had rolled in floating around him like perfume. At those times, he was most proud of himself then and could not resist getting onto her bed, between her and el doctor.

Tonight he paced. He moved from one curtained window to the next, sticking his big furry head through the fabric to look outside. Occasionally, he whined.

"I think he has to go out." Paloma slid into her robe and in her bare feet, walked to the front door. As she opened it, Oso sprang outside and disappeared into the dark. She could hear him bulldozing through the bushes. He stopped and the sound of his deep, meanacing growl reached her.

"Oso! Come here. Oso!" she called. The dog did not return but continued to growl. A sudden cold wind rattled the branches of the trees. She closed the door and waited a few moments. She knew he would bark to let her know when he had returned and wanted to come in. She returned to the bedroom, climbed into the warm, welcoming bed with Juan Pablo, and they both fell asleep.

The sun was up when they awoke. The first thing Juan Pablo did was dash into the shower. He knew his patients would gossip if he was late.

The first thing Paloma did was call for Oso. He did not come to her and she remembered he was outside.

She called to him but did not see him. She did not hear him either.

"No! No!" She sent up a silent prayer. She called him again. Still, he did not return.

She rushed back into the house, picked up the phone and called Domingo.

The big man sounded as if she had awakened him. She tried not to cry. "Oso is not here. I let him out last night and he has not come home. I am afraid he is hurt."

Again, Domingo hung up the phone without saying a word. She threw on the clothes she had worn last night and went to the door to wait. Juan Pablo joined her.

"I am so stupid! I should not have fallen asleep before he came in." She berated herself as he held her.

"No, you are not stupid. Oso will be okay. I know it."

Domingo and don Carlos arrived together. It was apparent that Domingo had come straight from his bed; his hair hung loose over his shoulders and down his back. Don Carlos, as always, was neatly attired.

Don Carlos hurried up to the house. He took in the wet hair and the bare feet of Juan Pablo and snapped at Paloma. "Paloma, why did you not call me?"

"Oh, shut up, Carlos."

Juan Pablo and Domingo both fought to refrain from smiling.

"I called Domingo because I knew he would call you and I did not want to have to explain anything. I just need to find Oso."

Paloma and the men moved away from the house and began calling for Oso. The new raven, the one that seemed to be always present when Paloma and the doctor sat at the fountain, circled over them, calling to them with shrill cries. As she flew, her circles tightened until she seemed to be hovering in the sky.

They all recognized the second larger bird that joined them. Cuervo took up the strident calling and agitated circling. He barrel-rolled from Domingo to Carlos to Juan Pablo to

Paloma, then returned to the smaller raven. Domingo called to the others to follow the black birds.

They found Oso deep in the woods, one large heavy paw holding down the head of a snake. He thumped his tail at them in greeting, but returned to his vigil. The skin of the snake rippled as it tried to extricate itself from under his paw.

"Oso, stay, do not move," don Carlos ordered. He and Domingo motioned to Paloma and Juan Pablo that they should stay back.

"A twenty minute snake," Juan Pablo whispered.

"What?" Paloma could not take her eyes off of her dog and its prey. The snake had red, yellow, and black colored banding. A coral snake.

"The venom from this snake is so lethal its victims die within 20 minutes of being bitten. That is all the time it takes for the venom to paralyze the breathing muscles. Even though this one is not so big, it is still extremely dangerous."

Large or small, Paloma knew Oso was in jeopardy. She and Juan Pablo became silent as they watched Domingo and don Carlos arm themselves. Carlos had a gun, Domingo a knife. Domingo had removed his sunglasses.

"Paloma, when I tell you, I want you to call Oso to you. Keep calling him until he moves away from the snake. Do not stop, no matter what." Don Carlos kept his eyes on the snake as he spoke. "Ready? Ahora! Now!"

"Oso, come! Good boy! Come here, Oso! Come!" She clapped her hands as she shouted. Juan Pablo joined in. He slapped his thigh as he called, "Oso! Oso! Oso!"

They could see that Oso did not want to leave his prey but the urge to obey was greater. Paloma knelt down and called to him over and over and over.

As the big dog rose and stepped toward her, don Carlos fired over and over and over into the body of the snake. It seemed to leap about in the dirt. As it writhed, it began to change. It grew larger, thicker, fatter, and in an instant Pamela

455

saw Taciano Zaragoza on the ground in front of them. Domingo fell on him with his knife and in one swift motion, slashed his neck. Blood spilled into the dirt and Taciano was still.

"It is over, Paloma. Te prometo. I promise you," don Carlos said.

"What happened? Was there a snake here? I do not understand," Pamela asked.

Juan Pablo stared at the dead man and shook his head. "There is no explanation for this, Paloma. He was a very bad man and now he is gone."

"But, I saw a snake. Oso had it pinned." Her voice began to rise as she spoke. She looked from Domingo to don Carlos. "I saw it! Where did Taciano come from?"

"Take her back to the house. We will attend to this," don Carlos instructed Juan Pablo. "Por favor. Please."

With the big dog at their heels, Juan Pablo guided her home. She hugged her dog while Juan Pablo examined him for injuries. There were none. The big dog appeared to be exhausted and very thirsty. He had stayed with the snake for many, many hours.

Pamela went to the kitchen and mixed up eggs and chorizo for them, making enough for don Carlos and Domingo, should they come back.

A strange smell reached her. She went to the front door and looked out. Domingo returned to his car and removed a shovel. The big man then lumbered into the trees and disappeared.

In the woods, black smoke plumed into the sky. The odor was nauseating and sweet. It was so thick she thought she could taste it: a disturbing perfume of copper, charcoal, and meat. She hurriedly closed the heavy wooden door.

When the men came back to the casa and knocked on the door, Pamela tried to act as if this were just a normal visit. "Come in. I have made something to eat."

"No, we cannot. We must go home and bathe." Carlos

said. Both he and Domingo were cloaked in the scent from the fire. It was a smell she knew would linger in her senses for a long time and was one that she could never forget.

Juan Pablo extended his hand to don Carlos, then Domingo. "Gracias." No other words were necessary.

PALOMA Y ESPERANZA

After that day, the smaller raven was seen less and less. She seemed to drop in to check on the goings on in Esperanza and then then she would disappear. The times between her visits lengthened until she became just a memory. The people who had seen her knew who she was and why she had come back. They also understood when she no longer appeared.

The gas station remained empty for several days. One afternoon, when Pamela drove by, Shebo, the PeMex driver, was up on a ladder, painting the building. She called to him.

"Shebo, what are you doing? "

He climbed down from the ladder and leaned into her open car window.

"I have bought the gas station! It is now the Medina PeMex." He radiated pride.

"How did you manage that?" Pamela was surprised.

"Don Carlos helped me. He is the one who suggested I buy the station. It is a very good thing for me and mi familia. I do not have to be on the road for weeks at a time. I can help my wife with los niños. And, I will earn much more money. It is, how do you say, a win-win situation."

Vibrant orange, purple, and red flowers had been planted in wooden barrels on each side of the door of the station. The lot was paved. A shiny, new red and white Coca Cola vending machine stood by the open doorway. In the clean front window hung a blinking neon sign, PEMEX MEDINA —ABIERTO, OPEN.

"Don Carlos, eh?"

Shebo nodded and as one, they said, "¡Tiene un corazón de oro!"

Pamela continued into Esperanza, following the sound of the bell of La Iglesia de la Santa Cruz. Parents and children shopped in the market. Young lovers strolled with their arms around one another, the chaperones following at a safe distance. The viejos, the old men, played dominos and sipped cerveza, beer.

Coming to Esperanza has been a fortuitous accident, she thought. I have friends of my own. My art is better than it has ever been, I have found myself here. I have built a new life and I have peace.

Overhead, Cuervo whistled and swooped low over the plaza. She turned down the volume of her radio so she could hear the rhythms of the mariachi band.

RESOURCES

a. Ernest Hemingway, El Viejo y La Mar, (Grupo Editorial tomo, 2010), 9.

b. Ibid., 21.

c. Ibid., 103.

a. Ernest Hemingway, The Old Man and the Sea, http://www.classic-enotes.com/american-literature/american-novel/ernest-hemingway/the-old-man-and-the-sea/full-text-of-the-old-man-and-the-sea-by-ernest-hemingway/

Made in the USA
Middletown, DE
20 October 2018